DEARLY DEPARTED

Also by David Housewright

Penance

Practice to Deceive

DEARLY
DEPARTED

A HOLLAND

TAYLOR

MYSTERY

David Housewright

A Foul Play Press Book *W. W. Norton & Company New York London*

Copyright © 1999 by David Housewright

For information about permission to reproduce selections from
this book, write to Permissions, W. W. Norton & Company, Inc.,
500 Fifth Avenue, New York, NY 10110.

The text of this book is composed in Iowan Oldstyle
with the display set in Modula
Composition by A. W. Bennett, Inc.
Manufacturing by Quebecor Printing, Fairfield, Inc.
Book design by Chris Welch

Library of Congress Cataloging-in-Publication Data

Housewright, David, 1955–
    Dearly departed : a Holland Taylor mystery / David House-
    wright.
        p.   cm.
    ISBN 0-393-04771-7
    I. Title.
PS3558.08668D43   1999
813'.54—dc21
                                                    99-30031
                                                    CIP

Published by Foul Play Press, a division of
W. W. Norton & Company, New York

W. W. Norton & Company, Inc., 500 Fifth Avenue,
New York, N.Y. 10110
www.wwnorton.com

W. W. Norton & Company Ltd., 10 Coptic Street,
London WC1A 1PU

1 2 3 4 5 6 7 8 9 0

For Robert and Sharon Valois

For Renée

acknowledgments

Special thanks
to Dale Gelfand, Phyllis Jaeger, Lou Kannenstine,
Alison Picard, Michael Sullivan, Bob and Sharon
Valois, and Renée Valois

one

What I remember most was her voice. It was strong and clear and totally unafraid, even though the words she spoke gripped my heart with two icy hands:

If you are listening to this now, it is because I am dead.

At first I didn't want to listen. I did not know the voice, had never heard the name that went with it. But I knew the man who had invaded my office, who now stood in front of my desk, a stumpy index finger pressed hard against the play button of a cassette recorder, and it was all I could do to keep from knocking him to the floor and beating him about the head and shoulders. Hell, if there had been a wooden stake handy, I would have gladly driven it through his heart.

But that voice, that voice . . .

Hunter Truman was a man who preferred what Winston Churchill called "short, Anglo-Saxon words," words usually reserved for those moments when you hit your thumb with a hammer or stub your toe in the dark. He used them frequently. Probably the only words he used more often were these: "I'll sue."

Truman was an attorney, a fact that might have pleased his mother but few others. He took bragging pleasure in the sixty-some civil lawsuits he had filed on his own behalf over the past ten years—more if you added all the spin-off countersuits. Most were frivolous. The rest were vindictive and vengeful. He didn't care if he won, only that he crushed his victims with legal fees— a problem he didn't have since he always represented himself. I hadn't known this several years ago when I met Truman, and although I was still struggling to make a go of my detective agency back then, I like to think it would have made a difference.

At the time, Truman had insisted that enemies of a client he declined to identify had attempted to run him down just that morning. He gave me a description of the car and the first three digits of the license plate, then hired me to learn who had driven it. By late afternoon, I discovered that the car was owned by a middle-aged couple living in the Kenwood neighborhood of Minneapolis but usually driven by their teenage daughter. I also discovered that while several people might have wanted Truman dead, no one was actually trying to kill him. And he had known it. He had merely wanted the information I provided so that he could sue the teenager's parents for one hundred thousand dollars in punitive damages for having an "out-of-control" daughter. The teenager's crime? She had flipped him the bird when Truman cut her off on a downtown Minneapolis street so that he could claim a prime parking spot in front of the Federal Court Building.

Armed with the information I had gathered for him, Truman dragged the parents through the court system, vowing that if they wouldn't control their daughter, then—bigod!—he would. Eventually he lost the suit and was ordered to pay the parents a two-hundred-and-fifty-dollar judgment. Meanwhile, the parents had burned several thousand dollars defending themselves.

I hadn't liked being used so badly. Nor had I appreciated his lying to me. But I probably would have forgotten all about the incident if Truman hadn't tried to pull the same crap a couple of years later—this time with me as his designated victim.

I had just worked a case involving credit card fraud. A man had been contacting grieving widows. He'd get their names from the obituaries and call them and offer to switch their credit cards from their husbands' names to their names. All they had to do was provide him with the credit card numbers and expiration dates. And soon they would start receiving bills for televisions, stereos, microwave ovens, and airline tickets that they hadn't purchased. I had been drawn into the case by an older woman who didn't think the authorities were giving it enough attention.

It turned out the caller was an inmate at Oak Park Heights state prison. He had been using a pay phone to gather the credit card information and then sell it to accomplices on the outside. When confronted with the crime, the inmate grinned and said, "Don't shoot, I give up." He'd treated it all like a hoot—and why not? After his conviction, he drew a sentence that was to be served concurrently with the sentence he was already serving. He didn't lose so much as an extra day of freedom. Meanwhile, the money gleaned off the scam was pulling interest in a mutual fund somewhere.

Only that wasn't good enough for Truman, who had defended the lowlife. Annoyed because he couldn't shake my testimony on the witness stand, he sought revenge by bringing me up before the

Private Detective and Protective Agent Services Board, claiming I had abused my license, stating specifically that I had "engaged in fraud, deceit and misrepresentation while in the business of private detective." However, on the morning of the hearing, Truman withdrew his complaint—although not his claims—and the matter was dropped. But not before it had cost me several sleepless nights and the expense of hiring my own attorney.

When chance and the Minnesota Timberwolves put us at the same concession stand a few months later, I confronted Truman with a few well-chosen Anglo-Saxon words of my own and told him if I ever saw him again, I'd shoot him. He said he was going to sue me for defamation and assault but apparently found something else to become hysterical over because he never did.

Now he was in my office, and I found myself regretting that I'd stopped carrying a gun.

He set a battered briefcase on the floor, straightened slowly, and said, "I need your help." He looked it, too. I had never seen anyone who appeared as sorrowful or as dejected as Truman did outside a cancer ward. His hair was tangled from running his hands through it, and he had little patches of beard where he had shaved not too carefully. His eyes were bloodshot and tired. He looked defeated. It was because of that look that I didn't throw him out. But, then, I didn't invite him to sit down, either.

"Let me guess, the Office of Lawyers Professional Responsibility pulled your ticket," I said.

"Fuck, no. Why would they do that?" Truman answered without much enthusiasm.

"Jealousy."

Truman didn't reply. His eyes locked on an empty corner of my desk blotter, and for a moment he reminded me of a lawn ornament, one of those sad-eyed ceramic deer that people stick in their front yards.

"You have thirty seconds to tell me what you want," I said.

Truman's woeful demeanor didn't last long. "Thirty seconds, what's that shit?" he wanted to know in a voice that started low and increased in volume.

"Twenty-five seconds."

Truman must have figured out I was serious because at fifteen seconds he said, "I want you to find a woman for me."

"Try Lyndale and Lake Street; the girls who wave at passing cars are usually the most reasonably priced."

"Jesus H. Christ. This is serious."

"Five seconds."

In five seconds, Truman whipped a photograph out of his pocket and set it—ever so tenderly—in front of me. It was of a woman who looked like she should be advertising perfumes with dangerous-sounding names. She wasn't beautiful, exactly. Her hair was dark and so were her eyes, but her chin was too sharp, and her nose had a slight hook to it. Yet she had a presence, a confidence, that a camera could not diminish. Or perhaps the camera lent it to her—what did I know? I guessed her age at twenty-five.

"The police think she was murdered," Truman said.

That bought him an extra minute.

"What do you mean, they think?"

"Shit, the assholes can't find her body, and they can't find any conclusive fucking evidence of foul play."

I was puzzled and probably looked it.

"Listen to what I'm saying," Truman commanded. "The last time anyone saw her, she was leaving her office Halloween night. Remember that goddamn snowstorm?"

I remembered it well. Twenty-three inches of snow fell within twelve hours, and my snow blower wouldn't start.

"Her husband comes home, and she's not there. But here's the thing: Her car was in the garage, her coat and purse were on the chair where she usually left them, and the front door was open. I don't mean unlocked, I mean open."

"Maybe she went out for a pack of cigarettes and kept on going. It's been done before," I volunteered.

"In a snowstorm? Without her coat or boots? Without her fucking purse, her credit cards, her checkbook, her cash? Listen to what the fuck I'm saying! The cops thought she might have left, too, but changed their minds because nothing was missing from the house. No clothes, no jewelry, no nothing."

"Did the police sweep the house?"

"Shit, yeah. They didn't turn up jack. No sign of forced entry, no physical evidence, no witnesses. Christ, if they knew what the fuck was going on, you'd think I'd be standing here?"

I reached across the desk, grabbed a fistful of silk tie, and jerked it toward me. "You utter one more obscenity in my presence, I'll wash out your mouth with soap," I snarled. It was a good snarl, too—I practice it in front of a mirror.

He started to utter one of the seven words banned from network television, gulped when I yanked his tie, then nodded.

I released his tie. It's not that I'm particularly offended by obscene language. I've been known to mutter a few four- and seven-letter words myself. But Truman was beginning to annoy me, and since I didn't like him in the first place, I saw no reason to put up with his vulgarity.

"You're a straight shooter; I respect that," he told me. "A conscientious guy."

"Sure," I replied sarcastically to the hollow compliment.

"That's why I'm here," he continued. "I know you didn't like it when I dragged you in front of the board, but I was protecting the interests of my client; that's what lawyers do. If other people get hurt along the way . . . Hey, don't blame me, blame the system."

"Get out of my office," I told him.

"No, listen, this is important."

"Hit the bricks, pal."

"Taylor, Christ, listen. . . ."

"Truman, you're a jerk. A gold-plated, one-hundred-percent jerk, and I do not want to work for you. You haven't got enough money to hire me. You could be Bill Gates or Warren Buffett and still not have enough money to hire me. Go away."

"All I want is a minute—"

"You've had a minute."

"Taylor, c'mon, just listen to this," he said, producing a cassette recorder from the briefcase. He pressed the play button as I rounded my desk, reaching for him.

If you are listening to this now, it is because I am dead.

The voice stopped me. It was a woman's voice, and there was something about it, a characteristic I couldn't identify. It wasn't an accent, although it had an almost exotic resonance. And it wasn't the way the pitch of her voice rose and fell pleasantly like it was singing a ballad, something by the Gershwins. But there was something, a quality that I can hear even now. . . .

If you are listening to this now, it is because I am dead.

I returned to my side of the desk. Truman took a chance and sat in the chair that I reserve for guests. He sighed with the effort, like he'd remembered too many things at once. I swiveled away in my chair, looked out my window at downtown Minneapolis, and listened. . . .

"If you are listening to this now, it is because I am dead. (Long pause.) I realize that everything I'm about to tell you seems so . . .

unlikely. But I am frightened, and I believe I have good cause. I am tak-ing steps to protect myself. Unfortunately, there is only so much one can do and still maintain a life worth living. I am making this tape in case things do not go my way. (Long pause. Low barking of several dogs in the distance.) *I am sitting beneath an oak tree on a knoll overlooking the pond as I record this. There's a mist rising off the pond. . . . Oh, sure, Larry, ruin the whole scene.* (Loudly.) *Larry just ran into the pond for a drink. You can't bring these guys anywhere near water. . . . I have three black Labradors. I call them Larry, Moe, and Curly Joe, although I couldn't tell you why—I've never been a fan of the Stooges. I usually take my babies for a run in the morning in the wooden area behind my house. What's the appropriate word for a small forest? Glade? Grove?"*

"Grove," Truman answered.

"Stephen hates it here. But I love it. I told him if he wants to move he'll have to do it without me.

"(Deep sigh.) *I suppose if I'm going to do this thing, I'd best get to it. To be official, Hunter . . . my name is Alison Donnerbauer Emerton. I am twenty-seven years old. I am married to Stephen Emerton, and we live at 3747 Pioneer Trail in Hastings, Minnesota. I am making this tape for my attorney, Hunter Truman of Minneapolis, with the explicit instruc-tions that he deliver it forthwith to the appropriate authorities in the event of my death. . . ."*

"Stop the tape," I said.

"Don't you—?"

"Stop it."

Truman hit the pause button.

"Why did she come to you with this?"

Truman shrugged. "I was her attorney."

"Did she pick you out of the phone book? What?"

Truman hesitated; he studied the palm of his hand as if the answer was written there. "I was her husband's attorney before they were married. That's probably why she called me."

"Probably?"

Truman shrugged like he didn't want to commit himself.

"Go 'head," I instructed.

Truman pressed the play button.

"If I am dead, it is because Raymond Fleck killed me. . . . (Long pause.) Fleck is a convicted rapist who has been stalking me for the past six weeks.

"To begin at the beginning, I am a public-relations practitioner and marketing manager for Kennel-Up, Incorporated, a company based in Hastings that manufactures and sells conventional as well as electronic dog kennels. Raymond was one of the company's site managers. I was responsible for his dismissal from the firm for sexual harassment. I met him when I took the position with Kennel-Up last March. Prior to that I worked for a health-care company. I took the Kennel-Up job partly because I love dogs more than doctors and partly because it pays better. I now make more than Stephen, which doesn't sit too well with him. But, let that go for now.

"(Deep sigh.) From the first, Raymond was too . . . familiar. He held my hand too long after he shook it; he made periodic references to my appearance, telling me how attractive I was, how pretty my hair, how flattering my dress; he would linger at the coffee machine when I ventured for a cup. I am not an unattractive woman—"

"You're beautiful," Truman told the machine.

"—and over the years I've grown accustomed to this kind of treatment, so I let Raymond's behavior slide. That might have been a mistake. Perhaps he interpreted my silence as approval, even encouragement. (Brief pause.) I discussed the matter with Stephen. He wondered if my behavior and style of dress were leading Raymond on. He also suggested that I would be branded as a whiner or a troublemaker if I took the matter to my employers. Typical Stephen. However, when Raymond's behavior became even more objectionable, when he began to massage my shoulders or rub my back when our jobs put us in close proximity, when he began making pornographic references, I told Mr. Selmi about my concerns.

"Mr. Selmi is a great old teddy bear of a man. Everybody loves him. He started Kennel-Up in his garage when he was thirty-five. Now he's seventy-something and rich. Only I get the impression he wishes he was still working out of the garage.

"Anyway, Mr. Selmi seemed quite upset. He questioned Raymond in my presence. Raymond, of course, denied everything. Said it was all in my imagination. Even suggested that subconsciously I wanted him to do the things he described. Mr. Selmi asked me to leave his office, and he and Raymond spoke for a long time—several hours at least. Later, Mr. Selmi informed me that my problems with Raymond were over. But he was mistaken.

"Later that evening, I discovered Raymond's car parked in front of my house. I could see the burning tip of a cigarette behind the windshield. I called the police. I was impressed by how quickly the officers responded, but not by their kid-glove treatment of the man. It was as if they were afraid to offend him.

"Raymond told the police he had done nothing wrong, and legally speaking I suppose that was true. He also claimed I had invited him. He said I had promised to sneak out of the house after Stephen was asleep and meet him. He was lying, and I said so. The police and Stephen—damn Stephen—weren't sure what to believe. That is until they ran Raymond's name through their computer and learned that he had been convicted of raping a woman about seven years ago. Apparently Raymond had satisfied the conditions of his parole because the police said there was nothing they could do but warn him off. Raymond left, and after he drove away, so did the police.

"The next morning I went directly to Mr. Selmi and told him what had occurred. He fired Raymond before Raymond had a chance to remove his overcoat and then stood watch while Raymond cleared his personal effects from his office.

"Stephen . . . I nearly left Stephen that night. He said I had no business getting Raymond fired. He said Raymond had paid his debt to society and had as much right to a job as I did. He said if I didn't like it at Kennel-Up, I should have quit instead.

"I encountered much the same reaction from my co-workers. One woman accused me of fabricating the entire incident just to get Raymond dismissed, although she couldn't explain why I would do such a thing. Several others complained to Mr. Selmi, saying they did not want to work with me— apparently I was the only one to receive Raymond's special attention.

"Then the telephone calls started coming: at home, at work, night and day. Usually the caller would hang up when I answered. Sometimes a loud whistle would be blown in my ear. Sometimes nothing would happen as I repeated 'Hello, hello, hello' like an idiot. A box filled with dead roses was left on my desk. A dead cat was stuffed in my mailbox at home. A few days ago the tires of my car were slashed in a supermarket parking lot, which means someone followed me there, right? I knew it was Raymond.

"I bought a gun. A .22. I asked for something bigger, but the man said a .22 was plenty big enough. I had it with me yesterday while I was in downtown Minneapolis. I was gripping it inside my purse when a homeless man came up and handed me an envelope. 'Person paid me to give you this,' he said and then walked away before I could ask him who. I opened the envelope. There was a piece of paper in it. On the paper someone had written the word Soon in crayon. Nothing else, just Soon.

"Mr. Truman, I know he's out there. I know he's coming for me. It's just a matter of time. The police can't help me, and Stephen won't. So, all I can do is wait. But I refuse to panic. And I refuse to run. . . .

"It's Wednesday, October sixteenth. I request that you accept this tape; lock it in your safe. A year from now, if I discover my fears have been greatly exaggerated, I'll ask you to return it, and we'll go to lunch, and you can charge me an exorbitant fee for your patience. Thank you for your consideration. Hey, you guys! Larry, Moe . . ."

———

We sat silently listening long after the tape had stopped playing. Finally Truman ejected the cassette from the machine. He held it in both hands like it was ancient parchment instead of plastic.

"Leave it," I told him when he made a move to drop it in his pocket. He placed the cassette on the desk blotter next to Alison's photograph.

"Tell me more," I said.

"Witnesses verify that Alison left Kennel-Up at five-fifteen. Give her fifteen minutes to reach her home. Her husband arrives at six-fifteen and finds Alison missing. No trace of her. When I learned about it, I gave the original cassette to the cops; this is a copy. They checked Raymond Fleck. He had an alibi. A woman who worked with him at Kennel-Up claimed that from about five till seven, they were fucking each other's brains out. Excuse me, having carnal relations."

I waved off the apology; the color of his language no longer concerned me.

"The cops thought that was awfully convenient and wouldn't eliminate him as a suspect. Only, eliminate him from what? There's nothing there, Holland. Nothing at all. No prints, no fibers . . . They put Alison's photograph on TV, in the newspapers— *'Have you seen this woman?'* They even put her on those goddamn milk cartons. That was two hundred and twelve days ago."

"You counted the days?"

"Every fucking one."

"What do you want me to do, Hunter?" Strange how we were suddenly on a first-name basis, the best of friends.

"Find her."

"Find her?"

"Find out what happened to her. Listen to what I'm saying: I know she's dead, but I don't know, I mean . . . I have to know what happened to her. I have to know. Even if there's nothing we can do about it, even if—I have to know, Holland. Please. . . ."

Why did it matter so much to him? I wondered. *What was Alison to Truman besides a client? Was that the extent of their relationship? Or was there something else?* I was betting on the something else. I had no reason to draw that conclusion except that Hunter Truman was the most unreasonable, unsympathetic, mean-spirited man I knew who wasn't in jail. As far as I could tell he had never displayed so much as a modicum of concern for anyone. Yet he seemed to care deeply for Alison Donnerbauer Emerton. And suddenly, so did I.

"There's not much I can do that the cops haven't," I told him.

"Give me your best guess. I'll settle for that."

It was ten o'clock Monday morning, the first week in June, and the phone hadn't rung for a few days. I told myself, what the hell, a buck's a buck, and Hunter Truman wasn't such a bad guy. . . . Yeah, right.

"I'll look into it, see if I can generate a few new leads. If not . . ." I shrugged.

"You will?" Truman asked gleefully.

"I get four hundred a day, plus expenses."

two

Anne Scalasi was my best friend—maybe my only friend—and she proved it by ignoring my presence at her desk until she finished reading a memo that was one paragraph long. It took her several minutes.

The office of St. Paul Police Department's Homicide Unit hadn't changed much since I labored there. Hell, except for the occasional computer terminal, it hadn't changed much since 1972. Detectives still sat in metal chairs at metal desks, separated from each other by movable soft-sided walls. Empty metal coatracks stood guard outside each cubicle.

From where Anne sat, she had a clear view of the erasable white plastic marker board covered with rows of names. It was a roster of this year's homicides. Red was active. Black denoted cases where a suspect had been charged. There were only a few reds.

"What do you want?" Annie barked at last.

"I can always tell when you're upset."

"Why would I be upset?"

"Beats me."

"You're sick, Taylor," she informed me. "Sending a dozen long-stemmed roses to a woman on the anniversary of her divorce is a sick thing to do."

"I thought it was a kindly enough gesture," I replied in my defense. "Telling a dear friend who's down that someone cared."

"Oh, then that explains the card," she said.

"The card?"

"The *unsigned* card. 'Oh, baby, oh, baby, oh, baby, thank you for last night and all the nights that came before.' Remember?"

"I was joking about you going to the baseball game with me on such short notice," I protested.

"Yeah, right. My oldest—who isn't too thrilled that I divorced her father in the first place—signed for the flowers. She read the card. She wanted to know if it was a message from my lover."

"What did you tell her?"

"I told her the truth. It was from a sick friend."

"Did she believe you?"

"Only when I told her the sick friend's name."

I ignored the insult and insisted that I was only trying to be considerate.

"Since when?"

"It's the new me. A man for the millennium: thoughtful, kind, selfless—"

"What do you want, Taylor?"

I held my thumb and forefinger in front of my eye and squinted through the quarter inch that separated them. "An itty, bitty favor."

Anne tried to look stern, eventually failed. Like most true friends, we had long ago surrendered to each other's faults and foibles; prolonged anger between us was impossible. She shook her head and smiled. It was a dazzling smile, rarely seen by anyone other than her children and, occasionally, a pal. A few months ago a photographer for a local magazine spent the better part of a morning attempting to coax that smile from her and couldn't, so zealously does she guard it. It was just as well. The headline above the accompanying article read: ST. PAUL'S ANGEL OF DEATH. It was not an image Anne approved of.

Lieutenant Anne Scalasi was commander of the St. Paul Police Department's Homicide Unit and therefore one of the most visible female law enforcement officers in the state of Minnesota. She rarely enjoyed the attention she received; press coverage of her divorce had infuriated her. Yet she loved the job. Many suggested—although they would not allow their names to be used in the article—that Anne's promotion was merely a public-relations ploy by an affirmative-action-conscious police chief and mayor. I spent well over four years working in Homicide, nearly all that time as Annie's partner, and I wholeheartedly disagreed. Anne Scalasi was the best cop I have ever known.

She began life as an elementary schoolteacher in Anoka, a fact the magazine found particularly ironic. Just for the giggles she decided to join the local Ride-Along program and went patrolling with Anoka County deputies. That was all it took. She was hooked. Anne quit teaching, got a job as a night dispatcher for a suburban police department that same week, and attended the police academy during the day. And she married a cop. After earning a law enforcement degree, she became the department's first female officer and, later, its first female detective. Eventually she was recruited by the state attorney general's office. That *was* a political appointment, and as soon as she realized it, Anne quit, taking a position with the Minnesota Bureau of Criminal Apprehension. The BCA liked her so much, they sent her to the FBI's training center in Quantico, Virginia, where she was taught by the Behavioral Science Unit to investigate mass murders and serial rape killings. She scored first in her class. When she returned to the BCA, she requested that she be allowed to work with other law enforcement organizations that might require her expertise— which, of course, is why the agency was created in the first place. But the BCA began placing various bureaucratic restrictions on her, making her play second, third, and often fourth fiddle to their field agents. So she joined the St. Paul Police Department, which was happy to give her free rein.

I remember when she arrived. We gave her the cold shoulder, my colleagues and I, calling her "Miss Betty" behind her back— Miss Betty being the name of the woman who taught *Romper Room* on TV. One day she leaned across my desk, smiled her dazzling smile, and announced: "The more violently the face of a murder victim is battered, the more likely the killer and the victim had a close relationship."

I told her I knew that.

"And now you know that I know it," she told me. "I know a lot of other things, too. So, you want to catch bad guys with me or what?"

We caught a lot of them together.

"Do you know the Dakota County sheriff?" I now asked.

"Yes. Ed Teeters. Nice man."

"Nice enough to let a PI snoop around one of his investigations?"

Anne gave me one of those here-we-go-again eye rolls and asked, "What are you into now?"

"Alison Donnerbauer Emerton," I told her. "She disappeared seven months ago. I was just hired to learn what happened to her."

"Good luck," she said. "I worked the case. . . ."

I don't know why I was surprised. Solving unsolvable murders is, after all, Annie's specialty.

"Teeters asked me if I could give him a fresh perspective. I couldn't," she admitted.

She opened a lower desk drawer and took out a huge family photo album—her murder book, a grisly, gory, gruesome account of every homicide investigation she had ever worked, the investigations presented in chronological order with the most recent in front. Each account contained before-and-after photographs of the victim, a detailed description of the killing, a synopsis of the investigation, and final disposition of the case. Homicides that were solved had a blue tab; those that remained unsolved had a red tab. There were only a few red tabs, and most of these were near the front. Anne turned to the tab labeled #197. Case #197 differed from the others in that it was skimpier and didn't feature a photograph taken after the victim's body was discovered. The "before" photograph was a reprint of the one Hunter Truman had given to me that morning.

"Theories?" I asked.

Anne shrugged. "Assailant knocks, Alison answers; assailant pushes a gun in her face, forces her into a car, drives off. I put a stopwatch on it. From the mouth of the cul-de-sac to the driveway to the front door, back to the car and out; add thirty seconds waiting for Alison to answer the door: one hundred and sixty-seven seconds total. And that's conservative."

"Who?"

Anne consulted her notes. "Raymond Fleck."

"Based on what? The tape?"

"No, his MO. He was convicted of rape eight years ago; what he did was knock on the woman's door in broad daylight. When she answered, he pointed a gun at her, shoved her in, raped her, left."

"Does one conviction constitute an MO?"

"He was convicted for one, but the arresting officers figured him for a half dozen others they couldn't get positive IDs on. Victims wouldn't come forward."

"Why take Alison with him?"

"The one time he was convicted, he stayed in the house for five hours. Made himself lunch between attacks. This time he didn't have five hours to enjoy himself; the husband was on his way home."

"If he did it for revenge, why not simply kill her and leave?"

"Where's the sport in that?"

She had a point. Still, did she have anything that made it more than a theory?

"He's free, isn't he?"

"I asked a stupid question." I admitted.

Anne studied Alison's photograph for a moment and then closed the album with a resounding thud. "Teeters brought me in because he was looking for an angle his people might have missed. I could convince him to let you in for the same reason."

"Would you?"

Anne pushed herself away from the desk. Her swivel chair was on wheels, and she rolled it slowly to a bank of beige-colored metal filing cabinets. From the third drawer of the middle cabinet Anne retrieved a file maybe three inches thick, the pages held together with a metal fastener. The label on the file cover listed Alison's name and the date of her disappearance. Anne dropped the file in front of me and started rummaging through the bottom right-hand drawer of her desk. She came up with a brown grocery bag and slipped the file into it, but not before I peeked under the cover and read the first page: Case #97-050819 Dakota County Sheriff's Department Alison Donnerbauer Emerton TABLE OF CONTENTS FELONY MURDER. The word COPY had been stamped in red several times across the page.

Anne folded the bag and tossed it for me to catch, explaining that since technically it wasn't a St. Paul or Ramsey County case, technically she wasn't violating department regulations by lending me her file. Technically.

"But I want it back. Without any rocket ships or baseball diamonds doodled in the margins," she said. "Meanwhile, I'll try to grease the skids for you with Teeters."

"You're being awfully cooperative, Annie," I told her.

She leaned across the desk and spoke slowly between clenched teeth. "I do not like it when women are killed simply because they are women. It is UN-AC-CEPT-ABLE."

Now you know why Anne Scalasi is the best in the business. It's not the training; it's not the experience. It's the outrage. She never lost it. The rest of us had. We were afraid of it, afraid of how it twisted our perceptions of the *real* world, afraid of the pain it made us feel. So we hid from it—hid behind bad jokes and out-and-out goofiness, hid behind booze and drugs and sex and macho behavior that bordered on the self-destructive until the outrage went away, leaving us numb. Not Anne. Anne did not hide from her outrage. She drew it like a gun.

"I'll tell you another thing," she said but never did. That's because she was interrupted by a detective, a black man whose reputation was also unfairly marred by an affirmative-action label.

"Yo, mama!" Martin McGaney called as he danced toward us, waving a folded piece of paper like a baton before him.

"Yo, mama?" I repeated quietly.

"This better be good, Martin," Anne warned as the detective approached. The warning was unnecessary. You could tell by the smile on his face.

"Lookee what I have," he said, drawing out the words, handing Anne the paper. It was an arrest warrant.

"You finally found the guy who stole my ten-speed when I was in high school," I ventured.

"Taylor, you'll appreciate this. You used to be a good investi-gator."

"Used to be?"

"When you were young."

"Ahh."

"The bastard who raped and murdered that woman in front of her twelve-year-old daughter a couple weeks back? I got 'im!" He pumped his fist as he said it.

The case had made daily headlines since the crime occurred. A woman and her daughter had been driving home from a movie late at night when their car broke down. A "good Samaritan" stopped to offer assistance. Some assistance. He forced the woman and the girl into his car at gunpoint, drove to a secluded spot, and raped the mother, threatening to shoot the daughter if the woman resisted. When he was finished, he told the daughter she was next. The mother went to protect her child, and he shot her dead. In a panic, he shoved both mother and daughter out of the car and drove off. The daughter described the well-dressed assailant in detail but not the car, telling the police only that it was dark and "sporty looking."

"I took the daughter with me," McGaney said. "She wanted desperately to help us find her mother's killer. We cruised the car dealerships on the I-494 strip, looking for a model she might recognize. We found it. A Ford Taurus GL."

"A Taurus is sporty looking?!"

"She's a little girl, what does she know from cars? Anyway, I obtained a list of every black or dark-blue Taurus in Minnesota from DMV, concentrating only on those vehicles owned by men who fit the age and general description the girl gave us. I found nineteen within five miles of where the woman's car had stalled. I questioned each one, telling them I was investigating a hit-and-run and wanted to see their vehicles. One guy told me he'd sold his. Yeah, he sold it all right. The day after the murder he practically gave it away to a guy in St. Cloud. I drove the girl up to St. Cloud. She said it looked like the same car, but what clinched it was the radio. One of the buttons was still set for the station the guy was playing when he raped the mother—a station you can't pick up in St. Cloud. The new owner allowed us to impound the car, and I had forensics do a search. They found bloodstains and strands of hair in the back seat. The samples were identical to the victim's."

"Nice," I told McGaney, and I meant it; he'd done a helluva job. "Very nice."

"Where is the daughter now?" Anne asked.

"At home, waiting for me to call her about a lineup."

"The county attorney?"

"Licking his chops."

"And the sorry sonuvabitch named in the warrant?"

McGaney smiled. "At his place of business."

Anne grinned, too—grinned like she'd just learned her own daughter had been named class valedictorian. She took a small school bell from her desk drawer and rang it vigorously. "Ticket to ride, boys! We have a ticket to ride!" she shouted across the room. The detectives, smiling just as incandescently, literally hopped up from behind their partitions and started holstering guns, fastening bulletproof Kevlar vests, and donning dark-blue windbreakers with the word POLICE spelled out in huge white letters on the back. Conversations grew louder, jokes flew; it was like a party had suddenly broken out. This was why most of the detectives had come to this line of work—to get the bad guys— and they were loving it.

Anne told one of the detectives to arrange for uniform backup.

"Backup? We don't need no stinking backup," another replied in an accent that was supposed to be Hispanic, paraphrasing a line from *The Treasure of the Sierra Madre.*

They headed for the door en masse, Anne leading the way.

I hadn't felt so excluded since my friends won the softball league championship the season after I retired from the team.

Cynthia Grey always greeted me the same way, like an old friend she hadn't seen since the last high-school reunion. This time she gave me a warm hug and happy smile in her office suite, located in a former cloister not far from the St. Paul PD. Her office manager didn't approve—not of the hug and certainly not of me. Once again I had arrived without an appointment, distracting Cynthia from the task at hand, which was the practice of law.

Cynthia was known in the Twin Cities for her stalwart defense of DWI suspects, and her quotes were often sought by the local media. Like MADD, she wanted them off the street. But unlike those militant enemies of drunk drivers everywhere, she wanted the lawbreakers in treatment, not in jail. However, it was a stunning victory in a single civil suit that had recently thrust her into the public eye.

She had filed a complaint against a women's clothing manufacturer on behalf of a dozen female employees, alleging that the company's TV and print ads—which always depicted women in a sexual context—fostered an environment inside the company that condoned, if not encouraged, sexual harassment. Stories about the suit appeared in several local and national publications, usually accompanied by a photograph of the women and their lawyer. You could always tell which woman was Cynthia. She was the beautiful one in back who wasn't smiling.

Anyway, the clothing manufacturer settled. No one knows for how much because the settlement was sealed. But it was big time. You could tell by the quality of the cars the plaintiffs went out and bought immediately afterward. Cynthia bought a car, too. And gave it to me. True, it was only a 1991 Dodge Colt—it was all I would accept—but, still, when was the last time your girlfriend bought you a car?

Which brings me back to Miss Efficiency, aka Desirée Smith, the office manager. The phone had been ringing nonstop since the settlement, and without her, Cynthia wouldn't have time for all that media schmoozing. Without her, Cynthia probably would be late for most of her court appearances and client meetings, few of her motions would be filed on time, and her highly organized brigade of freelance attorneys and legal assistants would become a confused rabble. Chaos would reign, and the firm would fall. At least, that's how Miss Efficiency sees it. And whenever I come along, well, there goes the schedule.

Cynthia led me by the hand into her inner sanctum, away from the office manager's disapproving gaze, and cleared an empty space for me on her file-cluttered leather sofa. She sat in a matching chair across from me.

Cynthia was wearing a black two-piece suit. The jacket was double-breasted with a shawl collar, the skirt was tight without being too tight and came to the top of her knees, and her blouse was white silk. Lately, that was all she wore. Black and white. I asked her about it once, and she said she was establishing a "definitive image all her own." More likely it was the definitive image of the consultant at the store where Cynthia bought most of her clothes. Not that I'm complaining. She looks stunning in black and white, with shoulder-length brown hair and matching eyes, with long, shapely legs. I've only known two women with more attractive legs. The first was my wife, who was killed along with our daughter nearly five years ago by a drunk driver who Cynthia, in fact, later defended. The second was a twenty-two-year-old murderer I fingered for the Minneapolis cops. She was killed while resisting arrest.

"So, are you working?" Cynthia asked.

It was an honest question. I'm a one-man band, and I usually take on only one case at a time, so I often suffer through periods of unemployment. Occasionally, when those droughts linger long enough to cause me financial distress, I'll obtain lists of unclaimed property from various government agencies and then locate the missing owners for a percentage of the property's value. Sometimes—when money is real tight—I'll do bounty work for a Minneapolis bail bondsman I know. Still, I can't kick. Last year—my best year yet—I worked one hundred and sixty-nine days and took home nearly thirty-six K after taxes, insurance, health care, and expenses. That might not sound like much. But when you live alone (without house or car payments) like I do, it's plenty.

"As a matter of fact I am working," I told Cynthia. "I'm trying to learn what happened to a woman who disappeared last October."

"I thought you didn't do runaways."

"This is a little different. The smart money bets the woman was murdered, but the police can't find a body or evidence of foul play. I was hired to come up with an explanation that the woman's attorney can live with."

"Who's the lawyer?"

"Ahh, well . . ." I stammered.

"Not Monica Adler?" Monica was Cynthia's most hated rival.

"No, no, no," I assured her. "I haven't seen Monica since— well, quite awhile. Why would I talk to her?"

"Good question."

"No, it's not her."

"Who, then?"

"He came to my office—"

"Who?"

"Hunter Truman."

"That piece of shit?"

"You've met?" I asked.

"Bastard works the court like a fucking whore; that's how he peels his banana."

"Do you eat with that mouth?"

Cynthia flushed a deep crimson and not just from embarrassment. I am always amused when Cynthia's carefully constructed facade of upper-class gentility slips and the street kid peeks over the top, but she certainly is not. She works hard—and pays a great deal of money—to make sure the facade never slips.

"I am surprised that you would deign to accept employment from that gentleman," she said, her voice calm and well modulated.

"A buck's a buck."

"If you are financially embarrassed, I could lend—"

"Oh, stop it," I told her. "It's a job like any other job, maybe a little more interesting than most."

"But Hunter Truman?!" Cynthia asked, making the name sound like a disease usually treated with penicillin.

"He's no worse than most of the lawyers I've worked for."

"It hurts me to hear you say that."

I have to admit it gave me a twinge, too, defending him.

"Will you forgive me if I buy lunch?" I asked.

"*I'll* buy lunch," Cynthia replied. "I don't want to be eating on that . . . gentleman's money." She opened her office door and announced, "Taylor and I are going to lunch."

"You're lunching with Judge Kennelly," Miss Efficiency corrected her.

"I am?"

"Twelve-thirty at Gallivan's. You need to leave in ten minutes."

Cynthia closed the door again. "Sorry," she said.

"It's okay," I told her. "Actually, I came over to invite you to the Twins game tonight. They're playing the hated Cleveland Indians."

"I have a meeting tonight."

"Who with?"

"My ETOS Club."

"ETOS?"

"It's a club several women and I started in law school. Once a month we get together and discuss the various sides of social issues. Exploring the Other Side, get it?"

"Yeah, I do. What kind of social issues?"

"Tonight we're discussing why men embrace sports so dearly."

"That's a social issue?"

"Why *do* men like sports? Give me an argument," Cynthia said.

"It's a better excuse for getting together than forming a lame club."

"I'm serious."

"So am I. Where are you holding this meeting?"

"Don't get angry."

"Why would I get angry?"

"One of the members arranged for a private suite at the Metrodome, along the third-base line."

"You're watching the ball game? From a private suite? With booze and food and instant replay on TV monitors?"

She grinned. "Want me to bring you a souvenir?"

three

The snow had killed them. Twenty-three inches of it. It had kept the heads of witnesses low and their eyes down. It had clouded windshields, giving drivers a colorless, out-of-focus view of the world. It had buried footprints and tire treads and any hope of deploying dogs. One investigator had suggested that Alison Donnerbauer Emerton could be facedown in her own backyard, and they wouldn't have known it until spring. But when spring finally came, Alison was not in her backyard. She wasn't in the grove behind her house. She wasn't in the fields bordering the street that lead to the cul-de-sac. She wasn't anywhere that the Dakota County Sheriff's Department could think to look.

All this was duly noted in Anne Scalasi's file. Hunter Truman was right; there wasn't much there. But the sheriff had obviously held back information from Truman—and the news media. As Edmond Locard, the great criminologist once said, "Every contact leaves a trace. The criminal must, of necessity, leave behind something at the scene of the crime." And this time what the criminal had left behind was a single surface footprint on the flat rubber mat just inside Alison's front door.

Anne's file contained a four-by-five photograph of the print. Forensics identified it as the design of an LA Gear Air System running shoe, left foot, size ten, men's. No wear could be detected on the tread, leading the detectives to conclude that it was new or little used. There was no depth to the impression and no second print, so the height and weight of the suspect couldn't be determined. However, Raymond Fleck wore size ten, and while no running shoes could be found among his possessions, that fact had excited the detectives to no end.

One piece of evidence that had been released to the news media was the small amount of blood discovered on the carpet just inside Alison's front door and the few drops found on the doorframe. Citing the shape of the drops and the laws of flow dynamics, forensics concluded that the victim was standing just inside the door when she was struck hard enough to cause instantaneous bleeding and that the force of the blow splashed the frame and carpet. The blood was Type A Positive. Same as Alison's. And it had been there less than twenty-four hours. It supported Anne's theory about a shove in. Other than that . . .

Officers had searched every room in the house three times, using spirals and zones and strip patterns, and came up empty. No hair samples that did not belong to Alison or her husband. No fibers that weren't accounted for. No unexplained dirt or stains. There were plenty of unidentified fingerprints, but most were in high-traffic areas where you would expect them: the kitchen, the living room. There were none on the door or the doorframe. And none that matched Raymond Fleck's.

The detectives who searched Alison's purse had found the note. The single word, SOON was printed with an ordinary crayon on common white typing paper and placed in a standard number-ten envelope; the examiners at the BCA laughed when they were asked for a handwriting analysis. The detectives had also found Alison's gun. It hadn't been fired. The detectives traced it to a sporting goods store in Bloomington. An employee there remembered Alison.

"She wanted a .357. Everyone wants a cannon these days," the employee recalled. "They see the cowboys usin' 'em on TV, so they figure they gotta have one. Only I knew she couldn't handle it, so I convinced her to go with the smaller caliber, go with the .22 Iver Johnson. She was disappointed, and I thought I might lose the sale until I explained that you hit a guy with a .22 and you're going to stop him, no doubt about it, but you probably won't kill him unless you take out a vital organ. She thought that was good."

There was nothing else in her purse that should not have been there. Each item was carefully logged. Truman had been correct; Alison's ID, cash, ATM card, credit cards, and checkbook were all intact.

And that was it. The photographer had taken his photographs, the sketcher had made his sketches, the measurer had taken his measurements, the evidence man had tagged and preserved his evidence, and the master notetaker had written down in shorthand the observations and descriptions offered by all the others. It all added up to zero. This lack of clues didn't surprise me. In a murder, it's the victim who supplies the most information—and our victim was not to be found.

As for witnesses: The bulk of Anne's file consisted of verbatim statements made by 137 people who had been interviewed in the course of the investigation, many of them more than once. Some of the reports were badly written and incomplete. Others were paragons of clarity and brevity. I read them all, listing the names and addresses of a dozen or so witnesses who had the most to say about the case in my own notebook. I would interview these myself.

I was sitting at my dining room table, the pages of the file freed from the fastener and organized in front of me. Ogilvy, my gray-and-white French lop-eared rabbit, lounged at my feet, munching day-old popcorn.

A photograph was included in the file, an eight-by-ten color glossy of two women dressed in period costumes. Turn-of-the-century European, I guessed. The woman in the background, dark hair, dark visage, seemed formidable but confused—anger without focus. Her hand rested on the shoulder of a younger woman in the foreground. The younger woman was Alison.

I set the photograph aside yet found myself returning to it several times while I read the file, picking it up and studying it and tossing it down again only to reach for it a few minutes later. This was a different Alison than the woman in the black-and-white photograph. This Alison was no mysterious femme fatale, a seductress framed in shadow. This Alison was soft and vulnerable and desperate. You could feel her throat tightening around some great, indescribable pain. And her eyes, her spectacular blue-green eyes, were almost too painful to contemplate, yet I kept looking into them, couldn't stop looking into them.

One of the women who'd been interviewed was an actress named Marie Audette. She had been close to Alison when they both toiled for the University of Minnesota theater company. I guessed that the photo was taken in connection with a student performance. I set it next to the black and white Truman had given me. Identical faces, yet it was hard to believe it was the same woman. One so confident. The other so fearful. I wondered which had been taken first.

I was debating whether to sift through the entire file a third time when the telephone rang. The Twins and Indians were on the radio, Hall of Fame broadcaster Herb Carneal doing the play-by-play, and I turned down the volume before answering the phone.

"Have it solved, yet?" Anne Scalasi asked.

"The butler did it with a candlestick in the library."

"Now, why didn't I think of that?"

"How'd the roundup go?"

"No muss, no fuss," Anne replied. "McGaney's pissed, though. The killer gave up without a struggle."

"So you had to take him alive, huh? Bummer."

"You believe it? He kept the gun! You *never* keep the gun. Any idiot who ever watched an episode of *Perry Mason* knows you never keep the gun."

"The declining grade of criminal we get these days, Annie; I fear for the future of the Republic. Did you speak with Teeters?"

"I did. He agreed to let you in."

"Great."

"Desperate men will do desperate things. He'll meet you at eight tomorrow morning at the scene; he doesn't want you seen hanging around the station. Only, keep it quiet. Teeters has taken a beating over this case. The last thing he needs is for the media to get involved again. Especially your friend Beamon at the Minneapolis paper."

"Beamon is no friend of mine."

"Then why does he keep asking about you every time I see him? He asked about you again this afternoon when we brought in the killer."

"He thinks we're having an affair."

"Set him straight, will you?"

"I have. But the more I tell him we're just good friends, the less he believes it. I don't know what else to do."

"You could marry Cynthia."

"There's a thought."

The other end of the phone went dead silent, and for a moment I thought we had been cut off.

"Annie?"

"I was joking," she said.

"So was I," I told her.

"I'm going home to bed. It's late."

"Thanks, Annie," I told her.

"One thing, Taylor," she said. "If you learn anything, anything at all . . ."

"I'll tell Teeters first and then you."

"Good night, Taylor."

"Good night, sleep tight, and don't let the pom-poms bite."

"Pom-poms?"

"Just something my daughter used to say."

four

Alison Donnerbauer Emerton had been a loner and not always by choice. It wasn't that she'd lacked charm or social grace; many of the 137 witnesses the Dakota County cops had interviewed testified that she'd had plenty of both. Her problem was IQ. She was tested at 172, 32 points above genius. She graduated high school at sixteen, earned her bachelor's at eighteen and her master's at nineteen. She was younger, smarter, and more attractive than most of her peers. What other reasons did people need to resent her?

This resentment permeated the statements made by the witnesses: *"You'd think she would have known better." "I guess she wasn't so smart after all." "She was always too smart for her own good."* Crap like that. According to the file, Alison had forged only two long-lasting friendships in her lifetime, both with women she hadn't seen or spoken with for at least one month prior to her disappearance. Which is why I found no irony in her choice of profession. Perhaps by working in public relations she'd hoped to gain what she seemed to lack in her private life: personal attachments. But that's just a guess, the amateur psychologist talking. And maybe I was projecting too much of my own life into the theory. I, too, was basically friendless—except for Anne and Cynthia and, truth be told, I wasn't all that sure of Cynthia. After my wife and daughter were killed, I shed my friends the way you would change from a summer wardrobe to winter: quitting the cops to work in a one-man office, retiring from playing softball and hockey, spending my days solving the problems of strangers. But unlike Alison, who seemed desperate to connect with other people, lately I was disconnecting, keeping them at long distance. Again, the amateur psychologist talking.

What I did find ironic was Alison's choice of homes. If you wanted to avoid people—and I don't think she did—this was a good place to live. The house was located well outside of Hastings, about a forty-minute drive from St. Paul, on a dead-end road that I missed twice, in a forest that resembled Itasca State Park more than a simple grove of trees. Only six homes shared the cul-de-sac, built at least an acre apart. I parked in front of a large colonial with cedar shakes. The one with the patrol car in the driveway.

Sheriff Ed Teeters approached me with an irritated expression and a clenched fist. He was bigger than I am, but who isn't? Size does not impress me, though. After nearly fifteen years of studying the martial arts, I learned that the maxim my father taught me while I was growing up small was God's own truth: *The bigger they are, the harder they fall.*

"Late!" Teeters yelled at me. "Nothing better to do but hang around here all morning?"

"I got lost," I informed him, and Teeters instantly calmed himself.

"Happens," he said, and I wondered if he had once taken the same wrong turn himself.

"Lieutenant Scalasi says you have her file," he said.

I waited for him to continue until I realized that he had asked a question. "Yes," I answered.

"Heard the tape?"

"Yes."

"Opinion?"

"Not yet."

"Good man," the sheriff said. "Lieutenant Scalasi said you were a good man. Said you worked homicide in St. Paul for four years."

"Closer to five," I corrected him.

"How many murders you catch?"

"Ninety-six."

"How many you clear?"

"Ninety-one."

"Which ones you remember most?"

"The five that got away."

Teeters nodded, sighing like a stage actor, and leaned against my car, his eyes fixed on the colonial. "Some people, they get killed, you say good riddance—know what I mean? It's a terrible thing, but that's what you say 'cuz . . . Hell, you've been a cop."

I nodded, understanding completely.

"This time around . . . this is the one that haunts you. You don't solve it, you don't bring the killer down, it haunts you to your grave. That's why you're here. Normally I'd kick your PI ass back up Highway 61 for interfering in an ongoing investigation. But Lieutenant Scalasi vouches for you, and what the hell, there's no investigation to mess up. We ain't got squat."

"If I learn anything, you're the first to know, even before my client," I volunteered.

"Be quiet about it. Don't come by the shop. Keep the phone calls down. Had it up to here with media types. Way some of them bastards act, you'd think I did it."

And that was all the sheriff had to say.

I accompanied Teeters to his car. He stared at the house as he walked, then lingered in the driveway. He seemed reluctant to leave.

"I became a cop after I got my honorable from the army because I couldn't think of what else to do," he said bitterly. "Still can't." Then he climbed into his car and drove away.

I peeked through a window. The house was empty of furniture. Only the bare walls and carpet were on display behind the glass. That's when I noticed the FOR SALE sign protruding from the center of the front lawn. I had been there fifteen minutes, and that was the first I noticed the sign.

You've got a real eye for detail, I told myself and circled the house twice, forcing myself to concentrate on every little thing.

Behind the house was a large kennel, maybe thirty feet long and fifteen feet wide, surrounded by a high cyclone fence. The kennel was empty, too. I went past it and followed a path deep into the grove. The grove was denser than I expected, and several times I was forced to wrestle with trees and bushes that snagged my sports jacket. The undergrowth was brutal, and I began to think, *Yeah, the county cops searched the grove but how thoroughly?* I finally stopped at the small pond Alison had described on the cassette and sat under the oak tree on the knoll overlooking it. "How deep is the water?" I mused aloud and then dismissed the question. The cops had dragged the pond as soon as the ice went out.

I sat under the tree a long time, thinking it over. Teeters's investigation was solid, and whatever cracks there were Anne Scalasi had already filled in. What was left for me to do, besides waste Hunter Truman's money? I was ready to quit the case, and I hadn't even started.

C'mon, make an effort, I told myself.

I began thinking about Truman. And the tape.

The tape.

The footprint.

The problems at Kennel-Up.

The report from the officers who questioned Raymond Fleck outside Alison's house.

Fleck's record.

It all pointed to Fleck, and in less enlightened times he probably would have been strung up by now. Still, ignore the tape and what do you have? You have Stephen Emerton. Yes, the Dakota County cops would have learned about Fleck eventually, but would he have been the number one suspect? No. It would have been the husband. At least he would have been first on my dance card. We always kill the ones we love. At least we do eighty percent of the time. And based on the cassette recording, Alison and Emerton didn't seem all that close. Think about it.

The house.

Stephen Emerton was selling it. Alison had said he didn't like living there. Could that be a motive for murder? Hell, I knew a guy who murdered his wife for pouring melted cheddar cheese over his broccoli. "She knows I like colby," he'd confessed.

The timing.

Emerton had left his office at five P.M. Say it usually takes him forty-five minutes to drive home; assume the snow slows him down, add another fifteen, twenty. During that long drive he gets an idea, or maybe he already had the idea and the snow merely gives him an opportunity. At six he meets Alison at the door, clubs her with the proverbial blunt object, tosses her body into the grove, knowing the snow would hide it soon enough, knowing he could dispose of it at his leisure, knowing the cops would suspect Fleck. Then he reports Alison missing. Could he do all that in a quarter hour? Sure, he could. And the Minnesota Twins might win another World Series in my lifetime.

Still . . .

He could have hired it done. Teeters had examined Emerton's financial records, but he didn't find any suspicious movements of money.

Still . . .

If you were going to clutch at a straw, Stephen Emerton was as good as any.

I had brought Alison Donnerbauer Emerton's photograph with me. Not the black-and-white job Truman had given me but rather the colored glossy from Anne's file. I don't know why I'd brought it, but I had. It was in an envelope. I slipped it out and stole a look at it, starting at the bottom, moving up over the bodice to the lace collar around Alison's throat to her pointed chin to her thin lips to her slightly crooked nose to her brilliant blue-green eyes filled with pain and—now I saw—a kind of hopelessness. No matter how I handled the photograph, no matter what angle I held it at, those eyes seemed always to stare right at me. After a few minutes I shoved the photograph back into the envelope and turned toward the house. Teeters was right. Some cases do haunt you.

Eventually I made my way back to the house, stopping at the empty kennel. "What happened to the dogs?" I wondered aloud.

"Gonna call me every time you have a brainstorm?" Teeters wanted to know.

"No, I just wanted—"

"Taylor, I read Sherlock Holmes, too. The neighbors did not report hearing the dogs bark the day Alison disappeared, but that's not necessarily significant. The dogs were well trained, they rarely barked at anyone. A couple of the neighbors didn't even know Alison kept dogs, they were that quiet."

"Where are the Labs now?"

"Doggie heaven. Emerton put 'em down six months ago."

five

"This sorta thing never happened when I was a boy," Arlen Selmi informed me in his office at Kennel-Up, Inc. "People didn't have to be afraid of strangers, didn't have to lock their doors."

That was nonsense, of course. When Selmi was a boy, Al

Capone, John Dillinger, Machine Gun Kelly, Baby Face Nelson, Pretty Boy Floyd, and the Ma Barker gang had turned the Midwest into a free-fire zone, slaughtering citizens with the same ferocity as street gangs and drug cartels do now. Kidnapping had been a cottage industry. And sensational murders—Sigmund Freud explaining to a jury why a man would slice his wife into tiny pieces with a razor blade and feed her to the fish—occurred with the same numbing regularity that we see today. But I didn't question Selmi's recollections. Nor did I doubt that he actually believed the decade of his childhood was somehow safer, simpler, and less foreboding than our present era; lots of people who spend more time looking backward than looking forward—especially the elderly—have come to the same conclusion. Still, I wondered if it was the circumstances of his youth that he recalled or just his own optimism.

Arlen Selmi had adored Alison, loved her like she was his own daughter. I know because he told me so. Several times. His eyes glossed over and his throat tightened around the words as he spoke, and I thought about Hunter Truman and began to wonder what was it about Alison that made grown men all misty-eyed and introspective. Yet it soon became apparent that if I had asked, Selmi would not have been able to identify the color of Alison's hair. Oh, he could've described in wistful detail the virtues of a WAC lieutenant he was sweet on when he was stationed in North Africa. Or the curves and lines of a female welder he'd shacked up with for three weeks following VE Day. But Alison, "that sweet child," was only a blur in his mind's eye. Time had zipped by Arlen Selmi like a comet, taking the present with it and leaving only the past.

"His senility—I'd guess you'd call it that—it became pronounced soon after Alison disappeared," Sarah Selmi advised me. "I don't know if there's a connection; maybe so. He partly blames himself for hiring Raymond in the first place."

Arlen still carried the titles of president and CEO at Kennel-Up, but it was Sarah, Arlen's granddaughter, who actually ran the company, gladly taking on the responsibility when the rest of her family showed no interest. More than that, she lived with her grandfather, took care of him, brought him to work each day, and ferociously fought her family's efforts to have the old man committed—despite the fact that she was not mentioned in his will, only her father.

"My father does not love his father," she confided in me. "I understand that because I do not love my father, either. But I love that old man. Why is that? How can love skip a whole generation?"

I told her I didn't know and quickly urged her back to the subject. It's not that I didn't care. It's just that her problems had nothing to do with my problems. Okay, I admit I don't always rate high on the sensitivity meter, but I make it a practice never to visit other people's lives unless I'm paid for it. I don't like to get involved.

I asked Sarah about Raymond Fleck. I still preferred the husband, but since I was already in Hastings, I decided to ask a few questions at Kennel-Up first and interview Stephen Emerton that evening.

"Talk about love and hate, I hate Raymond Fleck's guts, yet I've never met him," Sarah replied. "I hate what he did to Alison, and I wish they would put him away forever."

"Do you think he killed her?"

"I don't know. The papers say he did and so does Grandfather. But most of the people around here say no," Sarah replied. "Yet, even if he didn't kill her, he did stalk her. Men think they can treat women however they wish, and that's crap. And they do it to all of us. *All of us.* I don't know of a single woman who wasn't frightened or harassed at least once in her life by a man. Not one. When

I was going for my MBA, I had this professor; he called me into his office, said I should be nice to him, put his hands on me, tore my blouse when I pushed him away. I took it to the administration, but nothing happened, nothing changed. He's still there, and I had to transfer to the U. Bastard."

"Did Alison tell you about Fleck?"

"No, Grandfather did. Alison, she didn't speak very much. After my grandfather fired Raymond, I tried to be Alison's friend. Went out of my way to be her friend, mostly because she didn't seem to have any other friends around here. One woman, a secretary, actually drew up a petition to have her dismissed. I intercepted it before it reached Grandfather. But Alison, she kept her distance. She didn't even mention the phone calls or the dead roses; I didn't learn about those until the police came to investigate. Poor Alison. Lord, I hate Raymond Fleck."

"What about the woman, the secretary?"

"I hate her, too. Give me an excuse to gas her, any excuse that won't piss off my other employees."

"What's her name?"

"Irene Brown."

I recognized the name instantly. Raymond Fleck's lover. His alibi.

Irene Brown reluctantly agreed to speak with me in the employee's cafeteria, which was little more than a cramped one-window room filled with two round tables, a dozen chairs, and a bank of vending machines. She didn't want to be there and probably would not have been if Sarah Selmi hadn't hovered over her like a grade-school principal. As it was, she remained defiant, answering questions with questions, giving me the same story she'd given the

Dakota County deputies, daring me to contradict her. And when Sarah left the cafeteria to attend to business, Irene announced, "I'm not talking to you anymore."

I pumped a couple of quarters into a vending machine and pressed the button marked Dr Pepper. "Want anything?" I asked as the can rolled into the tray.

"Didn't you hear me? I said I'm not answering any more questions."

I opened the can and drank a generous portion of the sweet liquid. When I finished drinking I asked her, "How big are your feet?"

"What?"

"How big are your feet?"

Irene looked at me like I was a few raisins short of a cookie.

"You love Raymond, don't you?"

Irene Brown was a large woman, six feet and overweight, with about as much sparkle as a cubic zirconia that's gone through the washing machine a few times. She took a chair and pushed it violently across the room, and for a moment the chair became Alison. "Yes, I love him," Irene answered, the clattering chair punctuating her remark.

"And you would do anything for him?"

"Anything."

I took another slow sip of the Dr Pepper.

"So tell me, how big are your feet?"

"Why is that important?" she asked, and when she did, I suddenly realized just how important the question was. I couldn't even tell you where it came from except my wife used to wear my discarded Nikes when she worked her garden, and they fit her fine.

"After Raymond was fired, Alison began receiving harassing

phone calls. She also received some rather unsavory gifts, like a dead cat—"

"Raymond had nothing to do with that."

"One day she found dead flowers on her desk."

"I told you, Raymond had nothing—"

"How did the flowers get there, Irene? Who put them there?"

"What are you saying?"

I drained the remaining Dr Pepper and tossed the empty can into a recycle bin. *Wait for it, wait for it,* I told myself as I surveyed the candy bars behind the glass face of a second vending machine.

"Are you saying I put the dead roses on Alison's desk?"

"I never said they were roses," I answered, feigning disinterest.

Irene didn't miss a beat. "Everyone knows they were roses," she told me.

"I guess," I said taking the change from my pocket and counting it. "Do you have a dime I can borrow?"

"No I don't have a fucking dime," was Irene's curt reply.

I sighed heavily and slid the change back into my pants pocket. "So, Irene," I asked casually. "How big are your feet?"

"Goddammit, there you go again."

"It's like this, Irene," I told her. "I think you're lying about being with Raymond between five and seven the day Alison disappeared."

"I don't care."

"The cops don't believe you, either."

"I don't care!"

"But you see, unlike the cops, I don't think you're lying to protect Raymond, no ma'am. I think you're lying to protect yourself."

Irene didn't have an answer for that.

"You hated Alison, didn't you?"

Irene nodded.

"You hated her because she was so much more attractive and so much smarter than you are."

"She was a bitch."

"And Raymond wanted her, didn't he?"

"It wasn't like that."

"You and Raymond were lovers, weren't you? And then Alison came along and that changed. Isn't that why you hated her so much?"

"No! No, I hated her for what she did to Raymond."

"What did she do to Raymond?"

"She ruined his life."

"You mean she ruined *your* life."

"No, that's not what I mean."

"How big are your feet, Irene?"

"Go to hell!" she retorted and strode swiftly from the cafeteria.

I chuckled quietly and made a few notes in the pad I carry, enormously pleased with myself. I had made it up. All of it. Made it up as I went along without thought or consideration, and damned if I didn't uncover a viable suspect both Teeters and Annie had missed.

"Must be divine inspiration," I mused.

"Beginning to annoy me," Ed Teeters said over the telephone.

"Are you running surveillance on Irene Brown?" I asked.

"No."

"Maybe you should put a team on her for a couple of days."

"Why?"

"In case she tries to unload some incriminating evidence. A pair of running shoes, for example."

There was a long pause on the other end, and I could almost hear the wheels turning inside the sheriff's head. "Thought of that," he muttered. "Tried to get paper for a search. Judge said no go. Said he doesn't authorize fishing expeditions. I'm listening," he said more loudly, and I told him of my conversation with Irene, told him that originally I hadn't suspected her at all.

"I was trying to get her to open up about Fleck. Usually, you accuse someone of a crime they didn't commit, and they'll fall all over themselves trying to prove they're innocent. I was hoping she'd talk about Fleck. She didn't."

"Means nothing," Teeters concluded.

"I know. But here's the thing. I pressed her for her shoe size. She wouldn't tell me. Instead, she kept asking why I needed to know. I wouldn't say, and that made her angry. Now, she's going to think about it. She's going to think about it long and hard. She's going to realize we have a footprint."

"Guilty, might try to dispose of the evidence. That the bet?"

"It's a long shot," I agreed.

He chortled. "Couldn't possibly be that easy."

SIX

I found Raymond Fleck kneeling in the dirt with a knife in his hand. He was trimming a roll of sod and using the strips he cut to fill a hole next to the sidewalk. Laying sod, digging holes, clearing brush piles: grunt work for a landscaper in North Minneapolis. Apparently it was the only employment he could find.

The knife blade reflected the sun as I approached. Despite the knife, Raymond did not look like Mr. Stranger Danger. He looked small and harmless in his dirty T-shirt and jeans, almost childish. And although he worked every day in the sun, his face had a gray tint you don't see on a well man.

"Raymond Fleck?" I asked.

His whole body sagged at the question. He dropped the knife atop the sod and wiped his hands on his shirt. "It's never going to end, is it," he said in a sad voice. It wasn't a question. It was a declaration. He was a man resigned to his fate, more pitiful than frightening.

Raymond was calm but watchful. His eyes looked around me, never at me, as if he were expecting someone else to come for him. He assumed I was a cop, but I corrected that assumption right away. In Raymond Fleck's world, the cops were bad guys. I wanted him to believe I was the Lone Ranger riding to his rescue. So after showing him my ID, I told him I was working for a client who was convinced that Stephen Emerton had killed Alison. Fleck's demeanor brightened considerably. At last, someone who believed.

"Alison hated her husband," Raymond said. "She wanted a divorce, but she couldn't get one because she came from a very strict Catholic family."

"She told you that?" I asked.

"Yes."

"When?"

He shook his head.

"Tell me about your relationship," I urged.

"We loved each other."

"Did you?"

"I thought we did."

"You're not sure?"

"I'm not sure of anything anymore."

"Tell me what happened, Ray." I gave his shoulder a reassuring pat.

"There weren't any lightning flashes or fireworks or anything like that," Raymond confided. "It happened slowly. She would touch my hand or look at me without speaking and then look away. I thought it was just my imagination; she couldn't possibly be interested in a guy like me. Except she was. She told me so at lunch that first time, the first time we went together. She had invited me to lunch. She said she wanted to talk about—I don't know—some project, only we didn't talk about work. We talked about . . . I guess we talked about us. She told me she was unhappy in her marriage, but she didn't know what to do about it, and I told her I was seeing Irene Brown, but I didn't really care about her, and then she smiled and squeezed my hand and said at least we had each other, and we began to see each other on the sly. Mostly lunches. A lot of lunches, okay? Nothing came of it. I mean, they weren't nooners or nothing. We didn't make love. But the talking, it was almost better than sex. She was so fantastic. I couldn't wait to see her, couldn't wait to hear her voice, and when I did I couldn't take my eyes off her, couldn't stop listening."

"Did Alison know about your prison record?"

Raymond shook his head sadly. "It's not something you talk about," he admitted.

"But she found out."

"Yeah, that night."

"Tell me about that night," I prompted.

"She told me to park outside her house, and she would meet me after Stephen went to bed. I told her that was a dangerous idea, but she insisted. She said she had to see me. *Had to see me,*" he repeated as if he could scarcely believe it even now. "So I parked in front of her house, but Stephen saw me and called the police."

"Stephen did?" I asked, knowing that Alison had made the call; she said so on the tape, and the police report confirmed it.

"Yes, and when they came—well, Alison had to deny she had

invited me; she had to protect her marriage and her reputation; she was Catholic, you see. She told Mr. Selmi what happened for the same reason."

"What did Selmi tell you?"

"He fired me. Had to, I guess. After what happened before."

"What happened before?"

"People . . . people around the office, they suspected that Alison and I were having an affair, you know, and that was hard on her—a woman trying to make it in a man's world, people talking behind her back, I mean. One day people were talking about it, around the coffee machine, I guess. I don't know. And old-man Selmi overheard and asked Alison, 'What's this?' What could she say? A good Catholic girl. So she said, you know, that I was harassing her, said it to protect herself. I understood that. Anyway, Old-man Selmi decided to have one of his fireside chats with me."

"What did he say?"

"Said I shouldn't dip my quill in the company ink well."

"There's leadership for you," I said sarcastically. Raymond didn't catch it. "What happened next?"

"Then Alison invited me over to her place; told me she wanted to explain why she said what she did. But Stephen called the cops. See, when the cops came that night, they checked my record, and Alison found out about—Anyway, that's why she turned on me. God, how long am I going to have to pay for that? One mistake, one lousy mistake . . ."

Raymond began to sob at the injustice of it all. I was grateful for the chance to step away, to pretend to give him some privacy. How long would he have to pay for raping a woman? At least as long as she did, I hoped. I'd read the report; I knew what he had done to her. How he rang her doorbell, and when she answered, he punched her in the face with the barrel of a gun and knocked her down and tied a gag over her mouth and raped her for five long hours, removing the gag only when he wanted her to wet his dick. Raymond had been arrested soon afterward, and when it became clear that the victim would testify, he pleaded down to second-degree criminal sexual conduct. He was sentenced to twenty-one months and served fourteen—it was his first conviction. And while in prison Raymond finished his education; several job interviews were waiting when he got out. He was fine. The woman still hasn't recovered.

During the first few years after the attack, she was paralyzed with fear, actually carrying two knives with her when she moved through her apartment. She sold her home; she couldn't live there anymore. Her TV was never off because she didn't want anyone to know if she was awake or asleep. Her lights were never off, either. She slept with them on—not just one or two, but all of them—averaging about three to four hours' sleep a night. She would get anxiety attacks driving home from work, panicking at every stoplight, desperate to reach her apartment before sundown. She never went out after dark. Never. Instead, she had holed up in her apartment with its reinforced doors and half-dozen locks and furniture arranged so that it was impossible to walk in a straight line, furniture with bells attached that rang when you bumped into it.

She found support from a small group of women who had also been raped. That had helped. And eventually time worked its magic, and she began to heal; she started to put that terrible day behind her. She started to go out. She started socializing again, although she still viewed each man she met as a potential threat. Then Alison disappeared, and Raymond Fleck's photograph became a regular feature on TV and in the newspapers, and she was right back where she started.

And Raymond? Raymond got treatment. Raymond learned how

to control his anger. In an effort to deflect accusations that he had killed Alison, he agreed to a newspaper interview. In the interview he talked about the therapy he underwent, the Transitional Sex Offender Program, and how it had made a new man of him. The reporter was very sympathetic and pointed out that the average rapist is charged with three or more sex crimes. But not Raymond. Raymond was cured. The system had worked. Praise the Lord.

Raymond was still weeping when I went back to him and put my hand on his shoulder. I was unmoved by his tears. I know a guy, whenever his contact lenses become dry, he forces himself to cry to rewet them; that's how much I believe in tears.

"It's okay, Ray, it's all right," I told him. What was it the political adviser said? *"Sincerity is everything. If you can fake that, you've got it made."*

Raymond rested his hand on mine for a moment and then brushed away his tears.

"What happened between you and Alison after you were fired?" I asked him.

"Nothing."

"You didn't tell Alison you were going to get her?"

"No, of course not."

"She received harassing phone calls."

"Not from me," Raymond insisted.

"The police pulled your telephone records. You called her several times at her home, at her office."

"I called her only a couple times. I had to—you know—talk to her, but she always hung up."

"You called her twenty-two times," I reminded him.

"No, I didn't," he insisted. "I only called her a couple times. Three times, four times."

"The records say twenty-two."

"The records are wrong."

"Could anyone else have called her from your phone?"

"No."

"Irene Brown?"

"Why would she call?"

"I don't know, why would she?"

Raymond didn't answer.

"You were seeing her when Alison came along," I told him.

"Yeah," Raymond confirmed.

"And you started seeing each other again after Alison had you fired."

"Irene was very kind to me; I didn't know how good I had it."

"Irene hated Alison," I told him.

"No, she didn't."

"That's what she said."

"You spoke to her?"

"I have a question for you, Ray. When Irene volunteered to provide you with an alibi for the time that Alison disappeared, when she said she was going to protect you from the police, did it ever occur to you that she was actually providing an alibi for herself, that she was protecting herself?"

"What is this? You said Emerton did it. Why are you accusing Irene?"

"I didn't say Irene—"

"You're accusing Irene! You're trying to get me to rat out Irene!"

"You have to consider—"

"Get away from me! I don't have to talk to you, you're not a cop. You just get away from me. Go on!"

Raymond scooped up the sod knife and threatened me with it. Oh, I was tempted, God knows. But I liked how this investigation was turning out, and I didn't want to endanger it by breaking every bone in Raymond Fleck's face.

"Some other time, Ray," I told him as I walked away.

seven

"Only in Minnesota."

I shook my head and stood dumbfounded outside the large and handsome split-level office building before me, home of the Metropolitan Mosquito Control District.

"Only in Minnesota," I repeated.

Only in Minnesota, a state well-known for its ability to marshal together whatever resources were necessary to solve the least of our problems, would the legislature budget over ten million hard-earned tax dollars to kill mosquitoes. I am as opposed to the evil insect as the next fellow. But ten million bucks? Seventy-five full-time employees? A shiny new office building? Cars and trucks and helicopters? Say it ain't so, Joe. But it is. Some well-meaning quality-of-life researchers discovered that on any given summer evening, the average Minnesotan is assaulted by four to five mosquitoes per five minutes. Upon hearing this news, our normally fractious state politicians rose as one: Forget the economy! Forget the environment! Forget the declining educational system! All work at the state capitol ceased until a bureaucracy was created— the seven-county Metropolitan Mosquito Control District—for the sole purpose of reducing mosquito attacks to only two bites per five minutes. Good Lord, how they must have celebrated that piece of legislation. Then they had the temerity to level the Midway Car Wash on University Avenue in St. Paul (where I worked as a kid) to make room for the damn thing. Is it any wonder that I was one cranky pup by the time a bored receptionist pointed me toward Stephen Emerton's office?

I stood beside Emerton's open door for a few moments, playing mental tricks to improve my disposition before I started questioning him. Anger and frustration creates a tense atmosphere, and a witness, sensing those emotions, will tighten up and shut up. It's a problem I've grappled with most of my career. It's the reason why Anne Scalasi conducted most of our interrogations while I stood in the background, looking surly.

"Mr. Emerton?" I finally asked, rapping softly on the open door and addressing the man inside.

"Aww, man!" he said, tossing a pencil on a map spread out on his desktop. "Not again!"

"Sir?"

"You're a cop, ain'tcha?"

"Private investigator," I replied and showed him my photostat.

"You work for that insurance company, don't you?"

I would have told him no if he had given me the chance, but he didn't, so I figured what the hell.

"What more do you guys want from me?" he continued.

"I'd like to ask you a few questions concerning your wife's disappearance."

"More questions? Christ, that bitch is gonna haunt me forever, isn't she? Aww, man, I'm tired of it. I'm just so fuckin' tired of it."

I tried to mask my disapproval of him, convinced people would not say such stupefying things if they could hear the sound of their own voices.

"We can speak another time," I suggested, although I made no move to leave.

"No, no," he answered, waving me toward a chair. "Now's as good a time as any."

Stephen Emerton was not the sharpest knife in the drawer by any means. Insulting a murder victim in front of an investigator wasn't the brightest thing a suspect could do, for example—it tends to arouse suspicion. Still, he was tall and handsome and splendidly tanned; he looked like someone who measured his biceps twice a week. I could see how a lonely young woman might find him attractive. And then there was the paper displayed in frames behind him. Diplomas from the University of Minnesota. BA. MA. And a certificate declaring his membership in Phi Beta Kappa. Only he didn't speak like a key holder. He spoke like a guy who spent his spare time calling talk radio programs.

"I don't mean to be rude," Emerton told me. "It's just that I am sick and tired of answerin' questions about my wife, okay? I mean, I have problems of my own, okay? I can't sell my house unless I practically give it away. The insurance company won't pay off on my claim; one day it's because without a body I can't prove Alison is dead and the next it's because they think I killed her—shit, make up your mind. And my friends, suddenly they're all too busy to check out a ball game or go out for a beer, and you know why. It's because of Alison, damn her."

I felt the anger start in my stomach and work up. I fought to keep it down.

"Don't get me wrong," Emerton continued. "I'm sorry she's dead. But hell's bells, man, give me a break. People make out like she was Mary Poppins or somethin'. She was cheatin' on me, you know? Forget that sexual harassment shit. She was sleepin' with that little jerkoff, and when he started gettin' serious, she burned him. That's why he did her, man. Any idiot can see that. It's not like she didn't deserve it."

I envisioned Alison's photograph, which was sitting on the front seat of my car, and thought about the expression on her face, the look of incredible despair in her eyes. Then I thought about how much fun it would be to pop Stephen Emerton in the mouth. I stood up.

"What? You leavin'? I thought you had questions to ask."

Self-control. You need self-control in my business. I reminded myself of that as I moved to the large map hanging on the wall, a map of the seven counties that make up the Minneapolis–St. Paul metropolitan area. About two dozen pins were stuck in it. Red flags were attached to the pins.

"What do these represent?" I asked.

"Targets of opportunity," Emerton explained. "Quick lesson: A female mosquito—the female mosquito is the only one that bites, did you know that?—a female mosquito bites you and sucks your blood so it can lay eggs containin' about three hundred baby mosquitoes. Follow? The eggs then turn into larvae. Now, larvae live in water. A tablespoon at the bottom of a beer can is enough, but the more the better. Are you still with me? Okay, a larva is transformed into what we call a pupa. A pupa is like a cocoon. It's in a pupa that the mosquito becomes a mosquito. What we do is, we gas the suckers while they're still in the larval and pupal stages. Those flags, those are low-lyin' swamp areas where we're takin' 'em out."

"What is this blue flag?" I asked, pointing to a pin surrounded by red.

"Oh, that's what this guy works for . . . Where does that jerkoff work?" he asked himself, searching his desktop, finding a business card. "The Mosquito and Fly Research Unit at the Medical and Veterinary Entomology Research Laboratory of the Agricultural Research Service of the U.S. Department of Agriculture. He's a wimp. He thinks he can get rid of mosquitoes with genetic engineerin'. Good luck. Man, there are one hundred trillion of the little buggers out there. I say gas 'em all."

"Gas them all?" I repeated. "One hundred trillion?"

"Hell, yeah. Why not? That's what insecticide means, okay? Kill insects."

"A man's gotta do what a man's gotta do," I told him, and he laughed.

"That's funny," he said. "I gotta remember that, that's funny. A man's gotta do what a man's gotta do. . . ."

"Sidesplitting," I agreed.

I went back to the chair. Emerton sat on the corner of his desk.

"Why are you convinced Alison was sleeping with Raymond Fleck?" I asked.

"A guy knows these things, okay? You can tell. Besides, it's not like it was the first time."

"It wasn't?"

"Hell, no. She was screwin' some guy at the health place, some doctor I think."

"Huh?" My internal computer sifted through Anne Scalasi's entire file in about two seconds flat, and all I could come up with was, "Huh?"

"Not long after we were married, neither."

"Are you—?"

"Sure? You were goin' to ask me if I'm sure? I told you, a guy knows these things. They say the husband's the last to know. Forget that. The husband is the first unless he's a dumb shit. Anyway, she didn't deny it, okay? I told her I knew she was whorin' around, and I was going to divorce her pronto. That was like the magic word with Alison: divorce. Her family, man, divorce was like worse than death. They'd rather you died than get a divorce, okay? So, she starts wailin' and pleadin' with me, sayin' she was sorry, and the next thing she ups and quits the health place and gets a job at the dog place."

"Why didn't you tell the police this?" I asked him.

"What for? Man, they already thought I did her, okay? I'm gonna be the jealous husband? I'm gonna give 'em a motive?"

"Why are you telling me?"

"You're not from the cops. You're from the insurance . . . Shit!" Emerton jumped off his desk, walked around it, and fell into his chair like he had been pushed there. He covered his face with his hands. "I'm never going to see my money now, am I? God, I can't believe I said that."

I believed it. I've seen stupid before. Especially in killers. It's like the act of murder freezes their brain cells. The mystery writer Dashiell Hammett, who once was a Pinkerton, called it "blood simple." On the other hand, despite the degrees hanging on his walls, maybe Emerton was just plain simple.

"Who do you suspect?" I asked.

"Huh?"

"The doctor Alison was . . ." I couldn't get the word out.

"Fuckin'?" Emerton finished.

"Involved with," I substituted.

"I don't know. I'm just guessin' it was some doctor. Coulda been a janitor for all I know. Hell's bells, man, I wouldn't be surprised if she was with him right now on some beach in Bermuda, laughin' her ass off at how badly she fucked up my life."

"Wait a minute. First you say she's dead. Now you say she's alive."

Emerton stared at me for a good ten seconds, his jaw muscles working but nothing coming out of his mouth. Then, "She's dead, man. Don't go sayin' she ain't. You ain't usin' that to deny my claim. She's dead."

"If you think she's alive . . ."

"I didn't say I think . . . I didn't say . . . What I'm sayin' is, wherever she is—in hell, man; she's probably in hell—I'm sayin' she's laughing at the joke she played on me."

"The joke she played on you?"

I wondered if it was too late for the Phi Betas to take their key back.

Stephen Emerton annoyed me. He annoyed me even before I met him. And I sure didn't like the way he spoke about his wife, discussing her like she was a major appliance that had broken down a week or so after the warranty expired. Except I wanted his story—I wanted it complete and unabridged—so I tried to ignore the blood pounding in my head and listened, encouraging him when he became bored with the topic. I pumped Emerton for more information about the doctor—if it was a doctor—he claimed was "getting into Alison's pants," but he turned into a dry well. I gave it up after about an hour and made my way back through the now deserted offices to the front door.

I reached my car and removed Alison's photo from the envelope. Her eyes spoke to me as they always had. Now, though, along with the despair there was something else, something I hadn't seen before. It was like her eyes were pleading with me. But for what? Justice? Revenge? Or maybe it was just the gathering twilight that was casting soft shadows across the glossy surface. I returned the photograph to the envelope and started my car.

Emerton's revelation that he suspected Alison was cheating on him with the phantom doctor and later with Raymond made him an even more likely suspect than before; Teeters would put him through the grinder again and so would the insurance company— and so would the media once they all heard. I looked forward to telling them. Only I didn't want to annoy the sheriff with yet another phone call. It could wait until the morning.

eight

I greeted Cynthia Grey with a bouquet of assorted flowers. I didn't know what kind; the florist had put them together for me. But they looked good and they smelled good and besides, it's the thought that counts.

Cynthia hugged me and kissed me and thanked me for the flowers and asked, "What are these for?" as she arranged them in a vase.

"Consider it an apology."

"An apology? For what?"

"I've spent most of the day listening to tales of the abuse of women. I've heard from a woman whose college professor expected her to trade sexual favors for a degree. I've spoken with a rapist who can't understand why people mistrust him. And another man is upset because his wife's murder is causing him great inconvenience."

"Taylor, Taylor," Cynthia said with a sigh. "That's nothing. I could tell you stories that would bring bitter tears to your eyes."

"Yeah, well, it all left me believing that as a whole, men are a pretty shabby lot."

After filling a vase with water, Cynthia used it as a centerpiece for her dining-room table. "This is very sweet," she told me. "But you don't have to apologize for the way other men treat women."

"I'm not. I'm apologizing for myself, for the way I treated you. Remember when you told me you were taking that sexual harassment case, the case against the women's clothing manufacturer with the slutty advertising?"

"Yes."

"Remember, I said it was silly?"

"Yes."

"Well, I was wrong. I'm glad you crushed the bastards."

Cynthia smiled brightly. "My goodness."

We watched each other, awkward in our silence. It was not one of those talk-about-sexual-harassment-and-then-go-into-a-clinch moments, so I slapped the tabletop and bellowed, "Woman, where's my dinner?!"

———

Cynthia made a dish of braised chicken and sweet peppers. Or rather she reheated it in the microwave. A personal chef had created it, a woman Cynthia hired to come to her home once a month and whip up about a dozen different menus for two and put them in the freezer. She's a helluva cook. The personal chef, I mean. And the price, about three hundred bucks and expenses, isn't so much when you compare it to a decent restaurant. But the idea of someone coming to your home and making your meals left a sour taste in my mouth. I told Cynthia so, and she very calmly explained that, unlike me, she was too busy to cook for herself much less for both of us. Besides, she didn't know how to cook.

Her mother hadn't been around to teach her; an alcoholic, she had run off when Cynthia was just six, leaving her daughter in the care of elderly—and brutal—grandparents who died within months of each other when she was twelve, leaving her a ward of the state. Cynthia drifted between foster homes, halfway houses, and the streets, unloved and unloving, with drugs and alcohol her only friends. After attempting to take her own life on her seventeenth birthday, Cynthia was mandated by a court-ordered detention into a local snake pit with some major-league crazies. It might have been the best thing that ever happened to her. The experience shocked her into a kind of sanity and ignited in her a passion for survival that still burns red hot. Upon her release, she embraced the straight life with both hands. She earned her GED, put herself through a three-and-three program—three years of undergraduate studies and three years of law school at the University of Minnesota—on strength of will alone and finishing tenth in her class. Along the way she taught herself how to view life critically, becoming what my father calls "a woman of substance" as well as a lawyer. Believe me, if Cynthia could hang ATTORNEY in neon above her town house, she would.

As for the rough edges, she pays a woman to teach her manners, how to walk and talk and present herself in nearly any social situation. She pays a woman to select her clothes, making sure she's always fashionable. She pays another woman to buy her furniture. And she pays a woman to cook gourmet meals. These women obviously care about their work, creating for Cynthia a look of quiet elegance, and only someone who knows her well could sense that it doesn't quite fit. I know because I've spent a lot of time with Cynthia over the past eight months. I had met her while working a case. Re-met her I should say. She had defended the man who had killed my family with his car years earlier. At first that fact bothered me a lot. Then, not so much. Now when I'm not with her, I'm alone.

After we ate, I helped Cynthia with the dishes—partly because I'm a warm, sensitive, caring man for the millennium and partly because she gives me *that look* when I don't.

Later, stretched out on Cynthia's expensive Ethan Allen sofa, I sipped the red wine the sales clerk at the liquor warehouse recommended to her while Cynthia drank Catawba juice. She hasn't had an alcoholic beverage in—what?—nearly eight years now. We were listening to a Nicholas Payton CD. The CD belonged to me. Mostly Cynthia listens to heavy-metal junk played by bands I've never heard of—a direct contradiction to the image she so carefully cultivates. I once offered my opinion of her taste in music. But only once. She responded with language that would make the most obnoxious rap artist blush. You can take the woman out of the street, but you can't take the street out of the woman.

The phone rang, and Cynthia got up to answer it. My eyes followed her as she removed the cellular phone from its cradle, extending the antenna with one quick motion. I listened to her side of the conversation, watching her as she paced the dining and living rooms, absentmindedly caressing the furniture with her hands, reminding herself who it all belonged to.

"Hi. . . . No, I'm not busy. How are you? . . . Sure. . . . Oh, you'd think we could, wouldn't you? My office is only three blocks away. . . . I have an office manager who would shoot me if I did that. . . . Yeah, I sometimes wonder who's working for whom, too. . . . Your schedule has to be worse. At least I don't get calls in the middle of the night. . . . True, but it's never a matter of life or death. . . . I wonder about it all the time, don't you? . . . Yes, I can do that. I'd be happy to. . . . Yes, he's here. He's sitting on the couch, drinking wine and listening to his beloved jazz. . . ." Cynthia held the phone away from her mouth and told me, "Anne Scalasi says you're a sonuvabitch."

"Now what did I do?"

"He wants to know what he did," Cynthia said into the phone. After a brief pause she exclaimed, "Don't tell him that! He'll be harder to live with than ever."

"What?" I asked.

Cynthia handed me the telephone.

"Hi, Annie," I said.

"You're a *lucky* sonuvabitch, Taylor," she clarified.

"How so?"

"Your tip to Ed Teeters, it paid off."

"No way!"

"He put a team on Irene Brown. She left her house an hour after sunset and drove to a Dumpster behind a fast-food joint. They have a videotape of her throwing a box into the Dumpster. Guess what the box contained?"

"No way!"

"A pair of LA Gear Air System running shoes, size ten."

I started to laugh at the improbability of it all.

"We're working on this sucker for seven months, and you break it in one day," Anne said.

"Actually, I did it in half a day," I told her and laughed some more.

"You're a lucky sonuvabitch," Anne repeated.

"Hey, I'm a trained professional. Luck had nothing to do with it. As the great pioneering criminologist Edmond Locard once said—"

"Give me a break. I lend you one lousy book on forensic detection, and all of a sudden you're quoting dead Frenchmen."

"I thought he was Belgian."

"Trust me. Anyway, Irene Brown had been waiting seven months for someone to catch her. Winnie the Pooh could have done it."

"Tsk, tsk, tsk. Do I detect envy? Jealousy, perhaps, of my unparalleled skills?"

"Screw you, Taylor."

"God, I'm loving this, Annie."

"It's not over yet. Teeters said that Irene Brown confessed that she followed Alison home the evening she disappeared. Brown said she was going to give Alison a piece of her mind."

"Does she have any to spare?"

"She said Alison met her at the front door with a small gun in her hand. She said Alison told her to leave, and that's what she did. Brown insists Alison was alive when she left."

"Well, she would, wouldn't she?" I told Anne.

"Brown claims that she didn't tell the police because she was afraid they would accuse her of killing Alison."

"Did she admit to making the harassing telephone calls?"

"Yes, and the flowers and dead cat, too. She also claims that Raymond Fleck had nothing to do with any of it."

"I wonder."

"Yeah, I do, too. Is she still protecting Raymond?"

"The running shoes. They were men's shoes," I reminded Anne.

"Teeters said that Brown insists they were hers, that they fit her better than women's shoes."

"Why did she keep them all this time?"

"She said she had no reason not to. She said she never imagined that she left a print."

"Unbelievable. What does Teeters say?"

"Teeters is ecstatic. He's so happy, he's actually speaking in complete sentences. He figures this will get the media off his back."

"Now the big one: What does the Dakota County attorney say?"

"I'm getting this all secondhand, you have to remember. The way I hear it, Dakota County is impounding Brown's car and having forensics conduct a search. If they find any blood, any hair samples, any physical evidence at all that puts Alison in the car or in any area where the suspect had access, the CA will go for a murder indictment even if he can't establish corpus delicti. If not, I don't know. Without Alison's body, without corroborative physical evidence, he'll have a helluva time proving that a homicide was even committed. The defense could argue that Alison decided to become a blackjack dealer in Vegas—"

Or take a trip to Bermuda, my inner voice whispered so softly that I barely heard it.

"—and you know juries; they like to see a dead body in a murder case."

"Still, if he pushes it, Brown might cop a plea, go for manslaughter," I suggested.

"Depends on her attorney."

"Or Fleck might open up."

"Yeah."

"Let me know?"

Anne sighed deeply. "How 'bout I buy you lunch tomorrow. W. A. Frost."

"Annie, my gosh."

"Yeah, well, you did a nice job."

"Thanks, Annie. But like you said, she spent the past seven months teetering on the edge, waiting for someone to shove her over."

"Probably, but you're the one who nudged her, not us. Make it eleven-thirty?"

"See you then."

I turned off the phone, collapsed the antenna, and set it on the coffee table. Cynthia was watching me from a wing chair, smiling.

"All right, I'm waiting," she said.

"Waiting?"

"For the self-congratulations."

"Cynthia, you wound me."

"Uh-huh."

I locked my fingers behind my head and leaned back. She continued to watch me, continued to smile.

"The other day you asked why men enjoy sports," I reminded her. "It's for the same reason I enjoyed being a cop, the same reason I like being a private investigator now. Yeah, there's plenty of greed and fraud and ignorance and stupidity and corruption, and sometimes you wonder why you're wasting your time. But if you stay with it, occasionally you'll be rewarded with moments of pure joy, like when Kirby Puckett hit a home run to win the sixth game of the 1991 World Series or when Black Jack Morris pitched a ten-inning shutout to win game seven—"

"Or when Holland Taylor solved a seven-month-old murder before lunch," she added.

I grinned. "God, I'm good."

nine

I was late to my office the next morning. It was such a beautiful day, I stopped at the University of Minnesota driving range on Larpenteur to hit a bucket of golf balls. It took me over an hour. I would have finished sooner except that I took time to admire the female golfer who was hitting seven irons from the tee next to mine. Absolutely gorgeous form. Her swing wasn't bad, either. Unfortunately, my ogling came with a price that I was forced to pay when I called my answering service.

"It is *un-ac-cept-able*," the operator told me, sounding a bit like Anne Scalasi in a bad mood. "We will not tolerate that kind of behavior from our clients. If there are any further incidents, we will terminate our relationship."

Gulp.

I tried to explain to the woman that it wasn't I who had called four times between eight and nine A.M., making angry references to various parts of the operator's anatomy when I wasn't there to answer the phone. However, she didn't see it that way, and I was forced to promise that I would "speak" with Mr. Truman. Either that or dig my old answering machine out of the closet.

But first I fortified myself with a cup of Blue Mountain Jamaican coffee—I grind my own beans—and sorted through my mail. Except for a large brown envelope from Publishers Clearing House, nothing excited me. I turned my attention to my newspapers. I get both the St. Paul *Pioneer Press* and the Minneapolis-based *Star Tribune*. Most people read newspapers starting with the front page and work in. I always start with the agate type listing the transactions in the sports section and work out. No particular reason; it's just how I do things. I noticed immediately that the Oakland As had brought up a middle-relief pitcher just in time for their series with the Minnesota Twins. They'll need him. My Twins were hot, having won nine of their last eleven, including a three-game sweep of Cleveland. It was still early, of course. Too early to get excited about a pennant race. And given the team's payroll . . . Still, every time my boys start playing well, I remember '87 and '91, and a little tingle creeps up my spine. True, '87 and '91 are starting to be a long time ago. But what has *your* team done lately? Not much I bet.

I was studying the stats of today's probable pitchers when the phone rang. I let it ring six times before I answered, knowing it was Hunter Truman.

"What the fuck is going on?" he wanted to know.

"Pertaining to what?"

"Goddammit, ain't you working for me? I gotta get my news from the fucking radio, from some greaseball on TV?"

"Are you referring to Irene Brown?"

"What the hell you *think* I'm referring to? Jesus, Taylor."

"If you'd shut up for a few minutes, I'll explain."

"Goddamn, Taylor—"

"Shut up Truman. Will ya?"

I told him all about Irene Brown, about how I spooked her into tossing the shoes, about what the Dakota County folks were going to do next. Truman surprised me by not uttering a syllable until I was finished.

"What do you think?" he asked at last.

"You asked me for my best guess. Well, my best guess is that Irene Brown is guilty of murder. Only I doubt Dakota County can make the charge stick even if forensics does discover corroborating evidence. Without a body, a good defense attorney should be able to clobber the county attorney. Hell, Truman, even you could win this one."

"Yeah, that's what I was thinking," he agreed. After a long pause, he asked, "Is that it?"

"That's it. I'll send you a bill."

"You're not looking into it anymore?"

"You wanted my best guess. Well, you have it. There's nothing more that I can do."

"Uh-huh."

"I'm having lunch today at W. A. Frost with someone involved in the case. If I hear anything new, I'll give you a call."

"Fine," he said and hung up.

"Yeah, pleasure doing business with you, too, Truman," I told the dead receiver.

"I should warn you before you order that I'm not buying after all," Anne told me as she perused her menu.

"You're not?" I asked, surprised.

She shook her head.

"What happened?"

"Raymond Fleck confessed to the murder after he learned that the Dakota County deputies arrested Irene."

"He did?"

"Irene Brown then confessed a few minutes after she learned that Raymond was in custody."

"She did?"

"Which means Irene did it and Raymond's trying to protect her, or Raymond did it and Irene's trying to protect him. . . ."

I stared at my menu, not really seeing it.

"Or worse," she added, "they both did it and this is just a nifty way to interject a reasonable doubt into their trials. Both had motive, both had opportunity, both confessed willingly. Who do you believe? Who will a jury believe?" Anne shrugged. "Without the body, neither Raymond nor Irene can prove that they're telling the truth. Without the body we can't prove that either or both of them are lying. And neither of them is willing to lead the deputies to the body."

"I just had a sickening thought."

"What?"

"What if they *can't* lead them to Alison? What if neither of them did it, but both believe the other did, and they're only confessing to protect each other? Call it the *Gift of the Magi* defense."

"People in love do amazing things," Anne agreed.

"Hell, I didn't catch anybody," I griped, tossing my menu onto the white tablecloth.

"Buy your own damn lunch," Annie told me.

We parted with a hug in the parking lot of the YWCA just down the street from the restaurant. Annie was parked in the first row, my car was way in the back. When I reached it, I found a folded sheet of plain white typing paper jammed under my windshield wiper. I unfolded it, expecting to learn that I was invited to the grand opening of a car wash or some damn thing. Instead, the note, written in black marker, read: STAY AWAY FROM THE EMERTON CASE IF YOU KNOW WHAT'S GOOD FOR YOU!

"Annie!" I yelled.

Fortunately her car window was rolled down to hear me, and she stopped just as she was about to exit the parking lot.

"What?" she called.

"Are Raymond and Irene still in custody?"

"Yes."

"Damn," I muttered, reading the note a third time. I *really* hadn't caught anybody.

Truman listened patiently as I told him of my discovery of the note.

"What does it mean?" he wanted to know.

"Just what it says. Someone wants me off the case, and it's not Raymond or Irene."

"Who?"

"Obviously someone who knows I was working the case. Stephen Emerton. The employees at Kennel-Up. I'm betting on Stephen Emerton, though."

"Why?"

"Yesterday he admitted to me that he believed Alison was having an affair with Raymond because he believed Alison had had an affair with an unidentified employee, possibly a doctor, while she was employed by the health-care organization. That makes him a stronger suspect, and it could be he's afraid I'll pass it on to the cops or his insurance company."

"That's bullshit," Truman insisted. At first I thought he was defending Emerton. A moment later I knew better. "That's absolute bullshit. There's no fucking way Alison would do that. He's lying."

"He has no reason to lie," I reminded Truman. "It hurts him more than it helps him."

"That's real bullshit."

"Maybe it's bullshit that Alison was having an affair"—I thought of the photograph, the black and white number that made her look like a cat on the prowl and the word caught in my throat—"but if Emerton believes it's true . . ."

"Yeah?"

"That's motive," I concluded. "He didn't admit it to the cops but he did to me, and now I'm thinking that last night he lost a lot of sleep over it."

"And put the note on your windshield?"

"It could have been someone else," I admitted. "But he's my only suspect right now." My inner voice was speaking to me again. It whispered, *Alison couldn't possibly have done it if she's in Bermuda.*

"You think we should look into it," Truman told me.

"Yes. But it's your nickel."

Truman made clicking sounds with his tongue; over the phone it sounded like the ticking of a clock.

"I don't know," he finally said. "If Irene or Raymond or both of them really did kill Alison, digging up another suspect could only help them at trial, am I right?"

"Possibly," I agreed.

"But you think we should look into it, anyway?"

"Yes." Although a small part of me wanted Truman to say no.

"Why?"

"Because someone doesn't want us to."

"There's a New York actress named Holland Taylor; pretty good one, too," Marie Audette reminded me when I met her in the lobby of a downtown Minneapolis recording studio.

"So I've been told," I said.

"Any relation?"

"No," I answered, without adding that I've always wanted to meet the woman.

After speaking with Hunter Truman, I located the names of Alison's two best friends in my notes. The first was Marie Audette. Her agent told me she was recording a voice-over for a TV spot, and I arranged to meet her before the session began.

"I heard on the radio coming over here that a woman was

arrested for killing Alison. Do you know anything about that?" she asked.

I told her that I did, told her I was partly responsible for apprehending the woman. If Cynthia had been there, she would have accused me of grandstanding. I assure you, my motives were pure. I wanted Marie's gratitude, yes, but only because I figured it would make her more receptive to my questions. The lovely, affectionate smile she bestowed on me was merely a bonus.

"Alison and I were very close while we were at the university," Marie confided in a throaty, sensual voice—yeah, I could see why people would pay her serious money to speak eloquently about detergent and fax machines. "She was like my little sister, which is kind of funny when you think about it. She was eighteen and I was twenty-two, but she was a senior and I was only a junior. God, she was smart. She could have been a great actress. She had this ability to totally immerse herself into a role, to actually become the character she was playing. Like Meryl Streep . . . Well, maybe not quite like Streep."

"I have a photograph of the two of you," I told her. "You're in costume. European, I think."

"*The Cherry Orchard?*"

I shrugged my ignorance.

"We did Chekhov for the university theater company. She was Anya to my Varya. She was wonderful; great reviews. The critic from the *Star Tribune* said Alison was, quote, 'an actor to watch.'"

"Why did she give it up?"

"I don't think it was important enough to her. We often spoke about acting, fantasizing about our careers. She told me she was going to change her name to Rosalind Colletti; it was going to be her stage name. But acting is an extremely punishing profession, and I don't think she was willing to take the rejection, the hammering we often get from agents, from casting directors, from critics. You know what her goal was? It wasn't the Oscar or the Tony. It was independence. She wanted to take only those parts that genuinely interested her and nothing else. Show me an actor with that attitude who gets work. Jack Nicholson, maybe, but first he had to pay his dues like everyone else. Ever see *Hell's Angels On Wheels?*"

"So she gave it up," I volunteered.

"We went to a few auditions together, then fewer and fewer until she stopped going altogether. It's too bad. I'm doing *The Merchant Of Venice* for The Acting Company; Alison would have made a great Jessica. Would you like a couple of tickets? On the house?"

"That would be very nice, thank you," I answered without hesitation. I used to glom onto freebies when I was a cop, too.

"Thursday night? I already gave away my weekend tickets."

"That'd be great," I said as she made a note to herself on a small pad.

"I write everything down," she told me.

"So do I," I replied, making a notation on my own pad. "When did Alison begin working for the health-care organization?" I asked.

"About a year after she earned her master's. First, though, she took a job with an advertising agency that had a public relations department. She was a junior account executive—or something like that—and the health-care company was her primary client. A year later she left the agency and began working full time for the health-care place. It upset a lot of people, too."

"How so?"

"First thing she did was fire the ad agency and hire someone else."

"Burning bridges," I suggested.

"She was like that."

"How did your relationship hold up?"

"Fine," Marie answered, shrugging. "We started to drift apart;

she was doing her thing and I was doing mine. We stayed in touch, though; met a couple times a month for lunch."

"When was the last time you saw her?"

"About a month before she disappeared."

"What did you talk about?"

"I can't even remember, it was so unimportant. She certainly didn't confide in me about what was happening in her life if that's what you're asking," Marie shook her head sadly. "I was supposed to be her friend—one of her *best* friends—yet she didn't confide in me. Now I wonder if we were friends at all. Sometimes it seems to me that we were only two people who knew each other for a long time."

I appreciated Marie's confusion. I am continually impressed by how little we truly know about each other, by how much we conceal. We often remain strangers even to those we're the most intimate with. I've known widows who learn more about their dearly departed husbands in the first week after they're dead than in forty years of married life. It makes one yearn for that lost age of formal introductions, that time in our society's evolution when our character was well known and even guaranteed by mutual friends, accepted customs, and shared institutions. Of course, there wasn't much call for private investigators back then.

"How did she meet Stephen Emerton?" I asked, nudging Marie slowly toward the question I most wanted to ask.

"I introduced them," she replied. "Stephen and I were seeing each other. Nothing serious, though. One day I introduced them over lunch. A week later Alison called and said Stephen had asked her out, did I mind? I said no."

"You didn't mind that your best friend was stealing away your boyfriend?"

Marie smiled. "Stealing him away? More like I was giving him away. And good riddance. Stephen's a good-looking guy, I admit.

But I've seen kiddie pools with more depth. 'An idiot, full of sound and fury, signifying nothing,'" she added, quoting *Macbeth*.

"Did you tell that to Alison?"

"'Friendship is constant in all other things, save in the office and affairs of love; therefore all hearts in love use their own tongues; let every heart negotiate for itself,'" she replied. I couldn't place the line.

"I recognized *Macbeth*," I told the actress. "The last quote?"

"That was Shakespeare, too. *Much Ado About Nothing*. Sorry. I know I can be annoying, quoting playwrights. Sometimes I can't help showing off."

"Forget it," I told the actress. "I've been known to show off on occasion myself." Then I asked, "Was Alison working for the health-care organization when she and Stephen met?"

"Yes."

"Did Alison see anyone else while she worked there?"

"Before Stephen? Probably. Alison was pretty enough; she could have had all the male companionship she wanted."

"Any names?"

"No," Marie answered. "None that I can remember."

"How about *after* she married Stephen?"

There it was—the high, hard one. Marie swatted it like it was a beach ball.

"I doubt it," she said. "I think you can tell if a woman cheats, and Alison just wasn't the type."

Alison wasn't the type: I was happy to hear Marie say it. Happy and relieved. So much for not getting emotionally involved in a case, so much for keeping an open mind. *Alison wasn't the type*. I wrote it down in my notebook.

"Although if she *was* cheating on Stephen, I would have been the last person she'd tell," Marie added. "Alison was very big on appearances. If she thought someone would disapprove of something she did, she'd have kept it to herself. I guess I know that much about her."

"Would you have disapproved?"

"Absolutely. You want to sleep around when you're single, go ahead, who cares—although these days I figure you're taking your life in your hands. But not when you're married. You have to be honest when you're married. Otherwise, why bother?"

"If Alison was cheating on Stephen and didn't confide in you, would she have confided in Gretchen Rovick?"

"The cop?"

"The sheriff's deputy," I corrected her.

"Maybe. She and Gretchen grew up together, went to the same high school. I met Gretchen only once, the weekend Alison was married. She was maid of honor, I was a bridesmaid. We were the only two standing up for Alison."

ten

Deer Lake, Wisconsin was A GOOD NATURED TOWN. It said so on the hand-lettered sign that marked the city limits. The sign listed the community's population at 1,557. It seemed larger than that. The parking lots of two supermarkets located across the blacktop from each other were packed with cars, and a considerable amount of traffic was moving in and out of King Boats, which I later discovered not only sold recreational boats but built them, too. Along the main drag a visitor could find a drugstore, bank, real-estate office, hardware store, several gift shops, two restaurants, a service station, a clothing store, a movie rental shop, an appliance dealer, a store that specialized in personal computers, and six—count 'em, six—taverns.

Gretchen Rovick was a Kreel County deputy sheriff, and apparently her beat included Deer Lake. She agreed to meet me at the Deer Lake Café after she finished her shift. I was an hour early, and it had been thirsty work driving three hours northeast from the Twin Cities—although I was familiar with the terrain since my wife's parents lived about forty miles south—so I stopped for a taste, parking in front of The Last Chance Saloon. The Last Chance Saloon was next door to The Next to Last Chance Saloon. It turned out to be the same bar with two entrances; a hokey gag, but I liked it.

All bars give off vibrations; you can tell what kind of joint it is just by walking through the door, and The Last Chance felt like a place where you'd best keep your wits about you. It was dimly lit and furnished with cheap Formica tables and metal chairs with torn cushions—the kind my mother had in her kitchen before Dad got his raise. The floor was grubby with sawdust that might have come from Washington's chopped-down cherry tree, and the remains of what must have been an impressive herd of deer hung from all four walls. A portly man wearing both belt and suspenders sat on a high stool behind a terribly nicked and battered bar, supporting his considerable bulk with his elbows, ready to speak but only if spoken to. He scrutinized my rate of consumption with a practiced eye, waiting for the opportunity to offer me another beer.

Had this been his life's ambition, this man who looked as though he had drunk too much of the profits over the years? Had he always wanted to run a broken-down beer joint in a one-horse Wisconsin town? I wondered what he thought of the idea now. What do you do when your dreams come horribly, hopelessly true?

I drained the glass, pushed it toward him. He refilled it, set it back in front of me, took my five-dollar bill, brought back the change. "Eldon," a voice called at the end of the bar, and he followed it. He did not speak to me. Didn't look like he intended to.

It was nearing four in the afternoon, and the bar was half filled with men—no women—who tossed rough jokes from one table to another, jokes that were politically incorrect to the extreme and fairly funny—jokes that they would never tell their wives and daughters. I was wearing a blue sports coat over my white button-down shirt and faded jeans, which meant I was overdressed for The Last Chance and therefore a figure of some suspicion. Several regulars regarded me carefully with the narrow squint of rural folk accustomed to strangers who talked fast and said little. I pretended not to notice.

However, I couldn't help but notice the argument raging at a nearby table. Two men spoke loudly as if they were in their own kitchen, not caring a fig who might be listening. I put the older man at sixty. Hard. You could roller skate on him. The younger man was twenty, twenty-five maybe, and soft, with a pockmarked face and a pale complexion. Life in the great outdoors hadn't done him any good at all. Jab a cigarette in his mouth and lean him against the lamppost outside the bus depot in downtown St. Paul, and he'd look just like any other punk you've ever seen.

"You don't believe me, you go on down to The Forks Casino and Restaurant. Take a look at the number of little kids locked inside the cars while their parents are gamblin' away the grocery money," the older man said.

"Can't stop folks from being shitty parents. Just look at you, old man," replied the younger. "But you can put money in their jeans. That's what a gamblin' casino does, gives people work. Looka what happened when the Indians built The Forks."

"What happened? What happened?"

"We got businesses movin' in."

"What businesses? The Forks ain't brought no business here exceptin' the pawnshop. Isn't that great? We got a pawnshop now. And the resort that bitch is buildin' on Lake Peterson, across from where they say they're gonna build a new casino? That's gonna take business outta town, not bring it in."

"Yeah? Well, it's good for whores," the younger man insisted. "Too bad your old lady croaked. You coulda put her out and made a fortune."

The older man wiped his face slowly and deliberately with his hand as if the punk had just spit on him and he was deciding what to do about it. He stood.

"You aimin' to try me, old man?" The punk jumped to his feet and gestured with both hands for the older man to come ahead. The older man took one determined step forward. As he did, the younger man reached into his hip pocket and brought out a knife. The blade sprang from the handle like a flash of lightning. The older man backed away.

The younger man giggled. "C'mon, c'mon, you've been asking for this."

"Excuse me," I said. While the punk was terrorizing the older man, I crept quietly behind him. He spun at my voice, the blade of the knife held low. I grabbed his knife hand, making sure my thumb was tight between his third and fourth knuckles, and then simply dislodged the switchblade with my knee. When he dropped the weapon, I pushed him backward, not enough to knock him down but far enough to be able to retrieve the knife from the floor unmolested. I went back to my stool and closed the switchblade, tossing it on the bar top.

"You may continue," I said.

What a smart-ass. No wonder the older man turned on me. "Any of this your affair?" he shouted.

Before I could answer, he was on me, covering the floor like a cat. I pushed myself off the stool and fell to my knees, ducking under his haymaker and punching him in the groin. I followed with an elbow to the jaw, and he went down. Only he didn't stay down long. He rolled and sprang at me again. Again I hit him and again he fell. I stole a glance at the punk. He watched for a few moments, grew bored, and turned his attention to a pinball machine in the corner as the older man struggled to his feet. It took him a little longer this time, but he made it, licking at the blood that now flowed freely from a tear in his upper lip. He smiled—actually smiled!—giving me the impression that he had been in many a barroom fight in his time and that he was enjoying himself immensely.

I almost shouted at him, "Hey, old man, you win, I'll go quietly"—anything to get out of that place in one piece. But I didn't have the chance. He charged at me again. This time I was able to brush him aside, letting his momentum carry him into an empty chair and table. "Jesus, how do I get into these things?" I asked aloud, shivering with the realization that I needed to hurt this big hard-ass and soon. Hurt him before he hurt me.

He was back on his feet, quicker this time, but the murderous light in his eyes flickered out as he looked over my shoulder toward the door.

"You just about finished here, Johnny, or do I have time to go out for popcorn?"

The voice was soft and low, but it resonated with the hard ring of authority. It belonged to a woman wearing a deputy sheriff's uniform. I turned just enough to see her moving toward us while still keeping a wary eye on the older man.

"Whoa, boys, it's Deputy Sweet Cheeks!" yelled a patron with a Green Bay Packers cap on his head.

"Sweet enough to use your balls for batting practice if you call me that again," she replied, looking at him without a trace of malice.

"Police harassment!" someone shouted.

"No, that's *sexual* harassment," she countered, smiling sweetly. Everyone had a good laugh, including the Packer backer, his buddy slapping him on the shoulder, saying, "She got you good that time." The tension in the room dissipated quickly. All those country boys, they were on her side now. How to Win Friends and Influence People with Humor. I wished I could do that.

Still, Johnny raised his fist as the deputy approached. She casually slapped it down. "Cut it out, you guys," she said for everyone to hear and then asked in a low whisper, "Are you really going to hit me in front of all these folks, Mr. Johannson? I mean, you could, but it ain't gonna look good, you know? 'Hear 'bout Johnny?' people will say. 'Punched hisself a little girl over to The Last Chance.' People around here be jokin' on you for a hundred years. They'd be sayin' you ain't no gentleman."

That last remark caused Johnny's head to flinch ever so slightly. And then he lowered his eyes. Cops are taught to read body language, and Johnny's told me that while he'd be happy to stomp *my* heart into the floor, he would never hit a woman. I wondered if the deputy had seen it. Apparently she had.

"Best you step outside with me. In private," she said to Johnny. "Later, you can tell these jokers that it goes against your upbringing to punch me out. You can tell 'em I remind you of your daughter. How is Angel, anyway?"

"She's doin' good," Johnny answered in a soft voice, wiping the blood from his face with his sleeve. "She's thinkin' of movin' up to Superior end of summer. Maybe finish school."

"Is that right? Good. Well, let's you and me step outside. You, too," she said, gesturing toward me with her chin. "Superior, huh?" she added as we moved toward the door. "Gotta remember to pay my respects before she leaves."

Gretchen Rovick had short, straight, sun-splashed hair tucked neatly under her wide-brimmed hat, eyes that nearly matched the mahogany trim of her deputy suit, a small, round face, and an athletic figure. She was one of the few women I've met who actually looked good in a uniform.

"It was my fault," I admitted when she asked the inevitable question: What happened? "I interfered in a private dispute."

"Dispute?"

"My boy got a little outta hand," Johnny Johannson said. "I guess this young fella thought he was doin' me a service. Weren't necessary."

"Your *boy*?! That was your *son*?!" I asked. He did not answer.

"Are you pressing charges, Mr. Johannson?"

"No, ma'am," he answered without looking at me.

"How about you?" she asked me.

"No ma'am," I replied.

"Now all we have to worry about is Eldon," Gretchen said, gesturing at the bar.

"Don't worry none about him, Deputy," Johannson said. "Him and me go way back. 'Sides, I don't think nothin' got broke."

"Well, maybe I should arrest you both, anyway. Can't have people fightin' in public places, know what I mean?"

Johnny nodded his head.

"If there's a next time . . ."

"Won't be a next time," Johnny vowed contritely.

"All right, then," Gretchen said, tossing her hands in the air, closing the incident. However, when Johannson headed back toward The Last Chance, Gretchen called after him, "You gotta do something about that boy, Mr. Johannson. He's headed for big trouble again, just like in Minneapolis. And no slick lawyer is gonna get him out of it this time."

Johannson nodded sadly, like he'd heard it all before.

Deputy Rovick watched Johannson's retreating back for a moment, and then she turned and studied me carefully. There was no hostility in her eyes. Just interest.

"I should have listened to my mother," I admitted. "She was forever telling me to mind my own business."

"She was right."

"That old guy, he likes to roughhouse."

"Johnny's all right," she assured me, leading me up the street. "Measures a man by how hard he throws a punch is the problem."

"Problem is the kid had a switchblade."

"Classic sociopath," she said in reply. "He was busted last year in Minneapolis for cutting a prostitute. Some shyster got him off." The deputy sighed audibly and looked back at the saloon. She knew she was going to have to deal with Johannson's boy sooner or later. But not today. Not alone. "Are you hungry? I'm hungry."

"Yes, I'm hungry," I told her.

"Good, you can buy," she said, leading me across the street to a restaurant called The Height.

"The height of what?" I asked sarcastically.

"The height of fine cuisine," the deputy replied. "People in the Cities aren't the only ones who like to eat well."

The restaurant was spacious and brightly lit. The furniture was obviously well cared for, and there was nary a deer rack in sight. The deputy led us to a table in the corner from where she could watch the door, the bar, and the stage. A rugged-looking thirty-something playing a twelve-string acoustic guitar rehearsed a

Blind Lemon Jefferson song from a stool on the stage. I was fairly amazed to hear the blues in Deer Lake and told the deputy so.

"We have music, too," she informed me.

I listened to him pick, a Native-American so far removed from his ancestors, from Crazy Horse and Red Cloud and Roman Nose and all those other badass warriors who would have pushed the White Eyes back into the sea if only they had better weaponry, that he could have dropped the Native, hyphen and all, and no one would have noticed. Except him. His name was Lonnie Cavander, and Deputy Rovick informed me that his greatest disappointment in life was that he was not allowed to carry a feathered war lance wherever he went. Instead, he settled for a buck knife the size of a buffalo horn.

"A blues-playing Sioux," I marveled.

"Dakota," Rovick corrected me. "Dakota means *friend* or *ally*. Sioux is what the Europeans called the Dakota. I don't know what it means. *Snake* or something like that. Anyway, Lonnie isn't a Dakota. He's an Ojibwa. Chippewa to the uninformed."

I listened to Lonnie Cavander practice, and when he finished the song I applauded. He smiled at me and nodded.

"Do you know any T-Bone Walker?" I asked.

He shook his head. "You have to be electrified to play Walker. Only way to get those wails. How about this?" he said and started playing a complicated riff that danced on the edge of my memory until I shouted out, "Charlie Patton!"

"Man knows his blues!" Lonnie shouted back.

I was so engrossed in the song that I didn't notice the waitress until she was at the table and Deputy Rovick said, "Hello, Ingrid." I looked up to find a woman with shoulder-length blond hair that had the effect of motion, sunset blue eyes, and skin the color of buttermilk. Of course her name was Ingrid. What else could it be?

Ingrid reminded us that The Height wasn't open for dinner yet but would be in a half hour if we cared to wait. We did, and she suggested the walleye special in a warm, pleasing manner that made her seem even more physically attractive than she really was, which is saying quite a lot. If she had recommended roadkill and a side of tree bark, I would have gobbled it up.

"Coffee?" she asked.

"Yes," I answered.

"Leaded or unleaded?"

"Leaded."

"Good for you," Ingrid said. "We take the fun out of everything these days. We take the caffeine out of our coffee and the sugar out of our chocolate and the alcohol out of our beer and then pretend we enjoy it. If something is unhealthy, we should stop using it altogether, not ruin it."

"I agree," I said a little too enthusiastically.

"Well, of course you do," Ingrid told me and smiled. I watched her as she walked across the restaurant, pausing first at the stage to give Lonnie a listen, her eyes closed to the music. I believe we all eventually reach a peak, a time in our lives when we are as smart and quick and strong and beautiful as we will ever be. Some of us reach it when we are in high school or college, others in middle age, still others just before they are ready to give it up. If we're lucky the peak will last a year or two. If not, only a few fleeting moments. I suspect mine had come and gone long ago. And as I watched the woman swaying gently to Lonnie Cavander's music, I wondered if this was hers.

"The most beautiful woman in Kreel County," Deputy Rovick informed me.

"Most beautiful woman in *any* county," I said, then caught myself. I hadn't realized I was going to say that. After a few embarrassed moments I said, "At the risk of demonstrating my ignorance yet again, what is she doing in Deer Lake, Wisconsin?"

"Ingrid owns the place."

"The whole town?"

"Just the part you're sitting in."

"I don't know what to say."

"You were expecting a bunch of inbred hicks dressed in overalls and sucking on jugs of mash, weren't you?"

"You have to admit that pretty much describes the clientele over at The Last Chance."

"Do I?"

"Perhaps it's my imagination, but your speech did seem to contain certain countrified colloquialisms that magically disappeared once you crossed the street."

"You've got me there," the deputy said and then presented her hand. "I'm Gretchen Rovick," she said as if we had just met.

"Holland Taylor," I answered, accepting the charade. Now we could start over.

We discussed Alison for an hour or more, Gretchen contributing extended anecdotes—like the time Alison embarrassed an American history teacher who couldn't see how the rivalry between Andrew Jackson and his southern-born vice president over Jackson's mistress, Peggy O'Neal, had contributed to the outbreak of the Civil War. Or the time she purposely answered all one hundred questions in a true-false test wrong to see how her teacher would react. (Alison argued it was impossible to get one hundred percent wrong unless you knew all the correct answers. The teacher gave her an F anyway.)

Often Gretchen would slip into the present tense. "I still can't believe Alison's gone," she'd say when she caught herself.

Gretchen and Alison had been childhood friends, growing up across the street from each other. Occasionally Alison would accompany the Rovick family on weekend retreats to Deer Lake, where they kept a cabin. And when Alison's other friends began to shun her after she was certified a genius, Gretchen remained steadfast and true.

"It wasn't her fault she was smarter than everyone else," Gretchen declared as if intelligence was a handicap.

The two friends didn't drift apart until the age of nineteen. Alison was at the University of Minnesota, completing work on her master's. Gretchen had enrolled in the Law Enforcement program at Minnesota State University in Mankato. After graduation, Gretchen moved to Deer Lake and took a job with the Kreel County Sheriff's Department. Still, the two women spoke at least three times a week by telephone. Inexplicably, Alison's last call, according to her phone records, was placed one whole month before she disappeared. About the same time Marie Audette had lost track of her.

"We spoke every other day," Gretchen said. "Our phone bills were outrageous. Then one day she stopped calling me, and when I called her, all I got was her machine."

I told her about the harassing phone calls and suggested that that was the reason Alison refused to answer the telephone.

"Doesn't explain why she quit calling me," Gretchen said. She turned away, and I was afraid she might start to cry. I hate it when women cry. There's never anything I can think to do about it except watch. Only she didn't cry. Instead she asked, "Is there anything else?" obviously anxious to end the conversation.

"Stephen Emerton claims Alison was having an affair with someone while she was working for the health-care company, possibly a doctor."

"Stephen is a jerk," Gretchen insisted.

"That's already been firmly established," I replied. "But is he also a liar?"

Gretchen breathed wearily. "The woman in me says Stephen is full of it. Alison would not have had an affair; she just wasn't like that."

"That's what Marie Audette said," I offered hopefully.

Gretchen nodded, then added, "The cop in me says it's a possibility, although Alison certainly never mentioned a doctor to me."

We had just finished our meal when the commotion started. A woman dressed in a wide flaring skirt and tight cotton sweater that was far too young for her was wobbling along the bar, a martini in her hand. She looked like the kind of woman who only drank with men. And there were plenty about, most of them competing to see who would be first to refill her glass or drag a chair over to her, all of them ogling her with a thirst that was both comical and frightening. One of the men pushed a second, who pushed a third, who pushed the first, and so on, while the woman laughed gleefully.

"Stay here," Gretchen commanded firmly in case I was contemplating a reprise of my performance at The Last Chance.

The deputy moved to the center of the group. Two men left immediately, leaving three and the woman. I couldn't hear what Gretchen said, but her words were effective. The woman responded with a high-pitched laugh, but the men all grabbed some bench except for the largest of the three. He grabbed Gretchen by the wrist. She did not pull away. She merely looked at his hand, then at him, and spoke a few, slow words. The man hung in there with as much tenacity as a professional ballplayer in the first year of a guaranteed multimillion dollar contract, which is to say he backed off quickly, sitting with the others, pulling the woman down into a chair next to him. After a few more words, Gretchen returned to our table. The four people watched her, huddled close together, and then left the restaurant.

"Are you married?" Gretchen asked me as she regained her chair.

"No," I said, without going into details.

"She is."

"Who is she?"

"Eleanor Koehn. She's a slush."

"A slush?"

"A lush who drinks and then becomes a slut."

"I take it her husband was not among Eleanor's admirers."

"Her husband is King Koehn. He owns King Boats."

"King Koehn?"

"That's what he calls himself, what he insists his employees call him. About half the people in Deer Lake work for him one way or another."

"And he doesn't have time for a wife," I guessed.

"Sure, he does. Just not his own."

"Compliments of the management," Ingrid announced, interrupting us with a bottle of Beringer white zinfandel and two wine glasses.

"This isn't necessary," Gretchen told her.

"Are you on duty?" Ingrid asked.

"No."

"Compliments of the management," she repeated, pouring a generous amount of the liquid into each glass. We both thanked her.

"You did that well," I told Gretchen after our hostess left.

"Breaking up the brawl?"

"No. Scamming the freebie," I said, and Gretchen laughed.

"Don't tell Bobby Orman," she said. "He's the sheriff. He takes a real dim view of deputies accepting gratuities."

"You did handle yourself well, though," I told her again. "Both here and at The Last Chance. You're a good cop."

"I don't know. I might be catching on. Finally. When I first started, I was in everyone's face. Always mouthing off, always threatening people until physical force became a necessity. I was the best baton twirler in Kreel County, you know?"

I nodded.

"I guess I was trying to overcompensate for being a woman, trying to prove I was just as tough as the male deputies. There was a lot of hostility and suspicion when I first started; the guys stood back to see if I could handle myself. Some of them didn't want to work with me. Others, when I called for backup, they'd take their own sweet time responding, stopping along the way to bag a speeder, stuff like that. So I was always asserting my authority, I was always playing it hard. And I never understood why no one complained. Oh, they'd scream a blue streak about some of the things I said but nothing when I beat them up.

"Then one day I started thinking, This is silly. It's silly for a deputy—man or woman—to start duking it out with some guy in a bar. What does it prove? That you're stupid, that's what it proves. I guess I've mellowed. I don't get in their faces anymore. I don't try to belittle them. Or challenge their manhood. I talk softly but firmly and directly, and people respond. They call me ma'am. They kiss my hand and they say, 'Can I tell you my side of the story first, ma'am?' Most people who give cops BS do it for effect, they do it for the crowd. But look at me: five foot six, one hundred twenty-five pounds. People who give me BS look stupid, and no one wants to look stupid in front of their friends. They'd rather go to jail. Besides, I bust someone, he figures he'll get treated right. He knows he won't have an accident on the stairs; you know, trip and bump his head eight or nine times."

"You're a peace officer," I volunteered.

"That's it exactly. A peace officer. I like the sound of that."

We finished the wine and listened to Lonnie Cavander's first set, and when it seemed the right time, I squeezed Gretchen's soft, warm hand and told her it had been a pleasure meeting her. She told me she had enjoyed herself, too, and I should call her the next time I was in Deer Lake. Neither of us spoke of Alison again.

eleven

The Donnerbauers lived in a house in an old-fashioned St. Paul neighborhood that harkened back to the days of F. Scott Fitzgerald and bootleg booze. But the house itself wasn't old-fashioned, merely old, with a spotty lawn and crumbling sidewalk. Mrs. Donnerbauer greeted me at the door, waving frantically. "Come in, come in," she urged, as if she were afraid the neighbors might see me.

I had called the Donnerbauers from a pay phone before leaving Deer Lake and asked if I could visit. They agreed. But it was well after ten when I arrived, and no visible lights burned in the house as I stood on the porch and stared at the front door, deciding whether I should knock or not. I figured they must have gone to bed until Mrs. Donnerbauer opened the door just as I was about to leave.

I stepped across the threshold into virtual darkness. An ancient floor lamp burned in the far corner of the living room, but the dim light it cast was supressed by a burnt-orange lampshade and didn't reach the door. The only other light in the room came from a seventeen-inch television mounted on a metal TV tray, also in the far corner; its flickering shadows gave the plastic-covered furniture an eerie sense of movement. A man that I assumed was Alison's father sat under the floor lamp in a chair facing the TV screen, his bifocals balanced on his nose. He was either watching the Entertainment channel or reading the *People* magazine that was opened across his knee. Mrs. Donnerbauer introduced me, saying, "The detective person is here." Mr. Donnerbauer didn't reply. Maybe, in fact, he was sleeping.

Alison's mother led me to the kitchen in the back of the house, where a single bare lightbulb burned overhead. She offered me a chair after first removing a large cardboard box from the seat. The box was at least fifteen inches square and filled with the small rubber bands that the delivery kids wrap around your newspaper. She set the box on the counter next to an impressive stack of wrinkled aluminum foil. "Would you like some coffee?" she asked. When I said I did, she filled a tall juice glass and handed it to me.

"Would you like some fish sticks?"

"Fish sticks?" I replied.

"We have plenty," Mrs. Donnerbauer said, confessing that she worked as a food demonstrator, enticing supermarket shoppers with free samples as they pushed their carts up and down the aisles. She always brought the leftovers home to feed her family, which now consisted only of herself and her silent husband.

I declined the fish sticks.

"That woman in the paper, are they going to make her pay for hurting my little girl?" Mrs. Donnerbauer asked abruptly.

"I don't know. There's not much physical evidence," I answered.

"It ain't fair," she insisted.

I agreed with her.

Mrs. Donnerbauer was a small woman on the downside of fifty, an age she hadn't reached without hard struggle. Any resemblance to the young woman in my photographs had been eroded by time. Without prodding, Mrs. Donnerbauer began speaking of her Alison—only not with the hallowed devotion you would expect from a grieving mother. Rather, she spoke of Alison as if she were the wayward daughter of an unpopular neighbor.

"Very peculiar child," Mrs. Donnerbauer said.

"How so?"

"Well, she wasn't like the other children."

"How so?" I repeated.

"For one thing, she was always reading," Mrs. Donnerbauer said as if she had caught her daughter drinking three-two beer behind the garage. "Reading at the dinner table. Reading in the car. Reading in front of the TV. Reading at night under the covers with a flashlight."

"Nothing wrong with that," I suggested. "I did much the same thing when I was a kid."

"*War and Peace?*" Mrs. Donnerbauer asked. "*The Selected Plays of Eugene O'Neill? Canterbury Tales?* In old English! Once I caught her reading *The Rise and Fall of the Third Reich*. She was eight years old. Imagine."

Imagine, indeed.

"And she would never answer when I spoke to her," the woman added from across the kitchen table. "I would chant her name: Alison, Alison, Alison. Nothing. At first I thought she was deaf or something. Then I thought it was because Alison hadn't been named until after she was three months old because of a family disagreement. . . . *His mother,*" she mouthed silently, gesturing toward the living room. "I thought maybe she didn't realize that Alison was her name. Of course, I now know that she was just ignoring me, like her father. Isn't that right, dear?" she asked the man in the living room. When he didn't reply, she shook her head. "See?"

"Maybe he didn't hear you."

"Oh, he heard me fine; he just doesn't want to say anything." Mrs. Donnerbauer sighed dramatically. "It's the cross I bear."

I didn't say anything, either. After a moment, Mrs. Donnerbauer sighed again. I took that as a cue.

"It must have been difficult raising a girl who was so intelligent," I said.

"Very difficult. And a little bit"—Mrs. Donnerbauer searched for a word, settled on—"frightening. Imagine trying to raise a child who's smarter than you. It was bad enough when she merely *thought* she was smarter. But then the teachers at the school told us Alison should be in special classes because she was a genius. They tested her—they never asked me if they could, but I guess they test everybody. Anyway, they tested her, and the tests results said Alison was a genius. A genius," she repeated as if the word made her nauseous. "It gave Alison a reason to ignore me. Suddenly I wasn't smart enough to tell her when to go to bed or to eat her vegetables or what clothes to wear. I wasn't smart enough to be her mother. 'Leave me alone, leave me alone.' Everyday it was the same thing until finally I just threw up my hands and did leave her alone."

Mrs. Donnerbauer took time out to stare at something way above my left shoulder. I sipped coffee from the juice glass. At last she said, "I guess Alison found out what happens when you think you're so much smarter than everyone else."

I was amazed by the statement and flashed again on the photograph in my car. In the end, Alison couldn't even depend on her mother.

"She used to say she was blessed," Mrs. Donnerbauer continued. "Well, I didn't see it. Where's the blessing in being so different from everyone else? You tell me. I remember when she was graduated from high school—graduated three weeks before her sixteenth birthday. I was so embarrassed. . . ."

"Really? I would have thought you would've been proud."

Mrs. Donnerbauer shook her head. "You don't know what it's like, having people look at you, stare at you. Having people ask you questions because your daughter is so . . . different. People asking how she was around the house, like if she ate strange food or something. People asking if I—if *I*—took vitamins or something when I was carrying her; if I listened to Mozart of something in the delivery room. Imagine! People. Sometimes I don't know what to think."

"Sometimes I don't know what to think, either," I agreed.

"And of course, she didn't have any time for boys," Mrs. Donnerbauer continued. "She was too busy doing *genius* things."

"What about Stephen Emerton?"

"That was the one time I put my foot down," she answered proudly. "Stephen was such a good-looking boy and smart, too. But the way Alison treated him . . . Well, I practically forced her down the aisle."

"Alison didn't want to get married?"

"Oh, of course not. That's what *normal* people did. But I knew marriage was the best thing for her. And so . . ."

"Was she happy do you think?"

"What do you mean by that?"

"Was she happily married?"

Mrs. Donnerbauer stared at me as if she had never heard the expression before.

"I heard that she might have been seeing someone else," I added.

"Committing *adultery*?!" Mrs. Donnerbauer was genuinely shocked.

"I heard—"

"No daughter of mine *ever* committed *adultery*. I don't know where you got your information, young man, but you better go back and get some more, yes sir. We are Catholics in this house. Roman Catholics. *We don't break commandments.*"

I was actually relieved to hear her denial. "I didn't mean to offend you."

"Offend me? Why should I be offended because a man comes into my home and calls my little girl a *trollop!*"

"Mrs. Donnerbauer, I deeply apologize, I truly do," I said, trying to defuse the situation. "But you have to understand that when we hear rumors like this, no matter how ridiculous, we have to look into them. It's the courts that make us do it."

"The courts," she repeated and looked around, like she was searching for a place to spit. No one likes the courts. That's why it's easy to blame them when you get into a jam.

I tried again. "This rumor says that Alison was involved with a doctor while she worked—"

"No. No. No. My daughter would never get involved with . . . A doctor, you say? No. I don't want to hear any more. I think it's time you left."

I rose from my chair.

"My daughter is no *adulteress.*"

I was happy to believe her.

"Thank you, Mrs. Donnerbauer."

She eyed me suspiciously. "My child never cheated on her husband, I don't care what that . . . that brute Raymond Fleck told the newspapers," she added slowly and carefully in case I was leaving with the wrong impression.

"I never thought she did," I agreed.

Mrs. Donnerbauer apparently had to think about that. And in the silence that ensued, Mr. Donnerbauer said one word very clearly from his chair in the darkened living room: "Holyfield."

The word hung in the air like an unpleasant odor.

"No," Mrs. Donnerbauer muttered.

"What was that, Mr. Donnerbauer?" I stepped toward the arch that separated the two rooms.

"Dr. Robert Holyfield," he said, without taking his eyes from the TV screen.

"What? What? What are you saying?" Mrs. Donnerbauer pushed past me, practically running to her husband's chair. "What are you saying? Do you know what you're *saying?*"

Mr. Donnerbauer refused to look at her. "She was a woman like all other women," he answered coldly.

"What is that supposed to mean?" Mrs. Donnerbauer demanded.

Mr. Donnerbauer turned his head maybe ten degrees and tilted it just enough so that he could see his wife's face. His upper lip curled into an ugly snarl. "You know exactly what I mean, woman." Then he just as deliberately resumed watching TV.

"You bastard!" Mrs. Donnerbauer spat at him.

Mrs. Donnerbauer's high-pitched whine was gaining in volume behind me as I walked rapidly from the room, out the door, and into the night. I didn't look back until my car door was open and I was sliding in.

twelve

Minnesotans, like most Americans, are summer people. Perhaps more so than most Americans because we spend such a large part of the year without its warmth, yearning for it, planning for it. True, few people have as much fun in the snow as we do. Yet, when we recall the joys of childhood, we always think of summer.

On this particular bright, cloudless summer day, I drove with all my windows rolled down, searching South St. Paul for the Holyfield Clinic. I found it just where they said I would, a few blocks off Lafayette. It looked like a pillbox, with white concrete walls, a flat roof, and only a few windows. The parking lot was spacious and contained an inordinate number of handicapped slots; they took up all the spaces closest to the building except for one. The slot nearest the front door was reserved for R. HOLYFIELD, M.D. A new Lexus was parked in the space. I was tempted to "accidentally" scratch the paint with my keys as I walked by—revenge for seducing Alison. I might have, too, if not for the woman watching me as she leaned against the building and sucked on a cigarette, banished from her place of employment by Minnesota's anti-smoking laws.

Normally the Lexus wouldn't have troubled me. I am usually indifferent to the wealth of other people. You need to be if you're a baseball fan. But I find it obscene that the average doctor grosses over two hundred thousand dollars a year along with five weeks of vacation, yet a third of the citizens of the United States can't afford their services, can't afford health care at all. Like the man said, there's something wrong. . . .

With that in mind, I was surprised to find a large number of elderly patients in the waiting room. That is until I remembered that the Holyfield Clinic specialized in caring for patients fifty-five years and older. Their arthritis, hardened arteries, and respiratory ailments were Holyfield's bread and butter. Besides, they probably all had insurance companies footing the bill, otherwise they wouldn't have been allowed through the front door.

Getting to see Dr. Holyfield was no easy matter. I had called earlier that morning. Before I even mentioned my name and purpose, the receptionist made it clear that no appointments could be had for at least two weeks. And when I confessed that it was a nonmedical matter, well, time is money, and Dr. Holyfield was not one to squander either. That's when I turned nasty.

"Look, lady. This is a murder investigation. Now, I can come over there at the good doctor's convenience and chat quietly in his office, or I can send a few officers to drag him over here in handcuffs. Which would you prefer?"

Most people, especially people who are accustomed to civility, are frightened by loud voices. They shouldn't be. Loudness, what's that? It doesn't mean power or strength or confidence. Usually it means the opposite. No, it's the guy who talks softly, who looks you in the eye and says what he has to say without looking away, that's the guy to worry about. Fortunately the receptionist didn't realize that. Instead of calling my bluff and telling me to stick it where the sun doesn't shine, she quickly put me on hold, forcing me to listen to a John Denver tune—how's that for payback? She was back in less than a minute to inform me that Dr. Holyfield would see me for fifteen minutes at eleven o'clock. Don't be late.

I wasn't.

Dr. Holyfield was what too much money, too much education, and too much deference to his title had made him: a snob, who had little respect or appreciation for life that existed beyond the comfortable confines of his daily activities. True, I hadn't seen him in action. No doubt he was all kindness and light. Yet I would wager my retirement fund that tree surgeons cared more for their patients than he did. At the same time, you just knew he was well loved and even adored by a whole throng of people who hardly knew him at all. Just the kind of guy to seduce a lonely, vulnerable woman like Alison.

I purposely used his first name, calling him Bob. It's an old cop trick. It removes a suspect's dignity and makes him feel defensive, inferior, and often dependent, like a child seeking a parent's approval; it also lets the suspect know who's in charge. I don't know why this is true, but personal experience told me that it was, especially among people who expect to be called Mister and Sir and Doctor.

"It's nice to meet you, Mr. Taylor. I hope you appreciate that I am on a tight schedule," Dr. Holyfield informed me after we shook hands and he examined my photostat.

"I do, Bob, and I hope to make this quick."

Dr. Holyfield waved at a chair in front of his cluttered desk. I sat before he had a chance to—another slight.

"I haven't much time to give you," he informed me again and smiled. I wiped the smile off his face with my first question.

"How long did your affair with Alison Emerton last?"

He hesitated, then answered, "We did not have an affair."

"Bob, I'm going to ask you that question again," I said calmly. "Think before you answer. How long did—"

"I answered your ruddy question. Now, get out."

Ruddy? Tsk, tsk. Such language from a respected medical man. "Have it your own way, Bob," I said, only I didn't leave the chair. Instead, I pulled a blank subpoena from my inside jacket pocket and started filling in the empty spaces. After my conversation with the receptionist, I thought it'd be wise to bring a few, just in case.

Dr. Holyfield, who was standing now, asked, "What do you think you're doing?"

"Preparing a subpoena," I answered. "I'll take it to the Dakota County sheriff, and he'll take it to the Dakota County attorney, and he'll take it to a Dakota County judge, who will stamp his approval on it, and by this time tomorrow you'll be answering questions before the Dakota County grand jury. Ever been to Dakota County? Nice place. Long drive, though. I hope you don't have anything planned for the day."

Dr. Holyfield considered my words for a moment, and I wondered if I had overplayed my hand. A private investigator issuing subpoenas? Yeah, right, happens every day.

"I don't have time for this," he declared and moved back to his chair. "Ask your questions and be quick about it."

"I already asked one," I reminded him, making a production out of returning the subpoena to my pocket, trying hard not to smile in triumph.

"Five months," he answered.

"Did it begin before Alison was married?"

"No. We had met at several health-related functions prior to her marriage," he answered as if he was discussing a brake job. "However, we did not become . . . involved . . . until much later. Not until after her wedding. I don't know what drew us together. Perhaps we both needed to spend time with someone who understood our problems. Alison had come to the conclusion that marrying Stephen had been a dreadful error, and at the same time I was having serious misgivings concerning my own marriage. Originally, that's all we did: spend time together, go places, go to the zoo—I've lived in this state my entire life, and I had never been to the Minnesota zoo. We did not become intimate until several weeks had passed. I'm guessing we were both caught up in a fantasy that our lives were somehow different when we were together—there was no Stephen, I had no wife. In our fantasy, we were starting over, beginning our lives anew, with no attachments, no past to encumber us. Alas, it was only a silly fantasy and it ended. It ended all too soon."

For someone who had refused to speak with me until I leaned on him, Dr. Holyfield was surprisingly forthcoming. I encouraged him, yet I didn't trust him.

"How did the affair end?" I asked.

"Stephen found out and threatened Alison with a divorce."

"I'd have guessed she'd have welcomed a divorce."

I thought I detected just a smidgen of regret when Dr. Holyfield answered, "No." But I could've been mistaken.

"She came from a family that was vehemently opposed to divorce," he continued. "She had been brainwashed long ago into accepting the fallacy that she was married forever."

"How 'bout you, Bob?"

"When Alison informed me that our involvement had to cease, I came to the realization that I owed it to myself to rescue my own marriage, and I pledged myself to that goal."

"Did you?"

"Did I what?"

"Save your marriage."

"Unfortunately, no. My wife also learned about the affair. I understand a *friend* told her all about it. Our divorce was final just over seven months ago. It was acrimonious, as you might expect. There was a great deal of name calling, finger pointing, and suspicion. When it was concluded, my wife had custody of my children, my house, two cars, several IRAs, and an enormous alimony and child-support settlement. Prior to the divorce, I had made several unwise investments, so there wasn't as much money as she expected, or she would have taken that, too. As it was, I was forced to undergo an audit; she claimed I had hidden a substantial amount of our financial assets. The court concluded that it was merely one of her unfounded allegations."

I didn't do the polite thing and tell him I was sorry. I wasn't.

Instead I asked, "Was your divorce final before or after Alison disappeared?"

"Before."

"Did you try to contact her after the divorce?"

"Certainly."

"And how did she respond?"

The good doctor shrugged. "The sun had set on that relationship."

"Oh?"

"As I recall," he said, looking up at the ceiling, "her exact words were: 'I do not believe the resumption of our relationship at this time would be productive for either of us.'"

"Her exact words?"

Holyfield nodded.

"How did that make you feel?" I asked.

He shrugged again.

"I would think you'd be pretty upset," I told him. "After losing your wife and children, after being put in debt for the rest of your life for wanting her. Yeah, I'd be pissed off."

"To be honest, I was relieved."

"Relieved?"

"I had just survived one relationship. I was unprepared to leap into a second."

"Yet you contacted her," I reminded him.

He had nothing to say to that.

"Where were you the night Alison disappeared?"

"I'd need to consult my calendar," Bob said.

"Why don't you do that," I encouraged him.

He smiled and shrugged. "Why bother?"

"It might supply you with an alibi."

"For what?"

Was he purposely being obtuse?

"For the murder of Alison Emerton," I answered too loudly.

"What makes you think she was murdered?"

That one caught me right between the eyes.

"Excuse me?"

"What makes you think she was murdered?" he repeated.

Dr. Holyfield smiled, and in that smile I saw his intentions. He was giving me a preview of his defense.

"What do you believe became of Alison?" I asked, the dutiful straight man.

"Alison was greatly disappointed in the life she was living with Stephen," he answered. "I have no doubt that, given her intelligence, her drive, her beauty, she naturally hoped to achieve more."

"More?"

"More money, more prestige, more power, more adventure, more . . . I once told her that the hardest lesson an individual can learn is to be content with who they are, to accept themselves for who they are. Alison was not prepared to do that. That's probably why she left."

"Left?"

"Do you always ask one-word questions, Holland?"

The sonuvabitch had turned the tables on me. Now I was the student, and he was the teacher.

"What do you mean, left?" I asked again.

"I believe she decided to become someone else." He smiled some more. "I appreciate that there are several unanswered questions concerning the circumstances of her disappearance. However, that does not alter my theory. In fact, I can appreciate how the difficulties she was forced to endure during those dark days might have motivated her to leave."

"Leave for where?"

Dr. Holyfield merely shrugged.

"Why didn't you inform the police of your theory?" I asked.

"I am under no obligation to do so. If Alison wants to start her life over, I say good luck."

I left Robert Holyfield's office exactly fifteen minutes after entering it, feeling I had been played like a Stradivarius. Anne Scalasi would have been appalled. Still, what would she have done differently? Dr. Holyfield had readily admitted to having an affair with Alison, and he confessed that the affair had contributed to his divorce, to his losing nearly everything he owned. And he had admitted that Alison had blown him off when he had attempted to resume their relationship. However, he couldn't have killed her for rejecting him because, ladies and gentlemen of the jury, Alison is not dead. Goodness gracious, no. She's pumping gas in Fayetteville, Tennessee, at a service station owned by Elvis Presley. And, as implausible as it might sound, that argument could just as easily be applied to Irene Brown's defense. Or Raymond Fleck's. Or Stephen Emerton's.

Damn.

Reasonable doubt. Without a body, there's always reasonable doubt—the criminal's best friend.

But in this case . . . *Was* she alive?

I removed her photograph from the envelope. The eyes had changed somehow. So had the rest of her face. She looked different to me now.

"Are you alive?"

She had committed adultery; she had cheated on her husband. Stephen Emerton had told the truth about that. But what about Raymond Fleck? Had he also been truthful? It was hard to believe. But not as hard as it had been fifteen minutes ago. Alison was not the woman I thought she was.

"You lied to me," I told the photograph.

I shove the glossy back into the envelope and drove back through St. Paul toward my office in Minneapolis, as depressed as I ever hoped to be. And angry, convinced that Alison had played me for a sucker.

"Ahh, nuts!" I shouted, slapping the top of my steering wheel. Two days ago I had it solved. Two days ago I was the greatest detective since Eugène François Vidocq, the nineteenth century crook-turned-crook-catcher who founded the French Sûreté. Which reminded me, I really needed to return Scalasi's book.

thirteen

Cynthia looked delicious in a black turtleneck sweater dress with a carefully fitted bodice and a long, sweeping skirt. You'd never have supposed that she had dressed in a feverish seven minutes flat while I monitored her progress on my watch as I paced her living room. It would have taken her six minutes except for the great "with pearls or without" debate. She went without.

The way Cynthia acted as we drove to the theater in Minneapolis, though, you'd have thought I never took her anywhere, and I told her so.

"Only sporting events and jazz clubs," she reminded me.

There's no pleasing some people.

"Actually, I'm amazed anything could drag you away from your precious baseball. Don't you have tickets for the St. Paul Saints tonight?"

"It's like Tallulah Bankhead once said, 'There have been only two geniuses in the world. Willie Mays and Willie Shakespeare.' Besides, the Saints are in Sioux Falls tonight. They'll be home tomorrow, though; they're playing Ida Borders and the Duluth-Superior Dukes. Want to go?"

"Oh, rapture."

Marie Audette played Portia in *The Merchant of Venice*, a typical Shakespearean heroine: tough, clever, resourceful, who confounds her rivals and generally saves the day—but only while disguised as a man. And, of course, she is never recognized until the final scene, even by her lover. I pointed at Marie when she ascended to the stage.

"She gave us the tickets," I told Cynthia.

"Shhhh!" Cynthia hissed.

She shushed me several more times during the performance, punctuating her entreaties for quiet with sharp jabs from her elbow. Yet try as I might, I could not stop fidgeting. I couldn't stop shuffling through the notes in my head—apparently making quite a racket of it—searching for the one clue that would determine who actually had killed Alison Donnerbauer Emerton.

I had liked Irene Brown. But that was yesterday. Today, Dr. Bob, the jilted lover, looked good, except there was nothing to tie him to the scene. And both Raymond Fleck and Stephen Emerton still rated high in my estimation.

"Nuts," I muttered under my breath.

"Shhhhh!" Cynthia hissed at me.

I tried hard not to believe Dr. Bob's theory. I didn't want to

believe it. Alison wasn't the kind to run away from her problems.
No way. She would have stared them in the eye and taken them
on. Yes, that's what my Alison would have done. *My Alison*. But
was my Alison the same Alison as the woman in the photograph?
I had seen things in her face, emotions that touched me. Yet were
they real? Was that the face of a woman who committed adultery?
Twice? Apparently it was.

I shook my head, tried to clear it. Instead, my mind's eye super-
imposed Alison's photograph over the stage; I was looking at it
and through it even as I watched Marie Audette going about her
business. And I knew. Of course the emotions weren't real; the
photograph had been taken to promote a play, to reflect a character Alison was playing. What was the line Jon Lovitz used to say
on *Saturday Night Live?* Oh, yeah.

"It's acting!"

"Sheeesh," a voice behind me answered.

Stop it, Taylor, my inner voice told me. *Get a grip. Start thinking
like a detective. Be objective, dammit.* "Be objective," I muttered.

Cynthia's elbow almost cracked my rib. I didn't blame her for
being miffed. We were at a critical juncture in the play, the scene
where Shylock the Jew is demanding his pound of flesh, and Portia, disguised as a hot-shot arbitrator from Padua, says he can
have it, just so long as he does not "shed one drop of Christian
blood." Shylock is a louse, of course. Yet I always figured he got
the shaft. I mean, no one put a gun to Antonio's head, made him
take the loan, and if he couldn't pay the vig, well . . . Still, I
enjoyed watching Marie, standing center stage like a gunfighter
waiting for the bad guy to slap leather, beseeching Shylock "to cut
off the flesh" if he dared. But my concentration wouldn't hold,
and soon I was reflecting on my list of suspects again.

Irene Brown. Raymond Fleck. Stephen Emerton. Dr. Bob. Hell,

all things considered, even Mrs. Donnerbauer could be considered a suspect.

I squirmed in my seat some more, asking myself, Who put the note on my windshield telling me to quit the investigation? Not Irene. Not Raymond. Both were guests of the Dakota County Sheriff's Department at the time.

Stephen Emerton? Had to be. Who else was there?

I sighed noisily, drawing more frosty stares.

Motive and opportunity. Motive and opportunity. I kept repeating the words in my head like a mantra.

Meanwhile, Portia, still disguised as a male lawyer, was now dancing around her befuddled husband, messing with his mind, diddling him out of the ring she had given him on the day they were married, the ring he vowed never to be without.

"I see, sir, you are liberal in offers: You taught me first to beg, and now, methinks, you teach me how a beggar should be answer'd."

Marie Audette was a good actress. *Wait a minute!* my inner voice shouted. *So was Alison!* My mind spun back to the first act of the play. What was it that Portia told Jessica when she took up her disguise?

"I'll hold thee any wager. . . . I'll prove the prettier fellow . . . and wear my dagger with the braver grace; and speak, between the change of man and boy, with a reed voice and turn two mincing steps into a manly stride; and speak of frays, like a fine bragging youth: and tell quaint lies, how honourable ladies sought my love, which I denying, they fell sick and died. . . . And twenty of these puny lies I'll tell, that men shall swear I have discontinued school above a twelvemonth. I have within my mind a thousand raw tricks of these bragging Jacks which I will practice."

Motive and opportunity.

"Alison really is a genius," I muttered loud enough to earn another punch in the ribs.

"Remember when you first came to my office?" I asked Truman the next morning. "Remember I said Alison might have gone out for a pack of cigarettes and kept on going? That it's been done before? Well, maybe she did."

"That's ridiculous," Truman answered, pacing my office floor like a caged cat.

"Hey, man, this is America," I reminded him. "It's always been easy for Americans to go somewhere else and start over. That's what our ancestors did. That's why America exists today. Remember the executive director of the Minneapolis City Council? She packed her bags, arranged for her attorney to pay off her debts, and—poof!—she was gone. Nobody knew where she went. Everybody thought she had run away with a lover or had been abducted or ripped off the city. Turned out she simply went to San Francisco to become a different person."

Truman was unimpressed. He pointed out that the police had had the same theory but rejected it because none of Alison's belongings were missing. She hadn't packed, as the executive director had; she hadn't closed her banking accounts and settled her affairs; she hadn't contacted an attorney—hadn't contacted *him*.

"All that means is that what she left behind didn't concern her," I told him.

"This is insane. You're saying Alison staged her own disappearance, the tape recording, the blood, everything?"

"Yes."

"Bullshit. There's no evidence of that; you haven't got any evidence. All you have is a self-serving theory from some bum-fuck doctor who might have been the one who killed her in the first place. I can't believe you're buying this shit."

"Dr. Bob doesn't have anything to do with it."

"Oh, no? Then where the fuck did this amazing theory come from?"

"Two things. One, the note on my windshield. Whoever put it there didn't want us looking into Alison's disappearance. I think it was Alison. That was a mistake because instead of quitting, it made us look harder."

Truman snorted at that.

"Yeah?" he asked. "What's number two?"

"*The Merchant of Venice.*"

Truman stopped his pacing and stared long enough to measure me for a white jacket that fastens in the back.

"You're shitting me," he said.

"No, I'm not," I assured him.

"I can't believe I'm paying for this," he groused.

"Think about it," I told Truman. "Raymond Fleck, Irene Brown, Stephen Emerton, Dr. Holyfield, her parents: They all wronged Alison one way or another. Now each of their lives has been turned upside down; each one is paying a price. Why? Because no one knows for sure exactly what happened to her. She got 'em. She got 'em all at the same time; a brilliant girl is our Alison."

"You're saying she staged her own murder just to get even?"

" '*If you prick us, do we not bleed? If you tickle us, do we not laugh? If you poison us, do we not die? And if you wrong us, shall we not revenge?*' "

"That's ridiculous," Truman replied to the line I had memorized the evening before.

"Oh, and you would never do anything like that. You would never go out of your way to stick it to someone."

Truman didn't want to hear any more. "Find her, goddammit!" he demanded, throwing his hands in the air. "You think she's fucking alive, find her."

I made an effort to explain just how long, tedious, and expensive a missing-person's search could become, especially if the missing person was working hard at not being found. I don't know if I was trying to talk him out of it or not.

"Find her," he repeated.

I quickly produced a standard contract. He signed it after reading it twice and then threw the pen down on my desk blotter.

"No one is to hear about this," he ordered. "Not your friends with the police, especially not the media. I don't want anybody getting away with murder just because you have a fucking hunch. Understand?"

I understood. I told him I would keep the investigation to myself unless Irene Brown or Raymond Fleck were indicted. If that happened, I would probably have to speak up. Truman disagreed and commenced to argue with me the fine points of Minnesota Statutes 326.32–326.339, the licensing requirements and procedures for private detectives and protective agents. He thought there might be a loophole. I disagreed.

"Just find her," he said at last.

fourteen

I retrieved a missing persons form from my desk drawer and started filling it with information. The form was basically a cheat sheet I had picked up at the last convention of private investigators I attended. Once complete, it would contain nearly every known fact about Alison, from her style of dress (lots of sweaters and natural-fiber blazers) to her hobbies (dogs, cross-country skiing), from the languages she spoke (French and Russian) to her driving record (three speeding tickets in two years) and spending habits (two credit cards, paid entire balance monthly). All this plus a *Portrait Parle*, noting in detail Alison's physical characteristics—everything from the size and shape of her ears to the quality of her walk.

Much of this information was already available in Anne Scalasi's file. The rest I would acquire through interviews with Alison's neighbors, co-workers, paperboy, hairdresser, investment adviser, high-school and college professors, veterinarian, insurance agent, travel agent, Marie Audette, her family, her husband, and so on. It was a complicated, tedious process. Not as complicated as a shuttle launch yet complicated enough to give me a headache.

The reason for all this work is simple: People are creatures of habit. After spending a lifetime doing a specific thing in a certain way, it is extremely difficult, if not impossible, to change. Consider the case of Christopher Boyce, the Falcon in the movie *The Falcon and the Snowman*. Boyce escaped from prison, where he was serving a life sentence for selling secrets to the Soviet Union, and disappeared. Completely. However, Boyce was a nut about falconry, thus his nickname. So the government staked out those locations frequented by people who shared Boyce's passion—there are only so many places where people go to hunt with falcons. Sure enough, Boyce was discovered in one of them, a small town in Oregon.

The past had led investigators to Boyce's new life. The past would lead me to Alison Donnerbauer Emerton.

"All right, darlin'," I told the photograph I taped to my office wall, the photograph of Alison and Marie Audette in costume. "Let the games begin."

———

As with all my missing persons cases, I tried to find Alison the easy way first. By telephone.

"How may I help you?" the operator asked in a machinelike monotone.

"That damn daughter of mine. My wife says we got a telephone bill with all kinds of long-distance calls on it that we didn't make, and she thinks my daughter has let her low-life boyfriend use our phone. I was outta town when we got the bill, and my wife kept the first page, which is the bill, but not the bottom pages, which lists the numbers. So could you mail me the bottom pages so I can get this kid to pay for his calls? Cause I ain't gonna pay for 'em."

"What is your home number and billing address?"

I gave the operator Mr. Donnerbauer's address and telephone number but added, "Could you send them to my office?"

Sure she could.

"Customer service," a pretty voice chirped.

"Yeah, this is Phil Gaffner over at WorldNet. We got a DNP and we're tryin' ta verify some toll charges. Could ya give me listings and returns on 666-2273?" I recited Stephen Emerton's telephone number.

"Just a second while I pull it up on my screen, Phil," the woman replied, much of her cheerfulness gone. Telephone companies hate people who don't pay and are usually more than willing to help even competitors get their money.

"Customer service, how may I help you?" a man's voice asked.

"This is the Ian Ravitch Agency representing Miss Marie Audette. Miss Audette will be out of town for the next forty-five days on an acting assignment, and she requested that we pay her bills until her return. Could you send Miss Audette's telephone bill to our office, please?"

"What is the telephone number and regular billing address, sir?"

I read them to the operator directly from the missing persons form.

"And what address do you want the bill sent to?"

After gathering their records, I discovered that Mr. and Mrs. Donnerbauer had not made any long-distance phone calls to their daughter—or to anyone else since her disappearance. All of Stephen Emerton's calls were to credit-card and insurance companies. Marie Audette had made sixteen long-distance calls, most of them to agents in Chicago and Los Angeles. One set of digits did interest me, however. She had dialed a Deer Lake, Wisconsin, number the day I spoke with her. I dialed the number myself after preparing a sure-fire pretext designed to obtain me the name and address of whoever answered. The pretext wasn't necessary. A tape recording told me I had reached the residence of Deputy Gretchen Rovick, please leave a message.

Framed in silver and hanging above my computer is a photograph of a ridiculous-looking man dressed in a trench coat and fedora and leaning against a personal computer. The photograph was accompanied by a long newspaper article explaining how a private investigator had squashed the hostile takeover of a beloved local firm. According to the article, the investigator—the female reporter described him as James Bond-handsome; I just thought you should know—used his computer skills to uncover several secret bank accounts in Nevada and the Bahamas where the corporate raider's chief officers had quite illegally stashed fifty million undeclared bucks. The IRS, SEC, and FBI had been quite impressed and leaked the news to the media. I would tell you who the investigator was except, well, modesty forbids me.

Truth is, I am not an expert with a computer, merely tenacious. I approach it like John Henry, that steel-driven' man. I ain't gonna quit. I'm gonna find what I need if it kills me.

Fortified with a fresh pot of Jamaican Blue Mountain and armed with my PC, hard disk drive, printer, modem, and telephone and source books, I started dragging databases. There are literally thousands of them, most created and maintained by the government, most free and easily accessed. The trick is knowing where to look. I looked everywhere. I conducted credit bureau sweeps and social security number traces. I accessed the U.S. Post Office's National Change of Address Index, another database containing names compiled from every telephone book in the U.S., and another filled with voter registration information. I searched the motor vehicle registration records of forty-nine states and the criminal records of every county in all fifty states. I hired an information broker to hunt through bank accounts. I personally examined the membership directories and subscription lists of every public-relations-related association and newsletter I could find as well as a database that recorded the names of executives who have moved from one job to another in the past year.

Days turned into weeks. And I learned only one thing: Alison Donnerbauer Emerton was hiding real, real hard.

"Why are you doing this?" Cynthia Grey asked in a tone that made me think of icebergs and polar bears.

"I'm a private investigator," I told her. I liked the sound of that so much I repeated the phrase—I'm a private investigator—a half dozen times with different inflections, making it sound like I was either a swashbuckling adventurer or I made my living repairing refrigerators.

"You're annoying me," she said.

"This is getting old, Cynthia. Ever since I told you I thought Alison was alive, you've been ragging on me to quit the case, telling me she didn't break any laws, telling me she has a right to be left alone. Fine. I get the message. Now quit it, will ya? I don't tell you what cases to take."

We were in bed—my bed to be precise—and for the first time since we'd become intimate, our bodies did not warm each other. She was lying on one side and I was lying on the other, and the few inches that separated us might as well have been the Grand Canyon.

"What's the big deal, anyway?" I asked.

"It's wrong."

"I'll tell you what's wrong. What's wrong is Irene Brown and Raymond Fleck sitting in the Dakota County jail because neither can make bail, waiting to see if they're going to be tried for killing a woman who's not dead."

"Since when do you care about them?"

"I don't," I admitted. "But I'm the one who put them on the spot—at least Irene—and that makes me responsible."

"If only I could believe that."

"What?"

"I think you're trying to find Alison because you want revenge."

"Revenge?"

"Yes, revenge. When you thought she was dead, you acted like she was the great lost love of your life—"

"Stop it," I told her.

"You kept staring at her photograph with such longing—don't tell me you didn't; I know you did—but then you discovered that she had an affair, and suddenly you don't like her anymore. Taylor, you act like she had cheated on *you*. Well, she didn't cheat on you. She didn't do anything to you. She didn't even know you. So why don't you leave her alone? She was treated shitty enough in her life."

"She gave as she got," I told her.

"How do you know?"

"I know. . . ."

"You know nothing about her except what some people told you, and even then you're only listening to the bad and none of the good. Why do you believe Emerton and that doctor? Why do you insist that they're right about Alison and not Marie Audette and Alison's other friend, the deputy?"

"Because—"

"Because you don't want to."

"Are you going to let me finish?"

"I'll tell you what I think. I think you hope Alison really is dead. That way you can recast her as the virginal innocent in the fantasy you've created in your head."

Something cold gripped my heart. Alison dead? No, I didn't want that. I most certainly did not.

"You might find this hard to believe, Cynthia," I said, working hard to keep my voice calm and level, "but I have no emotional investment in locating Alison."

"Yeah, right."

"If you want to argue that I'm trying to find her just to prove that I can, fine. Maybe there's something to that. But it's my job, you see. It's what I do for a living."

"It's wrong," Cynthia reiterated.

"Why? Why is it wrong? When I was trying to find her dead body, I was a good guy. Now, because I'm trying to find her live body, I'm a jerk. Why is that?" Cynthia didn't answer, so I added, "It's just a job, honey."

"And if someone gave you four hundred dollars a day and expenses to investigate me, you'd do it, wouldn't you?"

"Cynthia, please. This is not about you."

"But it could be. That's the thing. It could be. If somebody wanted to learn about my past, if they wanted to hurt me with my past—"

"I'm not hurting anyone," I insisted.

"—me or anyone else on the planet, all they have to do is pay you four hundred dollars a day and expenses."

And then I understood. Cynthia didn't want me to find Alison because she didn't want a detective to one day find her, the real her. The expensive clothes, the furniture, the store-bought manners, they allowed Cynthia to do what Alison was doing: hide. That was why she worked so hard at her profession, why she so enthusiastically embraced the media. She was building a life beyond reproach, strengthening her reputation against the day that someone—like me—would discover that Cynthia Grey, attorney at law, was once a drug addict, that she had danced topless for a living. I understood that, only I wasn't thinking. Instead, I let my mouth do all the work, my brain just standing there leaning on a shovel while I talked myself into a hole.

"I ferret out people's secrets," I replied, trying to make my voice sound just as icy as hers. "I do it for money. And most of the people who hire me? They're lawyers. You act like all this is new to you, Cynthia. But we both know it's not. You've worked with PIs before; hell, you've worked with *me*. You want information you can take into court, you come to us. You want dirt you can use to help your clients and hurt your adversaries, you don't even quibble about our fee. Well, what I'm doing now is no different than what you've hired done in the past. You're no different than Hunter Truman."

Cynthia had nothing more to say. She left the bed and dressed in the dark. The rustle of her clothes and the creak of floorboards told me she was near, but I couldn't see her, and when I reached out, I caught only air. I wanted to say something to her, but what? I'm sorry? Yeah, right, that would cover it. I'm sorry, Cynthia, I was only joking. Sure.

"I'm sorry, I didn't mean to say that," I told her.

She didn't reply.

"Cynthia?"

The floorboards creaked again.

"Cynthia, if you loved me, you would ignore me when I say stupid things."

"Taylor, you're a jerk," she answered softly. And then she was gone. I listened as she made her way down the stairs to the front door, slamming it behind her.

"Taylor, you are a jerk!" I agreed.

I had run out of coffee beans and was finishing my last Dr Pepper when Hunter Truman called. He wanted an update. I told him I had nothing positive to report and asked if I should give it up. He said no, and I sighed my relief. I had no intention of quitting the chase, but it was starting to get expensive. That's why so many skips and missing persons remain unfound because it's not worth the cost of finding them. And I would rather hunt for Alison on Truman's nickel than mine.

"What do you want 'em for?" Stephen Emerton asked when I requested all of his and Alison's canceled personal checks starting one year prior to her disappearance.

I convinced him that I was helping the Dakota County attorney strengthen his case against Irene Brown; told him that if she were convicted of killing Alison, the insurance company would be

forced to pay off on Emerton's claim. He gave me a box of canceled checks dating back eighteen months.

"What do you want them for?" Sarah Selmi asked when I requested
Alison's complete employment history at Kennel-Up, emphasizing those days when she did not report to work, plus a record of
all her business trips and a list of the long-distance phone calls
she had made.

I was bound by Hunter Truman's directive not to tell her the
truth, and I couldn't think of a viable lie, so I simply said: "Because
it's important that we have all the information correct for the
trial." It sounds absurd, I know, but it worked. It usually does. Half
the time when you start a sentence with the word "because,"
people don't even hear the rest of it. They hear only the word
"because," which they translate to mean, "It's all right, go ahead."
If you don't believe me, try it sometime.

Sarah Selmi gave me everything I requested except for the
phone information. Kennel-Up had a WATS line, and they had no
way of determining which employees called where. She said it was
an ongoing problem since her employees shamefully abused the
service, dialing up long-lost relatives halfway around the planet.

I got back to my office and started sifting through the information
I had gathered. Kennel-Up promoted itself as a national company,
yet in reality it was strictly regional, selling its products almost
exclusively in North and South Dakota, Minnesota, Iowa, and
Wisconsin. Alison had visited each of those states several times
in the months before she went missing. However, she wrote no
personal checks in any of them.

One personal check, though, did catch my eye. It was made out to Bosch Publications. The name sounded familiar, but I couldn't place it. I closed my eyes and let it bounce around for a while, but nothing came of it. When I opened my eyes again, I was staring at my bookcase, specifically at the volume with the blue cover and the title *Minnesota Sex Offenders* on the spine. The book listed the names and offenses of nearly everyone who had been convicted of a sex crime in the state of Minnesota, along with the criminal's current address and any other information that the author could secure. It was very popular among the "not in my neighborhood" crowd.

I went to the bookcase, slipped the volume out, opened it to the title page, and noted the publisher.

Bosch Publications, Minneapolis, Minnesota.

Stephen Emerton was becoming increasingly annoyed by my presence in his life. But he did remember seeing a copy of the book I described. It was probably in one of the boxes he had stuffed with Alison's belongings and stashed in a ministorage garage near the intersection of Highway 36 and I-694. And, yeah, he'd leave the key with his secretary if I wanted to take a look.

I did.

It turned out that Alison had a great many books. Maybe a thousand. At least it seemed like that as I rummaged through the boxes stacked inside the garage designated 54A. It took about two hours before I came up with *Minnesota Sex Offenders*.

I took it out of the garage into the light, leaned against my Colt, and flicked through it. The corners of seven pages were turned down. Alison had circled the name of at least one sex offender on each of them. One of the names circled belonged to Fleck, Raymond G. The copy under his name listed Raymond's offense, how long he had spent in prison, his record there, and his current address and place of employment.

Well, well. I put the book back, locked the storage garage, and returned to my office, stopping to drop off Stephen's key on the way. Once inside my office, I examined the canceled check, the one written to Bosch Publications. Alison had bought the book two months before she left the health-care organization to work for Kennel-Up, Raymond's employer.

She had known about Raymond's record before she even met him.

I smiled.

"Mistake number two, Alison," I said aloud. "You should never have kept the book."

I continued to search through Alison's canceled personal checks. Three more interested me. One was written for *Dog Universe* magazine and a second for *X-Country,* a magazine for cross-country skiers. I contacted both publications and arranged to purchase their subscription lists.

The third check had been made out to a print shop a few weeks before Alison began working for Kennel-Up. I guessed it was written to pay for copies of her résumé. I guessed wrong. . . .

The woman behind the counter at the print shop was confused, so she called on a co-worker for assistance. He was no help, so she summoned the manager. The manager inspected my photostat and the canceled check and asked, "Why do you need this information?"

"Because it's vital that we compare it to other information that we have."

Sounded reasonable to him.

After about ten minutes, the manager produced an invoice with Alison's name on it dated seven months before she disappeared. The check hadn't paid for the printing of résumés after all.

"It was a joke," the manager said. "I remember now. Mrs. Emerton asked us to make a plate of her birth certificate, burn off the name and date, then run off a few copies; it had something to do with her parents' thirtieth wedding anniversary."

I almost said it out loud: *You should have paid in cash, Alison. Third mistake.*

A birth certificate is the cornerstone for creating a new identity. It's the most widely accepted form of identification in the United States. And Alison had several on which she could print any name and date she desired.

Once she fills in the blanks, she leaves them in the backyard, letting the sun age them. She mails one stating that she's fifteen to the Social Security Administration, along with a note written in longhand on ruled paper saying, "Daddy is making me get a job." Wham, she has a bona fide social security number.

She brings a second birth certificate stating her age at anywhere between twenty-four and thirty, along with the social security card, to the Department of Motor Vehicles, pick your own state. If anyone should ask, she explains that after living overseas for ten years with her father, who is in the U.S. Air Force, she needs a valid driver's license. She takes a test. Bam, now she has the second most widely used form of ID, accepted by grocery store clerks and traffic cops throughout the nation.

Now she can get a passport, a bank account, credit cards, insurance; she can get a job, start her own business, borrow money. All she needs is time and patience—and Alison had both.

Perfect. Just perfect.

Spurred by yet another hunch, I fired up my PC and began conducting a credit-bureau sweep and a vital-information trace against Rosalind Colletti, Alison's erstwhile stage name.

It was a waste of time.

"She's good," I decided, depressed by the realization that merely throwing my glove on the field wasn't going to beat her, that she might actually beat me.

I'll get her yet, my inner voice vowed. She might have genius on her side, but I had experience

Only I wasn't encouraged. You can divide private investigators into two camps. The first will declare vehemently that the longer an individual goes missing, the harder she is to find. The second, a much smaller group, will insist that the longer an individual is missing, the easier she'll be to find. I tend to agreed with the first group.

fifteen

Scott Dumer was a bartender. Not a bartender who was studying the law or working on a graduate thesis. Not a bartender who wanted to be an actor or a musician or a writer. He was simply a bartender. It was what he liked to do, and he was good at it. He poured a Summit Ale without my asking for it and set it in front of me. He didn't recite the price and wait for me to pay it. He didn't ask where I had been lately. Nor did he tell me I was a sight for sore eyes. Instead, picking up a conversation we had left off nearly a month earlier, he said, "With their piddling payroll, no free agents, bunch of minor leaguers in The Show for the first time, I figure the best the Twins can do is fourth in the Central, and that depends on what Kansas City does."

Considering how badly they'd been crushed by Oakland before going on to lose five of seven to Seattle and California, fourth place looked good. Still, hope springs eternal.

"Second," I told him. "The kids will come around. Besides, it's early."

"More pennants are lost in June than in September," he reminded me, then moved down the stick to attend to another patron.

Hey, a good bartender is like a good mechanic: When you find him, keep him. Scott was the only reason I went into The Dusty Road. Well, that and its close proximity to my home in Roseville. It's where I go when I grow tired of my own company and can't find someone to impose myself upon. Like Cynthia.

The bar was about a third filled, a weeknight crowd, quiet. The most noise came from a table of expensive-looking college girls. The girls were clearly slumming. They had tried to dress poor, but, being rich, they couldn't manage it. They generated a lot of wistful glances from us older, blue-collar guys who frequented the bar. All that young, taut, college-girl flesh—a man is never immune no matter how agreeably attached he might be to another.

I tried not to stare, reminding myself that I was on the far side of middle-age. Because by my calculations, middle age is not forty-five or fifty and certainly not sixty. If a man's average life expectancy is seventy-two or seventy-three, middle age is thirty-six, thirty-seven. You're just kidding yourself to believe otherwise. And to think that these sweet adolescents would be interested in a man of my advanced years would be just vanity, pure and simple. Besides, I didn't need an adoring-coed fantasy. I still had Cynthia. Didn't I?

I wished she'd take my calls so I would know one way or the other; I thought it was unfair of her to keep me hanging. Were we through or weren't we?

I was debating whether to call Cynthia at home—maybe she would beat her answering machine to the phone this time—when a woman came through the door, moving with a clear sense of purpose. She was well favored, and if she had seen better days, it wasn't too long ago. Her hair was glossy and so were her eyes, and although she didn't look like her, for a moment I recognized Alison. I dismissed the image with a sip of beer. Lately I had been seeing Alison everywhere.

The woman's presence silenced the college girls. They stared at her and she stared back, and in the moment their eyes met something was exchanged. I have no idea what. Her past and their future, perhaps. She was older than the girls by a couple of decades. She could have been their mother. For all I knew, maybe she was. By my standards she was merely middle-aged.

The woman made her way to a stool and ordered a shot, water on the side. It wasn't until Scott left her that she began surveying the bar for likely prey. Her eyes fell on me, lingered for a second or two, passed by, then came back. My pulse quickened.

I nodded.

She nodded back.

I smiled.

She smiled.

When Scott served her shot, she asked him a question, gesturing toward me with her chin. Scott, looking like someone who had just lost his dog, spoke about six words in reply. The woman downed her shot and left the bar. I felt betrayed.

"What the hell was that?" I asked Scott.

"Just another woman looking for love in all the wrong places."

"Can the country-western shit. What did she say?"

"She asked me who you were and why you looked so unhappy."

"And?"

"I told her you're in mourning because your roommate just died of AIDS."

"You're an asshole, Scott."

"I'd hate to see you do something you'd regret in the morning."

"Shut up and pour me another beer."

Like I said, a good bartender. We spent the next hour or so talking sports, segueing from baseball to football to basketball while he filled the drink orders of his waitresses and the other customers at the stick.

How did I come to this? I wondered during one of his brief absenses. Alone in a bar, pretending that the man who served me drinks was a long-lost pal. When I was a cop, when I played ball and hockey, when Laura was alive, I had lots of friends. But after she died . . . It was four years, ten months, two weeks, two days ago. You'd think I'd have lost track by now. In fact, it's how I judge the passage of time: Before Laura. Laura. After Laura.

I had dated her for sixteen glorious months. Maybe a million times I came *this close* to asking The Question, only to lose my nerve at the last moment and leave it for another time. Then in exasperation she told me, "If you ask me to marry you tonight, I'd say yes. But if you keeping putting it off until tomorrow or the day after . . ." I didn't put it off. She did say yes.

We were together for seven years, one month, one week, one day. Then a drunk driver took her away; her and my baby girl, Jennifer.

The memory of it tempted me to chug my beer. Only I had

chugged so many beers—and anything else with alcohol in it—in the months immediately after her death that I purposely pushed it away just to prove that I could. My bout with alcoholism had been temporary. Temporary insanity. I'd gotten over it just as I had gotten over Laura's death.

I tested my willpower for about ninety seconds, then finished the Summit and ordered another.

I did a quick survey of the bar. I was the only one sitting alone. But that was okay. I like being alone. I like relying only on myself. It's so much easier.

I admit that sometimes—not often but sometimes—I regret quitting the cops, the teams; I chastize myself for neglecting to return the phone calls of my friends and refusing their invitations until they stopped issuing them; I regret being alone. When that happens I call Anne Scalasi. And if she's busy, I hang out with her kids, take them to ball games, listen to their troubles about school and girlfriends and boyfriends and such—things they probably don't tell their mother. And if they're too involved with their own lives for my Big Brother act I call . . . who?

There have been women to chase away the alone feeling. Not many. But some. Like Cynthia. No, not like Cynthia. She's more than a warm body to lie near. She's someone I could actually care about, whose troubles I'd take to heart. That's what love is all about isn't it? Caring about someone who cares about you? It's that simple. And that complicated.

I drank some more beer.

I was working on my fourth beverage when Freddie sauntered in. Sidney Poitier Fredericks was tall and black and as mean as a politician who's behind in the polls. Some time ago he pistol-whipped me in an alley, causing me a mild concussion and great

embarrassment. I returned the favor a few evenings later, breaking into his condo and shoving the business end of a nine mil-
limeter up his nostril, letting him know how bitterly disappointed
I was by his behavior. I was content to let it go at that, too—keep
your distance and neither of us will get hurt. But then a few
months later the sonuvabitch turned around and saved my life.
Twice.

Freddie made his way noisily around the stick to where I sat,
appraising the college girls as he passed their table. I was glad to
see him. If not a friendly face, his was at least a familiar one.

"Mr. Fredericks," I said happily in recognition as he sat next to
me. "Let me buy you a beer."

He looked at me like he was seeing me for the first time. "Why?"
he asked bluntly.

"Well, you did save my life."

"Don't get misty-eyed about it; it wasn't anything personal. I
was paid, remember? It's not like we're friends. Is that what you
think? We're friends now?"

I shrugged. "Why not?"

"Shit," he said, making the word sound like *sheet*.

"We are in the same business," I reminded him.

"Only as competitors."

Scott took Freddie's order. Pete's Wicked Ale. I insisted on paying for it.

"Call it professional courtesy," I told him.

Freddie gave me a look when he snatched the bottle from the
bar top, but there was no thank you in it. Yeah, me and Freddie.
Pals forever.

"What brings you down here?" I asked, just to be polite.

"Lookin' to git me an order of spare ribs," Freddie grunted.

"They don't serve spareribs here."

"Oh, man . . . Spare ribs, Taylor. Spare ribs. You know, like Eve
was made from Adam's spare rib."

"Do you make this stuff up, Freddie, or do you subscribe to a magazine or something?"

"Is this banter? Huh, Taylor? Are we supposed to be fucking bonding now?"

"Apparently not."

"Shit," he said, this time breaking the word into two syllables: shii-it.

Freddie had turned his back to me. He was watching one of the college girls, who was watching him while pretending not to. "You got business, Taylor, you need air cover, you got my card. Otherwise, fuck it."

"Whatever you say."

He smiled then. "I do believe supper's on the table," he muttered for my benefit.

"Ladies!" he shouted and juke-jived his way to the college girls. Sixty seconds later he had them giggling hysterically. In another sixty seconds he was kneading the shoulders of the girl who had given him the eye. In two minutes more he was sitting at the table next to her, gesturing wildly with one hand to the beat of yet another seemingly hilarious story. What he was doing with the other hand under the table, your guess is as good as mine.

I couldn't bear to watch anymore. *How come I can't do that? I have charisma!* I decided I hated Freddie. Decided I should have shot the surly sonuvabitch when I'd had the chance.

I quickly settled my tab and left, considerably drunker yet no more cheerful than when I'd arrived. I was in no shape to drive. But I drove anyway. If I was busted for DWI on the way home, maybe Cynthia would defend me.

The morning broke cold and gray and didn't hold much promise for improvement. The woman on the radio said eighty percent chance of showers. It was a good day to stay in bed, I decided, and drew the blankets close to my chin. What with my pounding head and unsteady stomach, I could use the extra shut-eye, anyway.

Besides, I was tired. So tired, it was difficult to even roll over and find a more comfortable position. Yet deep sleep did not come. Nor had it last night, despite the numerous beers. Nor the night before. Nor the night before that. I kept waking after only a few hours, from dreams that were all too vivid, filled with the shadows of ninety-six murder investigations, with the ghosts of men whose lives I've taken in anger.

Whenever a case disturbs me, it seems like all my past troubles resurface and crowd around it. And this case disturbed me. In the beginning my desire to find Alison, to find her alive, tingled throughout my body like lust, making me aware of everything: the way my fingers caressed the keyboard of my personal computer, the way my chest heaved up and down with my breath—Cynthia had been right about that. Only now, twenty-four days after convincing Truman that Alison was alive, my passion was spent. I found I had no enthusiasm for the day, no energy. The search for Alison had stopped being fun, stopped being a game. It had become work, hard work at that, and I had begun to challenge the logic of it. Alison had not broken any laws, unless some overzealous prosecutor wanted to hang an abandonment rap on her—Cynthia had been right about that, too. And if her abrupt disappearance had made life difficult for Raymond Fleck and Irene Brown and Stephen Emerton and the rest, well, golly gee, that just broke my heart.

Still, I was taking money for it, wasn't I? Four hundred dollars a day. And expenses. What was the meter at now? Ninety-six hundred? Something like that. I found myself wishing I was broke, that I needed the job, needed the money. At least that would have given me an excuse for dragging my sorry ass to the office to resume the chase. It would let me pretend that I wasn't looking for Alison for personal reasons.

I stayed in bed until my headache shrieked for relief and the nausea in my stomach forced me into the bathroom.

The yellow Post-it note said that two packages were waiting for me at the office next door; the receptionist who worked there had promised the UPS man she'd mind them. She was young and attractive and wanted to have her way with me. I could tell by the way she called me "mister" and interrupted her typing only long enough to point to the packages.

One box contained the subscription list of *Dog Universe* magazine printed on mailing labels twenty to a page. The other held a floppy programmed with the complete mailing list for *X-Country*. *X-Country* had 447,000 readers, which seemed like a lot to me and I wondered if they padded their list for advertising purposes. *Dog Universe* had only ninety-three thousand. I checked both for Alison's name, hoping she had been careless, hoping she had forwarded the publications to her new address. No such luck.

I started with *Dog Universe*, X-ing out every label with a man's name, every label with an address located outside North and South Dakota, Minnesota, Iowa, and Wisconsin—the states where she had traveled in the course of her business. It took me fifteen minutes to get through the As and another five before I paused at Michael Bettich, 4001 Capitol Street, #314, Deer Lake, Wisconsin.

It wasn't the name that stopped me, it was the address. Deer Lake, Wisconsin. The same as Alison's best friend, Deputy Gretchen Rovick. Then I assured myself, "Michael could be a woman's name. What was the name of that actress who starred in *The Waltons* on TV? Michael Learned?"

I fired up my PC, loaded the *X-Country* disk, reminding myself that fifteen hundred and fifty-seven people live in Deer Lake, and it shouldn't be surprising if one of them liked dogs. I quickly discovered that Michael Bettich, 4001 Capitol Street, #314, Deer Lake, Wisconsin, also liked to cross-country ski.

If you have a credit card, a mortgage, a car loan; if you've borrowed money from any business for any reason, you are listed with one of the major credit bureaus, probably all of them. Most of the information they've gathered on you, including your complete credit history, is restricted by the Fair Credit Reporting Act. Which means not a helluva lot. The government claims it is cracking down on people who abuse the privacy laws, but there's not much they can do about it. Still, conscientious fellow that I am, I try not to violate federal regulations unless I really, really need to. And this time I didn't. The Federal Trade Commission ruled not too long ago that noncredit information such as name, address updates, DOB, social security number, etcetera, didn't fall under the Fair Credit Reporting Act, and it went online for people like me to access, for a price. And when I accessed Michael Bettich's header information, I discovered:

Name:	Michael Bettich
SS#:	398-91-0038
DOB:	3/6/70
Sex:	Female
MS:	Single
Address:	4001 Capitol Street, #314
	Deer Lake, WI
Employer:	Rosalind Colletti Investments
	2035 Broadway Avenue
	Deer Lake, WI

"You couldn't resist it, could you, Alison?" I said aloud, rereading the name of Michael Bettich's current employer for the fifth time. "You just couldn't let it go."

I got up and removed Alison's photograph from the wall, careful not to leave adhesive when I peeled the tape from the corners. I examined it carefully. The eyes had lost their pain long ago. For some time now they had held a different expression for me—she looked like Bill Clinton had when he claimed he did not have sex with *that woman*.

"Gotcha!" I said, more in relief than in triumph.

Cynthia seemed surprised by the rain. After parking her car she glanced skyward, shook her head, turned up her collar, and trudged to my front door. I held it open it for her, and she came into the house. There was no warm hug, no inviting smile.

"What are you going to do?" she asked, slipping off her coat and folding it over the back of a chair.

"I'm going to Deer Lake tomorrow morning to make sure it's her."

"Then what?"

"That's it. Like I said on the telephone, it puts a period to the investigation."

"Is that so important?"

"It is to me. I like things to be just so. What motivates me, besides my four hundred dollars a day and expenses, is a sense of order. Things ought to happen in a certain way. Like in baseball. Every batter gets three strikes. Every team gets three outs. The team with the most runs after nine innings gets the W. There are no ties, and you go from first to third at your own risk. When things don't happen like that, when a player alters the rules to take advantage of another player, I feel compelled to do something about it."

Cynthia didn't believe me. She said my answer sounded like I had rehearsed it, and she was right.

"There is more," I admitted.

Her expression asked, What?

"The other night, you said I wanted revenge because I had felt that somehow Alison had cheated on me. That's not exactly true."

"No?"

"I don't want revenge. I don't want to hurt her. Truly I don't. I just want to ask her . . . why. And I want to see her face when she answers."

"Just like any man who's been cuckolded."

I smiled. "Cuckold? That's a little eighteenth century isn't it?"

Cynthia smiled back. "I've been working to improve my vocabulary."

We ate a couple of glazed turkey fillets I had simmered in ground ginger, Worcestershire sauce, and orange marmalade while we listened to the ball game on the radio. We didn't have much to say to each other. Afterward, we watched the rain from opposite ends of a wicker couch in my three-season porch. Every time the thunder boomed and the lightning flashed, we moved a little nearer to each other until there was no distance between us at all.

sixteen

The Northland had grown considerably greener in the three weeks since I last drove through it, and the natives were dressed as if they actually believed the rumors that winter was over. I, for one, was skeptical. Some areas in the Northland reported snowfall on Memorial Day. I didn't witness this event personally since

I was visiting my parents in Fort Myers, Florida, a place where winter never comes, and spring is marked not with rain and slush but with the arrival of catchers and pitchers at the training camp of the Minnesota Twins. Still, I believed the reports. In the Northland, a snowball's chance in July wasn't all that remote.

"The Northland" is the title given by advertisers—"Visit the Northland's number-one used-car dealership"—to a rather vaguely defined region in northern Minnesota and Wisconsin noted for its countless lakes and forests. And if you hail from Des Moines, I could see how the place might seem to embody the sense of wilderness that the sobriquet implies. However, if you hail from the true north, from Fairbanks or Prince Albert or even Edmonton, the Northland seems more like a suburb of Kansas City. Certainly the traffic jam I joined when I approached Deer Lake had an urban familiarity. It took twenty minutes to creep from the city limits sign to the intersection at the center of town.

"What's going on?" I asked the county cop who was directing traffic. He growled at me and waved me through the intersection. I drove in the direction his hand pointed, obedient as any driver's ed student, and followed the traffic without knowing where it was taking me until I came to the Deer Lake branch of the U.S. Post Office. I escaped the caravan and pulled into the parking lot.

I noted the post office's address: 4001 Capitol Street. I reread the address I had written in my notebook for Alison: 4001 Capitol Street, #314. A mail drop. Give the lady credit; she understood the value of a mail drop. Her mail comes to 4001 Capitol Street, P.O. Box 314. She then picks it up or it's forwarded on to her; her identity and location are known only to the postal employees, who are legally bound to keep it to themselves. However, like I said before, Alison had genius but not experience, otherwise she might have known that the U.S. Postal Service Manual contains a provision that clearly states that the post office must disclose the street address of a boxholder to someone needing the address to serve process. You can make good money as a process server. I've done a little of it myself.

I went inside and waited in the short line at the counter until it was my turn. The postal clerk spoke with a natural courtesy very few public employees possess. She was short and thin and black, probably the only African-American I've seen in the lily-white Northland outside of Duluth who wasn't on vacation. She laughed at my surprise at finding her there and explained that she was the only black *and* one of the few women to work for the post office in all of Kreel County. "If I were gay I would fill the district's entire minority quota all by myself," she said and laughed again, without malice or bitterness. Listening to her infectious laugh and working to keep from breaking up myself, I found I liked her very much, this stranger—liked her more than some friends I've known for decades. But the laugh quickly died when I flashed my ID and lied to her, telling her that I was a process server looking for a deadbeat that my client wanted to sue, reminding her that my request was entirely legal.

"I know my job," she coolly informed me as her long fingers danced over the keyboard of her computer terminal.

"Bettich, Michael J., 2035 Broadway Avenue, Deer Lake, Wisconsin," she recited quickly.

I didn't write down the address in my notebook. It was the same as Rosalind Colletti Investments, Alison's alleged employer. I waited for the clerk to look up from her computer screen.

"Something more?" she said.

"Where is 2035 Broadway Avenue?" I asked, wondering if she was this protective of all her addressees.

"Do your own dirty work, gumshoe."

Gumshoe? Now there's a word I hadn't heard for a long time.

"Sorry I ruined your day," I told her, and I meant it.

asked for directions from a pump jockey working the twenty-four hour service station on the corner, who looked at me like I was the dumbest human being alive. His directions consisted of shaking his head and pointing a greasy finger at the small building across the street and up the block. There was no address on the outside of the structure, only the sign: KING ENTERPRISES.

From a distance, it looked like an honest-to-God log cabin hewed with ax and saw. It wasn't until I was up close that I noticed the nailheads. And it wasn't until I opened the door to discover a polished interior filled with black leather, mirrored surfaces, and glass—not an earth tone in sight—that I realized the logs were merely a facade. Is nothing real anymore? Even the hair on the receptionist looked fake, a cascading waterfall of midnight that splashed over her shoulders and down her back. Against her pale face it looked like a wig displayed on a mannequin's head.

The name plate on her desk read ANGEL JOHANNSON, and perhaps there had been a time when the name applied. But no longer. Angel Johannson had lost the wholesome innocence usually associated with the species, her face taking on the mistrustful countenance of one who's fallen from grace. According to the inscribed date, the high-school graduation ring she wore was only two years old.

I guessed she was the daughter of the infamous Johnny Johannson and sister to the punk. How many Angel Johannsons could there be in Deer Lake?

"May I help you?" she asked pleasantly enough.

"I'd like to speak with Michael Bettich," I told her.

She hesitated before answering, "I'm afraid you must have the wrong office."

"Is this the address of Rosalind Colletti Investments?"

She repeated herself, never taking her eyes off me. "I'm afraid you must have the wrong office."

"This is where the United States Post Office sent me."

"Perhaps you'd care to speak with Mr. Koehn."

"Does he know Michael Bettich?" I asked sarcastically.

"Mr. Koehn can help you."

"Fine, I'd like to speak with Mr. Koehn."

"I'm afraid Mr. Koehn is not in at the present time," Angel informed me. "If you would care to leave a message . . ."

This is going well, I told myself. "When do you expect Mr. Koehn?" I asked.

"I really couldn't say. He's at the rallies."

"Rally?"

"Rallies," she said, emphasizing the plural. "Some folks want the casino, some don't. At the park," she added, gesturing vaguely west with her hand.

Along with my business card I gave her my best Arnold. "Tell Michael I'll be back."

"I told you, she isn't here," Angel insisted.

"How did you know Michael is a she?"

The church, a small brick affair with glass doors and a steeple topped with a crucifix, was rooted in a large field on the right side of the county road. It left me feeling a slight pang of nostalgia. I hadn't been inside a church since that bright autumn day when services were held for my wife and daughter, and won't I catch hell about that the next time I see them.

In front of the church was a small platform, perhaps two feet high. Not high enough for the anti-casino protesters in back to see the speakers, though, and many stood on tiptoe and craned their necks. What they didn't see were two men, one sitting on a metal folding chair, the other standing before a single microphone. The man sitting was a priest. From a distance, he reminded me of the priest who had heard the confessions of my teammates and I when we were in high school. Right after practice the day before every football game, he would hear our confessions, and no matter what our individual transgressions, each one of us was given the same penance: five Hail Mary's and five Our Father's. We called him Father Minute Wash.

The casino proponents were gathered in a park on the left side of the county road, the Augustus Eubanks Memorial Park, dedicated to the memory of the only Kreel County resident to fall in the Sioux Uprising of 1862—it said so on the metal plaque attached to the huge rock at the park entrance. The platform in the park was much higher, nearly ten feet. This time it was the people in front who had the most trouble seeing the speakers.

About two hundred fifty people were in each camp, many of them holding signs that I couldn't read from where I stood on the road. Dueling protest rallies in the heart of conservative Wisconsin. I had to admit, I was fairly impressed. They weren't in the same league as the 1960s civil rights marches or early 1970s anti-Vietnam War rallies, still . . . Come to think of it, I hadn't been this close to a protest rally since the Vietnam War, and even then I had only joined to meet girls. The draft had been abolished before I started high school, and I didn't personally know anyone who was over there, so what the h_ll.

From where I stood, I could hear the speakers who addressed both sides, their words wafting up from the amplifiers a full two beats behind the gestures that accompanied them. It reminded me of a badly dubbed Japanese movie:

"Hope, this time, is more than the fleeting, seasonal stirrings of spring. It is concrete, and is being poured by workmen just down the road. . . ."

"If gambling is our game, we should be ashamed. . . ."

"Look at them! They say no to gaming. I say, Where were you when the Kreel County Civic Center needed your support? . . ."

"They call it gaming. Gaming is softer and nicer than gambling. But it isn't the right word. Gaming is checkers and Monopoly and hopscotch. Gambling is when there is a bet on the outcome of a game. . . ."

"A casino will supply jobs. Many jobs. Real jobs. . . ."

"What's next? Hookers in low-cut sequined dresses on Broadway and drive-by shootings in the neighborhoods? . . ."

"Yes, some people will have a gambling problem. It does break up some families. So does alcoholism, but shutting down the bars wasn't the answer for that. . . ."

"What message are we sending to our children if we condone gambling in this community? . . ."

"It's a chance to pull ourselves up. It's a chance to make our community strong again, for us and our children. . . ."

I paid little attention to the rhetoric. What was the point? Whenever questions of morals and sin arise, factions quickly form and become so deeply entrenched that compromise usually becomes impossible. Just ask the people who have been warring over abortion for the past few decades. Besides, it wasn't my town.

Instead of listening, I watched a few Kreel County deputies as they sauntered quietly through the two crowds, looking for trouble; others were leaning casually against cars parked along the county road. I was searching for Gretchen Rovick, hoping I'd see her before she saw me. I didn't want her to know I was in town. Gretchen had lied to me. She had known Alison was in Deer Lake, of course she had. She'd probably helped her disappear in the first place.

I moved to a large oak tree and hid behind it. Two teenagers sought refuge in the same spot, both sporting hairdos that were quite the rage among young men in the Twin Cities about five years ago. They were passing a joint between them, telling each other what a bitch it was growing up in Deer Lake. Yeah, they knew where it was at, and it wasn't anywhere near them, no way. They had seen the world on Daddy's satellite dish, and they wanted a piece of it.

I plucked the joint from the taller teenager's mouth, dropped it to the ground, and squashed it beneath my heel. I've seen what drugs do to people, I've seen it up close and personal, and I'm no fan. Anyone who tells me grass should be legalized gets it right in the neck. They argue that alcohol is worse. Maybe so. But you can have a drink or two without getting drunk. You can have a glass of wine with dinner or a few beers at the ball game and not be any worse off for it. But you can't smoke a joint without getting high. And after a while you crave a higher high. Then a higher one still. Pretty soon you want to be up there all the time, until you crash and burn. Not everyone, no. But enough. I've seen them. I've arrested them.

The teenager stared defiantly, wondering what to do about me until his companion whispered to him, "Narc." They both smiled nervously and walked away without looking back. I did the same, retreating to The Height until the rallies broke up and King Koehn returned to his office.

Ingrid was wearing a white shirtdress with gold buttons that matched the color of her hair. She was sitting at a table with a calculator, ledger book, and a few dozen invoices stacked neatly in front of her. "We're closed until eleven," she told me without taking the pencil out of her mouth.

"My name is Holland Taylor," I announced, giving her a look at my ID. "Do you remember me?"

She looked at the stamp-sized photo and then at me. "Gretchen's friend," she said, taking the pencil from her mouth. "Good to see you again." She offered her hand. I took it, probably held it too long—a soft, pleasant current of electricity passed through it into me, and I didn't want to let it go.

"Do you have a moment?"

"Not really," she said, gesturing at her paperwork. "I'm trying to finish up before the rallies end. I'm hoping for a good lunch crowd. Give me twenty minutes?"

"Sure."

"Ginger!" she called.

A woman poked her head up from behind the stick like she had been squatting there, listening for her cue. "Ingrid," she answered back.

"Take care of Mr. Taylor, here, won't you?"

"Sure."

"Twenty minutes," Ingrid repeated, then went back to her calculations.

Ginger motioned me closer to the bar and asked, "What's your pleasure?"

"Summit Ale?"

I wasn't surprised when she said, "Sorry."

"What do you have on tap?"

"Pig's Eye pilsner—"

I raised my hand quickly to stop her recitation. "Sold," I said. A moment later she slid a glass of beer in front of me. Pig's Eye pilsner was named for one of St. Paul, Minnesota's, more colorful founding citizens, Pig's Eye Parrant, a rumrunner and all-around scoundrel who had settled in the area when it was still populated almost exclusively by Native-Americans and fur traders. In fact, the city was actually known as Pig's Eye Landing for many years until a visiting priest decided the name was politically incorrect.

Ginger returned with my beer, and I asked her if she knew Michael Bettich. Waitresses can be a terrific resource for information, especially waitresses in small towns who can actually put a name and occupation to the face of the customers they serve, who are aware of the emotions at the tables they're waiting. They know when a farmer is having a bad year, when a customer's balloon mortgage is coming due, when the weather is making people weird; they can point out the customers who are dating for the first time, who are escaping from the kids for an evening, who want to kill each other. Ginger proved to be more knowledgeable than I had hoped and happy to share.

"Michael Bettich? Sure. Deputy Gretchen's pal. We don't see much of her these days."

I took the photograph of Alison out of my pocket and showed it to her.

"Yep, that's her," Ginger confirmed. "I think she's prettier in person."

"You say you don't see much of her anymore?" I asked.

"Nah. This gambling thing has emotions running pretty high. I think she's trying to keep a low profile. Especially around Ingrid."

"Why?"

"I guess because she might become Ingrid's chief competitor."

Have you ever felt like you've just walked in at the middle of a movie?

"I don't understand," I said, and my face probably showed it.

"You're not from around here, are you?" Ginger said and laughed. "Okay, here's the story. There's this resort called The Harbor. Mostly it's a restaurant, but they have plenty of space for campers and such, and you can dock your boat, okay? Anyway, it went broke. The lake it's on, Lake Peterson, had winter kill some years back and lost all its fish. The DNR restocked it, but rebuilding a fish population takes years. Besides, it's way out on the highway, and hardly anyone went there. Somehow King Koehn got stuck with it—The Harbor, not the lake—and he's been trying to unload it for years. Now, along comes Michael, and she buys it for—I don't know—ten cents on the dollar. People tell her it's a bad investment, but she buys it anyway."

I took a long pull of my beer as Ginger continued.

"Now, the next day—I mean like the very next day after the deal is done—word leaks out that the local band of Ojibwa is, like, ultrasecretly trying to buy the old civic center from the Kreel County Board of Commissioners—I guess to revamp into an off-reservation gambling casino."

"You guess?"

"Well, they haven't actually come out and said it, the Ojibwa I mean, but that's what everyone thinks. Why else would they want it?"

"What does the civic center have to do with Alison?"

"Huh?"

"I mean Michael."

"The Harbor?" Ginger asked. "Because it's . . . Okay, here's the rest of the story. When the county decided to build the civic center as a way to generate convention business, there was a big fight over where it should be located, in Saginau or Deer Lake. The board settled on a compromise. They decided to build the civic center on a lake midway between the two towns."

"Lake Peterson," I volunteered.

"There you go," said Ginger. "It seemed like a good idea at the time. Only it didn't do any better than The Harbor."

"How close is the civic center to The Harbor?"

"Directly across the highway."

"My, my, my, my, my."

"Get it now?"

"Uh-uh."

Ginger sighed, exasperated.

"You don't think having a casino across the way isn't going to

be good for business?" she asked. "That's why Michael is keeping
a low profile. 'Cuz everyone is mad at her."

"Who? Why?"

Again Ginger sighed. "Okay, let me count the ways," she said.
"You've got your King Koehn, who figures Michael stole The Harbor out from under him, like, unethically, using inside information—"

"Did she?"

"You got Charlie Otterness," Ginger continued as if she didn't
want to be interrupted. "Charlie owns a bait-and-tackle store outside of town. Big place; you want minnows and stuff, you go to
Charlie's. Charlie is also a Kreel County commissioner. And he's
a widower who rumor has it—now, I'm not one to gossip, but
rumor has it he was keeping time with Michael until the day she
bought The Harbor and now has nothing nice to say about her."

"Charlie told Michael about the impending sale," I guessed.

"It's amazing what people do in the privacy of their own bed-
rooms. Oops," Ginger added, making a dramatic gesture out of
putting her hand over her mouth. "Did I say that?"

She laughed and I smiled, but I wasn't feeling particularly
happy. Alison sleeping with a county commissioner to get inside
information? I didn't want to hear that.

"Stupid! People are stupid!"

Ginger and I both turned toward the door. A tall, thin, bearded
man dressed in jeans, a flannel shirt, and an ANIMALS 'R US button,
glanced at us and then looked away.

"Hello, Mr. Thilgen," Ginger said.

"Do you know how stupid people are?" Thilgen asked loudly.
Ginger went along, playing straight man.

"How stupid are they?"

"They're so stupid, they're out there arguing about gambling,
about gambling casinos, but they refuse to see the big picture."

"The big picture?"

"The environment."

"Ahh, yes. The environment."

"Don't you care about the environment? Are you stupid, too? Are you one of the stupid people?"

Ginger took a deep breath and did not reply. Thilgen seated himself in the restaurant section. Ingrid smiled at him, gathered her materials, and disappeared behind a door marked EMPLOYEES ONLY.

Thilgen was obviously well-known and not particularly popular. The waitresses flipped a coin to determine who would serve him; the loser demanded two out of three.

"Nobody cares about the animals," Thilgen continued. "They're going to widen the roads and cut down the trees to make room for parking lots and bring their foul-smelling cars in here and their human pollution. Well, what about the animals, is what I want to know. What about the deer and the woodchucks? Nobody asked them if they want a gambling casino. Oh, no! They're expendable. So what if we destroy the wetlands, the habitats. So what if we turn Lake Peterson into a landfill. Just as long as everyone makes a buck, screw the animals, forget the environment."

A waitress handed Thilgen a menu and hurried off, not bothering to list the daily specials, not taking a drink order.

"Damn Indians," he continued. "Indians, not Native-Americans! Indians and their damn dirty money. They're supposed to be protecting the environment. Noble savages—yeah, sure! General Sheridan was right. The only good Indian is a dead Indian."

Ingrid, coming back through the door, had obviously heard him. She was visibly upset.

"I won't have that kind of talk in my place," she told Thilgen, her eyes flashing. "Do you understand?"

"Kill the Indians, and kill that Bettich bitch who's ruining Lake

Peterson!" he replied even more loudly, as if daring her to do something about it.

"Get out, Chip," Ingrid said, moving to his table.

"People are so stupid," he added.

"So I've been told," Ingrid replied, pushing a chair out of her way, nearly knocking it over. "Get out."

Chip Thilgen refused to leave his chair. He looked at her across the table and smiled like he owned the place and she was the intruder.

"Make me," he said.

I figured that was my cue. I left the bar with every intention of offering aid and assistance, but before I had taken three steps, Ingrid was leaning over the table, her arms supporting her weight, and speaking to Thilgen in a voice too low for me to hear. But Thilgen heard her—oh, man, did he. The blood ran out of his face, and his eyes became large and still. Ingrid stepped back, and Thilgen rose on shaky legs. His fists were clenched, yet he seemed more frightened than angry.

"You can't talk to me like that," he said softly.

"Put a sock in it," Ingrid told him.

Thilgen headed to the door, moving slowly enough to prove he wasn't running but quickly enough to get the job done.

"You'll see," he called over his shoulder as he left. "I'm not someone to mess with."

"Neither am I," Ingrid said softly before she disappeared back behind the EMPLOYEES ONLY door.

I returned to my table and looked over at Ginger.

"That's three people who are upset with Michael," I said. "Who is he?" I asked.

"Mr. Chips?" Ginger asked. "Thinks of himself as an animal-rights activist. They say he sometimes liberates farm animals—cows and hens and horses. That's what the activists call it when they sneak onto someone's farm at night and let the livestock go free. Liberations. Only no one has caught him at it yet. I know some farmers, they say if they do catch him, they're gonna shoot him."

"So, who else?" I asked.

"What?"

"Who else doesn't like Michael?"

"Well, there's Ingrid."

At the sound of her name, Ingrid reentered the dining area and hung a left for the bar. "What about Ingrid?" she asked.

"You don't like Michael," Ginger said.

Ingrid snorted a very ladylike snort—an Audrey Hepburn-like snort—and said, "I like Michael just fine."

"You do not," Ginger insisted.

"I've liked her from the moment Gretchen introduced us," Ingrid argued. "What's not to like? Very smart woman, very charming."

"She'll probably wreck your business when the casino opens."

Ingrid smiled and shook her head at the theory.

"Not going to happen," she said defiantly.

"Why not?" I asked.

"Several reasons," she answered, turning her brilliant smile on me. "Want to hear them?"

"Sure."

"First, for the Ojibwa to operate a casino out of the Kreel County Civic Center, the land the center is built on must first be put into the name of the U.S. government. Then, through the Bureau of Indian Affairs, the government must put the land in trust for the tribe, making it part of their reservation—and that's just not going to happen. The issue has been too divisive. Deer Lake is pretty much fifty-fifty on it, and Saginau is the same; that's what the protests are all about. What politician is going to take up the Ojibwa's cause knowing he's going to alienate half of his constituency?"

"That's what they said about The Forks down the road, and the Ojibwa built that casino," Ginger reminded Ingrid. But Ingrid ignored her.

"Also," she continued, "King Koehn is against it, and he carries a lot of weight. You want to get elected in northwestern Wisconsin, you pretty much need his support."

"Why is King against it?" I asked.

"If he still owned The Harbor, he wouldn't be," Ginger suggested.

"You're probably right," Ingrid agreed. "He's not so much against the casino as he's against Michael. Michael worked with King for a short time, watching over his investments. After a few months she offers to take The Harbor off his hands. He sells. News leaks out about how the Ojibwa *might* be considering a new casino—"

Ginger rolled her eyes at the word "might."

"—and King claims he's been cheated and throws Michael out," Ingrid continued.

"*Was* he cheated?" I asked.

"Depends on your interpretation," Ingrid reasoned. "King claims Michael was his employee and therefore obligated to inform him whenever she learned about a good business opportunity. Michael claims that she was *not* King's employee, that she was operating her own business and merely providing a service to King, and was therefore free to seize any opportunity she wished. Me? I'm on Michael's side."

"Doesn't matter," Ginger insisted. "The casino is a done deal."

"I promise you it is not," Ingrid told her.

Knowing her boss considerably longer than I, Ginger must have seen signals in Ingrid's body language that I had missed because she smiled broadly and said, "You know something, don't you? What?"

"Me?" Ingrid asked. "I'm just a saloonkeeper. What do I know?" Then, to change the subject, she beat a quick riff on the bar top and said, "So, Mr. Taylor. What brings you back to Deer Lake? Come to see Gretchen?"

"No," I replied. "Actually, I came to see Michael Bettich."

"Hmm?"

"You know where I can find her?"

"She used to stay with Gretchen, but I think she moved out," Ingrid said.

"A few months ago," Ginger confirmed.

"Where to?"

Neither of them seemed to know. But Ginger had a suggestion. "Have you tried The Harbor?"

seventeen

The Harbor was all blond wood and glass, surrounded by a gravel parking lot on one side and Lake Peterson on the other; wooden platforms where patrons could dock their boats extended into the water. At the far end of the parking lot were several slots for RVs, each with a bank of water faucets and electrical outlets protruding from the ground. A worn asphalt driveway led past the slots down to the lake, where a sign asked drivers not to block the boat landing with their vehicles. A half dozen pickups and 4X4s were bunched together in the lot.

"Is this it, Alison?" I heard myself ask as I parked my car. "Is this why you faked your death? So you could build a drive-by resort on a mud lake in rural Wisconsin? Is this your dream?"

A moment later I had to duck beneath a plank suspended between two ladders just inside the door. Three men stood on the makeshift scaffold, all of them examining a clump of multicolored wires hanging down from a false ceiling. Another pair was studying a floor duct on the other side of the room. A sixth man was crouched behind the bar, working on a sink, softly humming a country-western tune from the Hank Williams catalog as he fixed a heavy pipe wrench against a fitting.

"Excuse me," I said.

He turned his head but did not stop working.

"Is Michael Bettich here?"

He shook his head.

"Expect her anytime soon?"

"Couldn't say."

"Know where I can find her?"

He shook his head again. "Not my turn to watch her," he told me, trying to turn the fitting, meeting stubborn resistance.

"It's important that I find her."

"Not to me," he replied, grunting loudly as the fitting slowly turned.

The other workers were equally helpful.

I returned to my car and sat with the door open while listening to the public radio station out of the University of Minnesota-Duluth—the only station I could dial up that played jazz. After two songs I shut the door and fired up the Colt, deciding against waiting for Michael's return.

"It shouldn't be this hard, it really shouldn't," I muttered.

It wasn't.

Just as I was about to put my car into gear, a Chevy Blazer cruised into the lot sporting all the paraphernalia of a police vehicle; KREEL COUNTY SHERIFF'S DEPARTMENT and a six-pointed star were stenciled on both doors. It was driven by Deputy Gretchen Rovick. Alison Donnerbauer Emerton was her passenger. She had changed the color of her hair from brown to a deep auburn—women have always found it easier to change their appearance than men—but even through the windshield, her blue-green eyes were undisguisable.

I stepped out of my car as the vehicle stopped. Gretchen took a hard look at me. She clearly didn't like what she saw.

"What?" Alison asked. I couldn't hear her, but it was easy enough to read her lips through the glass.

"Taylor," Gretchen answered.

Alison seemed genuinely surprised that I had found her.

I waited until they exited the vehicle.

"Good morning, Deputy," I said to Gretchen. She didn't reply. I turned to the other woman. Ginger had been right. She was much prettier in person. "Alison Donnerbauer Emerton, I presume. I've been looking forward to meeting you."

Alison smiled slightly. "I must have screwed up."

I told her where. She tapped her forehead with the fingers of her right hand as if to punish herself for her carelessness. "I'd forgotten I told Marie about the name Rosalind Colletti," she confessed.

"We all make mistakes."

"And this one is going to cost me, isn't it? How much?"

A bribe? I thought it was beneath her and told her so. "Besides, I'm already being well paid."

"What then? What will make you go away?"

"Tell me why, that's all. Tell me why you went to all the trouble." I was desperate to hear her explanation, and it probably showed.

She smiled at me; it was a superior smile. "It's a long story, and quite frankly I see no reason to share it with you."

Gretchen chuckled. She was leaning on the front fender of her Blazer, watching us.

"I could make your life difficult," I told Alison.

She smiled some more. A threat? She thought it was beneath me and told me so.

I was contemplating a reply—and getting nowhere—when a desperate squeal of tires captured my attention. A white Buick Regal was cutting across the parking lot at high speed, spitting chunks of gravel and an impressive dust cloud behind it. Two men I couldn't identify sat in the front seat. Suddenly the car skidded to a stop thirty yards in front of us. The passenger was holding something at arm's length and pointing it out of the window.

"*Down!*" I screamed and tried to pull Alison to the ground.

Alison pushed me away and stood up, watching me and not the car, asking angrily, "What are you doing?!"

Bullets were already flying. Gretchen took a slug in the leg. The force of the blow spun her against the side of the Blazer and knocked her down. I rolled away from the Buick, more or less toward the Blazer; and rolled over a Smith and Wesson .38— Gretchen's gun. I grabbed it with both hands and continued rolling until I was on my feet in a Weaver stance, a shooting stance with good balance. The Buick was moving now, heading out of the parking lot. I squeezed off four rounds just as it hit the highway. The rear window shattered, littering the asphalt with tiny fragments of safety glass. The car fishtailed but didn't stop.

Her skin was a ghastly, ashen color, and her breathing was so shallow that for a moment I thought she might be dead. But she was warm to my touch, and I could detect a rapid, thready pulse. I gently rolled her onto her back, and she opened her eyes. They were filled with terror and confusion. I said something to her. I don't remember what. "You'll be all right, Alison." Something like that.

I tore open her blouse. The hole was slightly above and to the left of her right breast. I sprinted to Gretchen's patrol car and found her first-aid kit. I packed the wound with gauze, trying to prevent air from entering the chest cavity. I was fumbling with a compress when I heard Gretchen's voice.

"Officer down! Officer down!" she repeated. She wasn't quite screaming. I glanced up at her. She was in the Blazer, laying on her side across the front seat, favoring her right leg as she worked the radio. I could see a hole midway up her thigh. Blood was seeping out of it.

"Deputy Rovick, you've been shot," I told her.

"Don't you think I know that?!" This time she was screaming.

When we had talked over dinner three weeks earlier, Gretchen had accused her fellow deputies in the Kreel County Sheriff's Department of sexism, insisting that they were slower to respond when she called for backup than when male deputies called. Maybe so. But you couldn't prove it by me because an officer—a male—arrived within two minutes, and within five more it seemed the entire day watch had converged on The Harbor. The workers inside the resort studied us through the large windows. Some of them were eating their lunches.

The first officer to arrive went directly to Gretchen. His name tag read: G. LOUSHINE.

"I need a tourniquet!" he barked over his shoulder.

I tossed him one from the first-aid kit while continuing to maintain pressure on Alison's sucking chest wound with the palm of my hand. Her eyes were still open, but she didn't speak.

"Two suspects, white males I think, driving a white four-door sedan," Gretchen recited as the deputy applied the tourniquet. "They hit us with a MAC 10."

"A Buick Regal, Wisconsin plates W-ZERO-F-F-W," I added. "And it was an UZI."

"You're crazy! How do you know that?" Gretchen yelled at me.

"How come you don't?" I yelled back. Gretchen didn't relay even her incomplete information to dispatch when she called for assistance, giving the suspects a good five-minute head start, and it troubled me.

"W-ZERO-F-F-W?" Loushine repeated.

"Call letters for a ham radio operator," I told him. "Wisconsin allows hams to use their call letters in place of regular license plate numbers."

"That's right," Loushine agreed under his breath and sprinted to his own car to broadcast the information I supplied instead of using Gretchen's radio. Perhaps he didn't want to embarrass her.

While Loushine was making his call, the sheriff arrived. His name tag read: R. ORMAN. He didn't rush to his deputy's side, which is what I would have done. Instead, he moved directly to where Alison lay on the gravel in an expanding pool of her own blood.

"My God!" he said, sucking in his breath. "Mike!" He knelt next to her and took her hand in both of his. "Mike," he repeated. The woman looked up at him but otherwise didn't respond.

The sheriff's eyes glazed over until they resembled Alison's. They were both in shock. Loushine placed a hand on the sheriff's shoulder and said, "The bus is on its way." Orman didn't reply, and Loushine had to shake him. "Sheriff? Sheriff, the bus is on its way."

Orman turned to stare at his deputy, but it was a few moments before his eyes focused.

"Saginau to Deer Lake, thirty-seven minutes," he said shaking his head, regaining his senses. "The Harbor is midway—make it eighteen minutes. Another eighteen going back. Too long. Can't wait for the ambulance. We'll take her to the hospital in my car. Get a blanket." A few seconds later four of us gently lifted Alison from the gravel and slid the blanket underneath her. I insisted that we roll her over on her chest. *"Transport the victim with her injured side down,"* the first-aid manual says. Using the blanket as a stretcher, we gently placed the woman on the back seat of the sheriff's car. I rode with her. No one questioned this.

Sheriff Orman didn't speak, instead concentrating all his energy on driving the cruiser at high speed over the winding Wisconsin back roads, his siren blasting the woodland quiet to shreds, although we didn't overtake a single vehicle. He took one curve too fast, and Alison moaned. It was the first sound she had made since being shot. The sheriff tried to check on her through the rearview mirror, but she was too low on the seat.

"We're almost there, Alison," I told her.

We drove another mile before the sheriff said, "Did you call her Alison?"

I didn't reply. It wasn't a good time.

We were Code Ten when we rolled to the emergency entrance of the three-story Saginau Medical Center. Code Ten means sirens and flashing lights. It was a good thing we had them, too, because without them the hospital staff would not have known we were coming. No one had bothered to warn them—not the sheriff, not his deputies. Some people just don't react well to catastrophe.

Two doctors, male and female, and two nurses met us at the

door and helped us transfer Alison from the back seat to a gurney. I discovered later that the doctors were husband and wife. Both had agreed to work in a rural community for three years in exchange for medical school scholarship money. The National Health Service Corps sent them to Saginau, population 3,267, the seat of power in Kreel County. Here they met, married, and decided to stay after satisfying their obligations. He was from New Jersey, she was from New Mexico. She gave the orders.

"Goddammit Bobby, you should have told us you were coming," she scolded the sheriff as she examined Alison. Her husband was taking blood pressure and pulse.

"Can you hear me?" the wife asked Alison. "What's your name, honey? Do you know who you are?"

Alison's answer was just above a whisper: "Don't call me honey."

"Pulse is one twenty-two, blood pressure ninety-six over fifty-eight," said the husband.

"Okay, here we go," the wife warned her husband and the nurses. "Gunshot wound, right side, midlobe, no exit. She has blood in her mouth, she's vomiting blood. Hang a liter of D-5 and lactated ringers. Run it wide open. Wake up pharmacy. She needs to be dosed. I want an antibiotic that really cuts the pus. Call X ray. Tell 'em to bring the portable. I want a full set of chest films and a flat plate of the abdomen. She doesn't sound good. I want respiratory therapy down here right away. Put her on O-2. CBC type and cross-match for six units. Get an NG tube into her."

"Should we put in a catheter?" the husband asked.

"First things first. We'll take her directly to OR. Let's roll, people. Stat!"

I understood "stat." It's an abbreviation of the Latin word "statim," meaning "right fucking now!" The rest was all Greek to me. They wheeled Alison down a dimly lit corridor and into a room designated simply Room One, where we were not allowed to follow.

"She's in good hands," a nurse informed us. The sheriff apparently wasn't so sure and tried to stay with the gurney. The nurse stopped him, using both hands and all her weight to keep him from crossing the line of yellow tape on the floor that separated the receiving room from the rest of the emergency facilities. Reluctantly, he spun away and went to look out the door.

The nurse took a deep breath. "You can clean up in there," she told me and gestured toward a rest room with her head. That's when I noticed for the first time the blood that stained my hands, my jacket, my shirt, my jeans, my Nikes. I nodded and headed toward the rest room, stopping first at a water fountain. While I was drinking, the sheriff slapped a handcuff over my left wrist. I protested, but he wasn't listening. He pulled me to a set of metal chairs that were anchored to the floor and wound the other cuff around an arm. Well, at least I could sit down.

He abandoned me without comment and stood vigil just behind the yellow tape, the tips of his black boots toeing the line, his eyes fixed on the closed operating room door. He stood there, not moving, for nearly twenty minutes, until the ambulance arrived with Deputy Rovick.

The receiving nurse poked her head inside the operating room, and soon the woman doctor emerged and went over to Gretchen. She loosened the tourniquet and examined the deputy's wound.

"I know you're hurting, but there's someone else who needs me more right now," the doctor said "Do you understand?"

Gretchen nodded.

The doctor gave quiet instructions to the nurse and then told Gretchen, "We'll give you something for the pain, and I'll be with you as soon as I can. Don't worry. You're going to be fine. I wouldn't leave you otherwise."

The deputy nodded again, and the doctor directed the ambulance drivers to wheel Gretchen into Room Two. Orman clutched the doctor's elbow. She pulled away. "I need to scrub," was all she said. She returned to Room One.

A moment later Deputy Loushine burst through the door like he'd had a running start.

"The scene has been secured for CID; we have bulletins on the car," he announced.

"What about the plates?" I asked.

"They belong to a ham operator in the next county," he answered as if he worked for me. "The sheriff over there is moving on it for us."

"What about witnesses, Gary?" the sheriff asked his deputy.

"Just Gretchen, Mike, and him," the deputy answered, indicating me. "The workers inside The Harbor claim they didn't see anything." He said to me: "Gretchen said you got off four rounds at the vehicle."

"Hit it, too," I replied.

"You're under arrest," the sheriff told me.

Loushine caged me inside a large tiled holding cell that resembled a locker-room shower. It was empty of all furniture except a lidless toilet that was hidden from outside view behind a low wall in the corner. The floor sloped gradually to a drain in the center of the room. Overhead, fluorescent lights were protected by a metal grating. The sole window looked out across the corridor to the fingerprint station. A blind was on the outside of the window. I sat on the floor in the corner directly across from the door. My hands were cuffed behind my back. I sat a long time. And as the hours flowed away, I found myself doing something I hadn't done for years, not since my wife and daughter were killed by a drunk driver. I prayed. I prayed for Alison, beseeching God to intervene on her behalf. But just as hard, I prayed for myself—prayed that I wasn't responsible for bringing the shooters down on her.

The sheriff arrived several hours later—at least I was guessing it was several hours. I had lost all track of time. Using the wall for support, I managed to shimmy to my feet. My legs were stiff from sitting, and I tried to stretch them as best I could without the use of my hands.

"How is she?" I asked.

The sheriff closed the door to the holding cell, thought better of it, and opened it again. He stepped out into the corridor and drew the blinds across the cell's window. When he reentered the cell, I noticed that he was no longer wearing his jacket, Sam Browne belt, holster, gun, or badge.

"So it's going to be like that," I said.

"You're going to answer my questions," he told me.

"Gladly," I said.

Only the sheriff didn't ask any. Instead, he paced relentlessly in front of me, his hands clenched, then pointing, then resting on his hips. His face was red and twitching; his lips were pushed forward bearing his teeth; his breathing was fast and shallow. He was displaying all the classic signals of the first stage of aggression and ritualized combat—*assault is possible*—that I'd been taught to recognize while training to become a police officer. If I had been in uniform, with my hands free, I would have given him a good whiff of pepper spray.

"You brought them here," he said at last.

"Brought who?" I asked.

"'Brought who, brought who,'" he mimicked. "You know who. You brought them."

"No, no," I protested. I had thought about it a long time, and my brain—and my conscience—refused to accept responsibility. "It has to be a coincidence."

"No coincidence," The sheriff insisted. "They came with you."

And suddenly it occurred to me that he knew all there was about Alison—where she had come from and why. I told him so.

"Her name is Michael!" he shouted. "Michael Bettich!"

He was in the final stage now—*assault is imminent*. His face went from red to white; his lips tightened over his teeth; his eyebrows slanted forward into a frown. He closed his hands and started rocking back and forth. His eyes darted quickly to my groin, my jaw—target glances.

"Listen," I told him, talking loud and fast now, trying to reduce the threat verbally, "only two people knew I was going to Deer Lake and why. Neither of them knew about The Harbor, neither of them knew where Alison could be found. And I wasn't followed; there was no chance of that. No one followed me to Alison, so it had to be—"

"Her name is Michael!" the sheriff screamed and lunged at me, catching my jaw with his shoulder. His momentum pushed me against the stone wall, jamming my cuffed hands against my spine and knocking the breath out of me. One, two, three blows to my stomach and then one to my face. Then another. I turned my head with the next punch, and his hand caromed off my chin into the wall. The sheriff cried in pain as I pivoted out of his reach.

He turned quickly and swung at my head, but I bobbed and danced away. His knuckles grazed the wall. The miss made him even more furious. He moved toward me with measured steps, his hands held high. When he was in range, I lifted my right leg into the chamber and snapped a kick to his solar plexus. But with my hands cuffed behind my back, I was off balance. When he fell, so did I, landing on my shoulder. I think I hurt myself more than I hurt him. I tried to roll to my feet, but it was too late. He was on me in a hurry, pounding my head, throat, and upper chest. I used my knee to push him away but the relief was only temporary; he resumed smothering me with punches before I could even get to my knees.

I was fading fast.

"Jesus Christ!" a voice shouted. "Jesus Christ, Sheriff! What are you doing?! Jesus Christ!"

A pair of hands gripped the sheriff by his shoulders and pulled him off me. I didn't see who they belonged to until I was able to shake the sweat and blood out of my eyes.

"Deputy Loushine," I muttered, tasting blood in my mouth. "How good of you to come."

"Jesus Christ!" he repeated.

"Get 'im outta here!" the sheriff shouted.

"But, Sheriff . . ." Loushine protested.

"Get 'im outta here!"

"He's a material witness—"

"Get this sonuvabitch outta my county!"

I rode in the front seat of Deputy Loushine's white 4X4. A second deputy followed close behind in my car. My hands were free, and I dabbed at my swollen, cut lip with a white handkerchief now stained pink.

"What you're doing doesn't make sense," I told the deputy.

"You're telling me," he answered.

"Do you know who Michael Bettich is?" I asked.

"All I know about her is that she's been living with the sheriff for over two months now," Loushine replied. "And that's all I need to know."

I had to chew on that one for a while. Finally I said, "It doesn't make sense."

We drove without further conversation. Twenty minutes later Loushine stopped at an intersection of two county highways, crossed over, and stopped again.

It was nearing 8:50 central daylight saving time, and the sun was fading fast. Loushine sat with his eyes on the road ahead while the second deputy parked behind us, came around, and yanked open the passenger door.

"This is the county line," Loushine announced.

"I guessed," I told him.

I left the 4X4 and struggled to my own car. I hurt all over, and my head felt light and fluffy, but I managed to squeeze behind the steering wheel without fainting. The keys were in the ignition; the engine was running; the headlights were on. Suddenly Loushine was next to the door, squatting so that he could see my face through the window.

"Sorry 'bout this," he said.

"To serve and to protect," I told him. "Have a nice day."

I steered my car more or less south, driving on automatic pilot, not knowing where I was until I saw the sign: WELCOME TO MINONG. There was something familiar about it, even in the dark. That and the county blacktop where I turned left, the gravel road where I turned right, and the dirt driveway at the end of the gravel road that I followed to a large two-story lake house.

The pain was a flashing red beacon blinking a simple message: Lie still, don't move. I ignored the instructions and left the car, hugging my sides like a grocery bag that was threatening to burst open at the next hard jolt. I staggered to the door of the house in the light of my high beams. I immediately recognized the man who answered my knock. He recognized me, too.

"What are you doing here?" he asked, obviously confused.

"Dean, who is it?" a woman's voice called from behind him.

I moved past the man into the hallway. The woman was wearing a flowing white robe that my wife and I had presented to her on her birthday over five years ago.

"Excuse me, Phyll. I don't mean to intrude. . . ." then I collapsed at her feet.

Never let it be said that I don't know how to make an entrance.

eighteen

A bright ceiling light was in my eyes, and a cool washcloth was on my forehead. Voices filtered through the bedroom door.

"No police," one of the voices insisted. "Not until we know what happened."

"Why did he come here?" asked the other voice.

"I don't know. We'll ask him when he wakes up."

"Think he's in trouble?"

"That's my guess."

"He looks different."

"Honey, he's beat up. You'd look different, too, if you were beat up."

I heard nothing for a moment, then: "What are you doing?" my mother-in-law asked. The metallic sound of the hinge of a double barrel shotgun opening and closing punctuated her question.

"Think I'll just take a look around."

"Dammit, Dean, you haven't been in the service for good long time."

"Honey. Once a marine, always a marine."

I woke up tired and sore, remembering vaguely a dream in which I was running naked through the forest, chased by a bear wearing a sheriff's badge. I couldn't remember if he caught me or not, and then I moved. Oh, yeah! He'd caught me.

The washcloth was still damp and resting on the pillow next to my head. I carried it from the bedroom to the kitchen. Phyllis Bernelle was sitting at the kitchen table drinking coffee, a black briefcase opened in front of her. Her head jerked up at my entrance.

"How do you feel?" she asked.

"How do I look?"

"Like someone beat you up."

"That's how I feel."

I sat across from her, and she poured me a steaming mug of coffee, French almond, one of my favorites. It had been Laura's mother who first introduced me to the pleasures of coffee made from beans you grind yourself.

"Are you hungry? Do you want some breakfast?"

I shook my head. I doubted my stomach could handle the job.

Phyllis was dressed in a simple sports jacket over a white shirt and blue jeans. That was another one of the things I liked about her. She dressed like me.

"I'm sorry, Taylor, I have to leave. I'm showing some property in about twenty minutes. Guy from Chicago is thinking of buying five lots on the flowage. It's something I can't get out of. I'd like it if you stayed, though. Will you, please? Will you stay here at least until I get back? You could use the rest."

I could at that.

"Thank you," I said.

She smiled and cleared her coffee cup to the sink.

"Where's Dean?" I asked.

"Up at the garden."

I nodded. Dean Bernelle had studied horticulture at the University of Minnesota on the GI Bill, then inexplicably took a job in the accounting department of 3M. He retired the year I married his daughter with a pension I wished I could look forward to, moved to his Wisconsin lake home, and now has the most ostentatious garden in the state—an entire acre's worth. But while he is quite content digging in the dirt, his wife is not. So Phyllis, who had never worked outside the home while Dean was working, earned a realtor's license and now makes more money than he ever did, selling lakeshore property. Which was perfectly fine with Dean. "The more she makes, the more I get to spend," he liked to say.

"How are things, Phyll?" I ventured.

"I was going to ask you the same question."

"I've been better."

Phyllis Bernelle had a way of asking questions without uttering a sound. She would stare at you with clear green eyes, and you would fall all over yourself confessing to various misdeeds. "The trick," Laura once told me, "is not to look at her." But I was looking at her, and I couldn't resist.

"I was worked over by the Kreel County sheriff yesterday."

"Why?"

"I think I upset him," I told her. "Something to do with his girl-friend."

She stared at me some more.

"I've been looking for a woman who was supposed to be dead but apparently isn't. I found her, and then she was shot."

"By who?"

"I don't know, but I intend to find out," I vowed. *And please, don't let me be an accomplice,* I prayed.

Now she was nodding.

"You always had such interesting stories to tell," she told me. "I've missed them. I've missed you. I wish we could have seen more of you since Laura was killed."

I didn't know what to say to that.

My mother-in-law closed her briefcase and pulled it off the table. "I have to go."

"I appreciate your taking me in."

"Will you wait until I get back?"

"Yes."

"Will you tell me what happened in Kreel County?"

"In grisly detail."

"Don't let Dean put you to work."

"I'll try not to."

"Listen," she said, "if you're in trouble, I know a good lawyer."

"Thank you," I answered. "But lawyers are a dime a dozen. It's friends that are hard to come by."

"Where the fuck are you?" Hunter Truman wanted to know.

"Minong."

"Where is fucking Minong?"

"Wisconsin."

"Where in fucking Wisconsin? Goddammit, you were supposed to call me yesterday. I've been waiting by the fucking phone since—shit—since noon. What's going on? Didn't you find her?"

"I found her."

"And?"

"Hang on to yourself, Hunter," I told him. "I found Alison, and two minutes later someone shot her. She's badly hurt." The pause was so long, I was compelled to ask, "Are you still there?"

"How bad?" he asked. "Will she live?"

I told him I didn't know and why.

"The sheriff assaulted you?!" Truman was clearly outraged. "The bastard assaulted you?!"

"Kinda makes you wonder, doesn't it?"

"Fuck, yeah," he said. A moment later, he added, "Shit, Taylor, what's going on?"

I told him my only theory. "It wasn't Alison who was shot—"

"Not Alison?"

"What I mean is, I think whoever shot her was shooting at Michael Bettich, the person she's pretending to be."

"Why?"

"I don't know, but it might be connected to a small resort she's building across the highway from a proposed Indian gambling casino."

"She's building a resort?"

Truman was asking too many questions; my head started to throb violently.

"I'll tell you more after I have a chance to get back up there and poke around," I told him, hoping to end the conversation. "Assuming I can avoid the county cops."

"Fuck 'em!" Truman said so loudly it hurt my ear. "You get your ass back up there; I'm officially authorizing you to do that. You find out what you can about Alison, and if the cops get in the way, we'll sue the shit outta the whole fucking lot of 'em."

"Whatever."

I was pleased that Truman was still paying, but even if he had pulled the plug, I would have gone back.

"When are you leaving?" he asked.

"Tomorrow."

"Tomorrow?! Why not today?"

I told him I had to go and quickly hung up the phone. My head couldn't take any more.

"Hi, Desirée. Cynthia Grey, please," I told her office manager-cum-Doberman about an hour later. I hadn't been able to reach Cynthia at home, so I tried the office.

"Whom may I say is calling?"

"Holland Taylor." As if she didn't know.

"Miss Grey is in meetings all day. However, I will inform her that you called."

"Please don't do this, Desirée; I need her." I wondered if my voice sounded as pathetic to her as it did to me. Probably, because she put me through.

"Holland?" Cynthia asked. "Are you okay? Desirée says you sound funny."

"If you really want a laugh, you should see how I look," I told her.

"What's going on?"

I gave her the short version, lingering on my injuries only long enough to solicit her sympathy. When I had finished, she told me, "Come home. You did your job. You found her. Now come home."

"I can't," I told her. "I have to know—"

"If you're responsible?" she finished my sentence. "Don't give me any of that male-pride bullshit," Cynthia added earnestly. "And I don't want to hear how a man's gotta do what a man's gotta do.

You come home. Right now. You come home to me before you get hurt again."

"Will you take care of Ogilvy for me?" I asked. "Make sure he has plenty of alfalfa and water?"

Cynthia hesitated before saying, "Of course." Then she added, "I hope he eats your Nolan Ryan autographed baseball."

That hurt.

"I'll call you tomorrow," I promised.

"Please do."

"I'm sorry," I said.

"I know."

"It's personal now," I told her. "Maybe it always was."

"I know."

I hung up the phone and stared out the window. Every muscle and bone in my body hurt. Even thinking hurt. "Run it off," my coach used to say. That had been his cure for everything. "Run it off, sweat it out." During those few brief years when I had the audacity to consider myself an athlete, I would follow his advice like it had come down from Mount Sinai. I wondered what had become of him as I crawled back into bed and pulled the blankets to my chin.

Dean Bernelle can't cook. He was one of those older-generation gentlemen who bought into the theory that cooking, that anything to do with the kitchen, was women's work. But he made a valiant effort nonetheless, whipping up fried eggs, toast, and canned chili for a late lunch. I thanked him profusely even though the toast was burned and the yolks of the eggs were rubbery.

The death of his daughter, Laura, and his granddaughter, Jennifer, had hit him especially hard. Yet he never discussed it. At least not that I was aware of. But it was always there, just below the surface.

"I'm putting in a wall of blueberry bushes near the shed," he told me. "I remember Jenny used to love picking blueberries. She'd eat a berry for every one she dropped in the bucket, then come home with her mouth and fingers all purple. Laurie would get so angry at us."

"That was just for show," I told him. "Mostly she didn't mind at all."

"Guess you're right," he agreed, then rapidly changed the subject. "Are you in trouble?" he asked. "Do you need help?"

"I don't think so."

"You look it."

"I admit I could have used a hand yesterday."

"Cops beat you up, is that right?"

I nodded.

"They used to do the same thing when I was young. They see a guy they thought was trouble, they'd smack him around a little just to keep him in line. I saw that a lot when I was young. I bet you did the same when you were a cop."

"No, not at all," I assured him.

Dean just smiled. I don't think he believed me.

"You're going back, aren't you?" he asked.

"Back where?"

"Back where they beat you up."

"I suppose," I admitted.

"Yeah, I knew it. I remember telling Laurie when she first started bringing you around, 'One thing about Taylor,' I said. 'He's no quitter. He's not going to quit on you. He's like a marine. You can kill him, but he's not going to quit.'"

"Did you really say that?"

"Yes, I did."

"No wonder it took her so long to accept my marriage proposal."

"Don't give me that," he said. "If you only had the guts to ask, she would have married you the weekend after you two met."

"Really? She said that?"

Dean nodded.

The things you learn.

The warm sun played peekaboo behind white, fluffy, daydream clouds—perfect weather for lake watching. I descended the long, steep flight of stairs that led from the Bernelles' home on top of the hill to the lake below, carrying three cans of beer that I'd found in the refrigerator. About halfway down I realized I was overburdened and stopped for a half hour to drink one of the beers. My load reduced, I continued to the L-shaped dock, making myself comfortable on the bench at the base of the L.

Like most forms of human endeavor, lake watching can be elevated to an art form in the proper hands. Me? I'm the Monet of lake watching. I can do it for hours, thinking about nothing and everything, whereas less dedicated artists grow weary and bored after thirty minutes or so. The difference is that most people look for answers in the gently rippling waves while I search only for questions.

"I wonder how much that cost?" was one of the questions. It was directed at the sailboat moored to the stem of the L. I remember the day Phyllis had launched it. Dean and Laura had both asked, "Where did you get it?" I asked, "How much did it cost?" I wondered what that said about me.

I was tempted to pollute Phyll's lake with the empty beer cans, thought better of it, and set them on the dock. A short time later Phyllis herself came down the stairs. The sports jacket was gone. In its place were pink shorts and a white tank top. She was a fetching woman, my mother-in-law. Like her daughter.

She sat next to me and looked out over the lake. She asked me how I was feeling, and I said I was okay and asked her how the meeting went, and she said the customer bought all five lots. The exchange pretty much exhausted us, and we sat there without speaking for a good half hour. Finally, Phyllis took my hand, gave it a tug, and asked straight out, "Have you found anyone yet?"

"No." I answered quickly, without even thinking of Cynthia— and when I did, I didn't take the answer back. I guess that said something about me, too.

"I'm sorry."

"I can't imagine getting married again," I said.

"I wish you would," Phyllis told me. "Imagine it, I mean."

I shrugged, wincing at the pain the gesture caused me.

"There is a woman," I said. "Her name is Cynthia. My mom can't stand her."

"Why not?"

Because she defended the man who killed your daughter and granddaughter, I nearly said. "It's a long story," I told her instead. "Anyway, she's *somebody*. I just don't know if she's *someone*, if you know what I mean."

"I know. It's just that I see the loneliness in you. . . ."

I turned quickly to face her. How could she see that?

"It's in your eyes, the way you carry yourself. . . ."

Nonsense.

"Maybe I recognize it and others don't because I knew you before the loneliness came."

"I'm not lonely," I insisted. "Alone, okay, but not lonely. There's a difference."

A small cloud passed over the sun before Phyllis replied, "It's time to move on. Laurie would say so, too."

A few more clouds came and went.

"I want you to come visit us again real soon, and I want you to bring a girl with you."

"It's not that simple."

" 'Most people are just as happy as they make their minds up to be.' Know who said that?"

"Who?"

"Abraham Lincoln. Find a girl," Phyllis told me. "Start over."

I thought of Alison. She had tried to start over. Look what had happened to her.

"It's not that easy."

"It's not supposed to be easy. Loving someone is the hardest thing there is."

She got that right.

"Find someone. If not this Cynthia, then someone else. A life unshared is a life wasted."

"Yeah? Who said that?"

"Me."

I had to smile.

"Find someone to share your life with," Phyllis added.

I gave her hand a squeeze.

"How 'bout you?" I asked, waving at the sailboat and the lake and the house on the hill. "Let me take you away from all this."

Phyllis laughed. "Then who would feed Dean?"

The next morning I waited in bed as long as my conscience would allow. When I finally shuffled into the bathroom, I was appalled by what I saw in the mirror. I touched each bruise that marked my body from face to upper rib cage to belt line—connect the dots and see a gruesome picture. There was some physical pain, some stiffness, but nothing I couldn't live with. My mental health was a different matter. My hand shook when I borrowed Dean's razor to shave, and I caught myself humming the theme songs to movies in which the hero got killed—the part of my brain that decided I was going back there was having a hard time convincing the rest of me that it was a good idea.

Dean lent me a shirt, and to my great relief, Phyllis had run the rest of my clothes through the washer, so they were lemon fresh—she'd even managed to remove most of the bloodstains; it was a miracle. I put them on and examined myself in the mirror, full face and then profile. I was convinced I looked presentable if not downright handsome; pretended that no one would notice the dark splotch beneath my ear or my bruised lower lip or the blood clotted in my right nostril.

After a while, I stopped humming.

Dean was standing by the kitchen sink drinking coffee when I entered. Phyllis, dressed like she intended to skip down to the dock and jump into her sailboat at any moment, was sitting at the kitchen table and reading the newspaper.

"You're leaving now," she told me, looking up from the paper.

"Yes."

"Are you coming back?"

"When I can."

She folded the paper neatly before asking, "Is there anything we can do for you?"

"I need a favor."

"What?" Dean asked.

"I want to borrow the Walther PPK that I gave you that Christmas."

"My gun?"

"I'll make sure you get it back."

"No problem," he said and left the room.

"You didn't tell us exactly what happened in Kreel County," Phyllis reminded me.

"I'm not sure I know myself," I told her.

Dean put the gun down on the table in front of me. It was lightly oiled, in the box it came in. The Walther PPK weighed only twenty-three ounces but it felt heavy in my hand. My reason told me to leave the gun. But my instincts—and my bruises—told me to load the Walther and slip it into my jacket pocket. So I did.

"I have to go now. Thank you both for everything."

"Holland," Phyllis called, stopping me at the door, hugging me. "Remember what I told you." There were tears in her eyes.

"I'll remember."

Dean smiled at me. *"Semper fi,"* he said, reciting the Marine Corps motto. *Always faithful.*

nineteen

I announced myself at the reception area of the Kreel County Sheriff's Department, speaking to the secretary through an intercom on the other side of a bulletproof glass partition. If I was going to have more trouble with the sheriff, I wanted to get to it—I'd be damned if I'd spend the day looking fearfully over my shoulder for irate deputies. A moment later the secretary buzzed me through the door and led me to him.

Sheriff Orman's office was small and cluttered and dominated by a large canvas hanging behind his desk. It was an oil painting of a magnificent twelve-point whitetailed buck at sunset, the buck looking real enough to move, his reflection shimmering on the lake he was drinking from. In the bottom right corner of the canvas, the name R. ORMAN was painted with an unobtrusive brush.

Orman was sitting behind the desk. He took a good look at my battered face but said nothing. His face wasn't in much better shape: two days' stubble, bloodshot eyes, sagging cheeks. But I didn't say anything, either. Instead, I stood staring across the desk at him, trying to act like a pro boxer just before the bell rings. I wasn't desperate for a rematch but if he wanted one, I'd be happy to oblige; this time my hands would be free.

"I am a licensed private investigator from the state of Minnesota; I am here looking for a woman named Alison Donnerbauer Emerton who is going under the name Michael Bettich," I informed him defiantly, explaining my presence and purpose in an out-of-state jurisdiction to the proper authorities just like the handbook suggests, pretending the sheriff and I had never met before.

"Michael is in a coma," Orman said sadly, looking down at a framed photograph lying flat on his desk blotter—a photograph of Alison. "They took her by helicopter to Duluth General. They have a better-equipped trauma unit up there, better-trained staff. That's what they tell me."

"I'm sorry about Michael," I said and I meant it.

The slight smile that flashed and then disappeared suggested that he believed me. I also think he liked that I used the name Michael and not Alison.

"If there's anything I can do . . ." I added.

"Loushine!" he shouted so unexpectedly that I flinched.

"I spoke with the doctor," Orman told me in a softer voice. "She said whoever administered first aid at the scene probably saved Michael's life. I'm grateful.

"Loushine!" he shouted again.

"The other day, you didn't ask who I was or why I was here," I reminded him.

"I know who you are and why you're here."

"Want to tell me?" I asked. "I'm a little confused."

"Dammit Loushine!"

"Yes," the deputy said, coming through the door. He looked surprised to see me.

"Gary, this is Holland Taylor," Sheriff Orman said. "He's a private investigator from Minnesota. I checked on him. He did ten years for the St. Paul Police Department, four in Homicide. I've asked him to consult with us on the Michael Bettich shooting. If he's willing, you're to give him full cooperation."

Loushine clearly wasn't thrilled with the order. "Sheriff . . .?" he began.

Orman cut him off roughly. "Is that understood?"

"Yes, Sheriff." The answer came reluctantly.

Of me Orman asked, "Are you willing, Mr. Taylor?"

"Yes," I told him without reluctance. The last time a private investigator received such an invitation was never.

"Good." Orman rose from his chair. "I'm going to Duluth. I'll check in later." He brushed past us.

"Wait," I called to him. "I have questions."

"Ask Gary," the sheriff said and hung a left in the corridor, disappearing.

"It makes even less sense as it goes along," I told Deputy Loushine.

"What's the matter, Taylor?" he asked. "Haven't you ever heard an apology before?"

We were walking along the well-lit corridor of the Kreel County Sheriff's Department building, my Nikes making soft squeaking sounds on the tile.

"What have you got?" I asked him, flexing my new muscle.

"The Buick was stolen," Loushine said. "It was owned by the chief of the volunteer fire department down in Wascott. He reported it missing the day before the shooting."

"Where's Wascott?"

"About forty miles southwest of us," Loushine said. "We have bulletins out on the car. Also, you were right about the gun. It was an UZI semiautomatic carbine. We dug .41 AEs out of both Michael Bettich and Gretchen Rovick. A MAC fires only .45s or nine millimeters—"

"Chip Thilgen," I interrupted, just to prove how smart I was.

"Yes," said Loushine. "We know he made threats toward Michael at The Height Restaurant in Deer Lake about an hour before the shooting. We have several witnesses. Including you."

"Including me," I agreed. "What does Thilgen have to say for himself?"

"Nothing yet," Loushine answered. "We haven't found him. We have a man on his house; he hasn't been home. And we checked with his employer. Thilgen has been absent without leave since the shooting."

"Where does he work?"

"King Boats."

"He works for King Koehn?" I asked, surprised.

Loushine shrugged. "Why not? Everyone else does. Anyway, we're checking his family, his friends—actually, he doesn't have any friends—and we have bulletins out on him, too."

"What else?"

"Hmm?"

"What else have you got?"

"That's it."

I stopped next to a door marked EXIT.

"What do you mean, that's it?" I said, appalled. "You've had this case for almost forty-eight hours."

Loushine didn't answer, and I pushed my way through the door.

"I'm not going to lie to you, Taylor," Loushine told me as he followed behind. "I'm not an experienced investigator. I've worked as deputy sheriff for nine years now, and I've handled exactly two homicides, both of them slam-dunk domestics. On this case I've been following Bobby Orman's lead, and quite frankly he's not up to it, either. Man had exactly two years of law-enforcement experience before he was made sheriff—in the Highway Patrol."

That stopped me again. "Two years? How did he get the job?"

"Appointment. The former sheriff was caught shacking up with a prostitute. The county board wanted someone squeaky-clean and politically palatable. Orman's father and grandfather had both been sheriff, and people loved them—"

"So they went with the son."

"There you go."

"Does he know the job at all?"

"Bobby knows administration; he was the factory manager over at King Boats for a half dozen years after he left the HP—it's kind of a complicated story. I went to school with Bobby; we played ball together, so I know he didn't want to be a cop, didn't want to follow the family tradition. But he did, anyway; joined the Highway Patrol after junior college. His old man was still sheriff, and Bobby could have gotten a job here in Kreel, but he went away; people figured he just didn't want to work in the old man's shadow. Two years later the old man dies of a heart attack while pulling an ice fishing shack off the lake; Bobby quits the HP and goes to work for King.

"The county goes through three sheriff's in the next six years, and each is worse than the one before. People are pissed; the County Board of Commissioners is up against it; half of 'em are up for re-election, right? So they tap Bobby; they want his name. He takes the job. Surprised me. But he's been okay. Works hard. Goes to a lot of law-enforcement seminars. Takes care of his people."

"How long has he been sheriff?" I asked.

"Couple years."

"Turn it over to the Department of Criminal Investigation," I suggested bluntly. The DCI was the Wisconsin equivalent of Minnesota's Bureau of Criminal Apprehension, a statewide investigatory unit created to lend aid to local police departments that didn't have the resources to handle major cases.

"That's what I said," Loushine told me. "But Bobby doesn't want to give it up, and neither does the county attorney."

"Where is the county attorney?" I asked.

"Vacation in San Francisco."

I gave Loushine another stare.

He shrugged. "What can I say? Man likes his job; he wants to be re-elected next year."

My stare intensified. "Unbelievable."

"It's a sorry situation," Loushine admitted, and I sighed dramatically. But the truth was, I couldn't have been more delighted. Giving a police department *guidance* during an active criminal investigation? A free hand to do whatever I want, all with the department's support? That's like a PI's most forbidden fantasy come true.

"Okay," I said and continued walking.

"Okay," Loushine echoed, falling in step with me. "Where are we going?"

"What do you know about Alison Donnerbauer Emerton?" I asked in reply as we crossed the street and headed for the Saginau Medical Center.

"Never heard of her," he said. "You mentioned the name the day of the shooting. Who is she?"

"I assume Gretchen Rovick is still in the hospital?"

"Yes," Loushine replied, then added, "Who is Alison Donnerbauer Emerton?"

"Deputy Rovick's best friend."

We cornered the woman doctor at the Saginau Medical Center. I asked her if she had any updated information concerning Michael Bettich's condition.

"Still critical, last I heard," she said.

"What do you think her chances are?" I asked. I wanted the doctor to promise that Alison would be all right. But she was unwilling to commit herself. I changed the subject.

"How's Deputy Rovick?" I asked.

"She'll be fine," the doctor responded. "She should be on crutches in a few days and walking normally in ten more. The wound was superficial."

"Where is she?" Loushine asked.

"Second floor. Two-oh-two."

"Can we see her?" the deputy added.

"Be my guest."

We started toward the elevators.

"By the way," the doctor stopped us. She looked me in the eye and said, "It was you who administered first aid to Michael, right?"

I confirmed her suspicion.

"You saved her life," the doctor said and patted my arm. "For a while, anyway."

I was proud of the compliment, but the way the doctor phrased it sent an uncomfortable surge of electricity through my entire body.

We found Gretchen sitting up in bed, reading the latest mystery by Nevada Barr. Her leg was elevated under the covers, which were rolled to her waist, revealing a teal nightgown trimmed with lace that I found particularly alluring. Apparently Loushine agreed.

The way his eyes kept finding Gretchen's ample chest, you just knew this was a side of his colleague that he had never seen before.

"How are you feeling?" I asked.

"Fine," she answered cautiously before turning to Loushine. "What's he doing here?"

Loushine explained.

"No way!" Gretchen protested.

Loushine shrugged. "Sheriff's orders."

Gretchen returned her gaze to me. "But he could be responsible."

"Why's that?" I asked.

"There are people who wanted Alison found," she insisted. "You found her for them."

"Alison?" Loushine asked.

I silenced him with an upraised hand. "Why did they want her found?" I asked Gretchen.

"Because . . ." Her voice was high and excited, but something stopped her. After a few moments of reflection, she said, "No, you're right. They're probably all angry enough to kill her, but my understanding is that the people she left in the Twin Cities needed her alive; they wanted to prove that she was alive and that they had nothing to do with her disappearance."

I had come to the same conclusion the day before and revisited it several times since then. Nevertheless, it was comforting to hear it from someone else. Part of the reason I had returned to Kreel County was to prove that I had nothing to do with the assault on Michael Bettich—mostly to myself.

"Tell me about Alison," I told Gretchen.

"Who the hell is Alison?" Loushine asked again.

Gretchen sucked in her breath and started talking with the exhale, talking so low that Loushine and I had to move to the foot of the bed to hear her. From where I stood, everything she told him was the truth—except maybe why Alison had left the Twin Cities in the first place. She seemed as unsure about that as I was.

Gretchen told us that Alison simply appeared on her doorstep late one night eight months ago with a battered suitcase and a fascinating if not altogether heroic tale. She was seeking asylum and anonymity, and Gretchen agreed to provide both. The deputy was delighted that her friend had come to her, and if Alison now insisted on being known as Michael Bettich, that was just swell as far as Gretchen was concerned—although she did confess that her police-officer mentality had compelled her to take a keen interest in the goings-on in Dakota County, Minnesota, until she was satisfied that her friend was not fleeing criminal charges.

Michael soon settled in and began building a new life for herself. Her brilliant mind impressed King Koehn so much that he gave her a job overseeing his investments after their first meeting; the fact that she was also pretty probably didn't hurt, either—King liked pretty. And after dating around for several months, Michael settled on Sheriff Bobby Orman, moving in with him two months ago.

When Gretchen had finished, Loushine shook his head. "Nobody tells me anything," he muttered.

"It didn't bother you that Alison had left so many people in the Twin Cities holding the dirty end of the stick?" I asked Gretchen.

"The way Alison explained it to me, they all deserved it."

"Probably did," I agreed. Gretchen responded to my remark with a weak smile—she wasn't sure about her friend, I concluded. After all this time helping to protect Alison, she still wasn't sure. Hell, neither was I.

I smiled myself and removed a small notebook from my pocket and flipped it open. I read the names that I had written there the night before while sitting at Phyllis Bernelle's kitchen table. "Who in Kreel County had motive to kill Michael?"

"You ask that like she's dead," Gretchen protested. "Michael is *not* dead. Stop talking like she is."

Gretchen was right. From the beginning, I had been treating the case like a homicide investigation, when in fact there had not been a homicide—and saying so was like putting Alison's photograph on the cover of *Sports Illustrated*: It was a jinx and lessened her chances for survival.

I rephrased the question. "Who wanted to hurt her?"

"Nobody," Gretchen insisted.

"Nobody?!" I shouted, then checked myself. "Nobody," I repeated in a softer voice, waving my notebook. "I've been in town for only a couple of hours, and I can name at least six suspects. How 'bout you?" I asked, turning toward Loushine.

"I only have one. Thilgen."

Chip Thilgen looked good, I admitted; his was the first name on my list. But it bothered me that the car used in the shooting had been stolen out of town the day before Alison was shot. If the crime had been premeditated—as the theft would seem to indicate—it seemed damned unlikely that Thilgen would have announced his hatred for Michael one hour before shooting her. And if it wasn't premeditated, why did he steal the car?

"Sure, there's Thilgen," I said. "But how 'bout Ingrid?"

Loushine demonstrated his lack of experience when he shook his head at the suggestion, eliminating the owner of The Height out of hand.

"She stands to lose business if The Harbor is a success," I explained. "How many gourmet restaurants can this region support?"

Loushine still shook his head.

"How 'bout Charlie Otterness?" I asked.

Gretchen cringed at the sound of his name.

"Betrayed?" I continued. "Humiliated by the woman he loved?"

"That was before Michael became involved with Bobby Orman," Gretchen interjected, as if that made all the difference in the world.

Loushine shook his head some more. "Charlie wouldn't hurt a fly," he said.

Unbelievable. According to these two, nobody in Kreel County was capable of murder.

"King Koehn," I suggested.

Loushine held out his hand, wobbled it. "I suppose he's worth looking into," he agreed, bending just so slightly to the possibility.

Man, I thought. *If they didn't like those suggestions, they're going to hate the final two names.*

"Sheriff Orman?"

"Bullshit!" Loushine spit the word quickly and loudly.

"What motive would he have?" Gretchen queried.

"Did he know about Michael; that she was Alison?"

"I don't know," she admitted. "I didn't tell him."

"Maybe he found out. Maybe he didn't like it."

"Bullshit," Loushine repeated.

"He's sure gone out of his way to botch the investigation, hasn't he?" I reminded them.

The two deputies stared at me without speaking, but I could tell I'd struck a nerve. They looked at each other and then away.

"He just doesn't understand how things work, that's all," Loushine said. But his words didn't echo with the same vehemence as before.

"Who else?" Gretchen asked. "That's five suspects on your silly little list. Who's the sixth?"

I stepped next to the bed and showed her the name I had written last.

She read the name, blinking several times while reading it as if she feared her eyes were deceiving her. She was looking at Loushine, expecting him to say something, but he remained silent. He hadn't seen my list and didn't know the sixth name. Gretchen shook her head and closed her eyes more tightly than natural, then opened them quickly as if she expected me to disappear. I didn't.

"Fuck you," she said at last.

She was breathing hard through her nose; her mouth was clamped shut but only for a moment. When it opened again, she shouted, "How dare you?! Who do you think you are?"

She threw Nevada Barr's book at me, but fortunately it was a paperback and easy to dodge.

"What?" a confused Loushine asked.

"It's *me*!" Gretchen shouted. "*I'm* the sixth name!" Then to me: "Get outta here! Get outta my sight!"

I moved away from the hospital bed, ending up in the corner as far from her as I could get and still be in the same room. I studied her from my vantage point, my arms folded over my chest, pretending I could determine her guilt or innocence just by looking at her.

"What the hell, Taylor?" Loushine asked.

"Michael Bettich has no family, as you well know," I reminded Gretchen. "So if she dies, what happens to The Harbor? Who collects the little gold mine she was building for herself? Her best friend, I bet."

"You think I hired someone to shoot her so I could get her resort?" Gretchen demanded.

"People have been killed for less," I told her.

"I'm a *deputy*!" she shouted at me. When that had no effect, she added, "I was *shot*!"

"How convenient," I told her.

"You sonuvabitch," she hissed at me. She flung the covers off and attempted to swing her legs over the edge of the bed to come after me. But Loushine stopped her and rolled her back in bed— he seemed excited to have physical contact with his fellow deputy.

"Get out!" Gretchen barked at me after she was safely tucked in.

"We'll talk again," I told her and left the hospital room. Loushine followed me out.

"Is this how things are done in the big city," he asked when we were in the corridor, Gretchen's door closed behind us. "Is this how trained *homicide* cops conduct investigations?"

I didn't respond. Instead, I led Loushine to the hospital switchboard. "No calls in or out of Gretchen Rovick's room until we tell you," I instructed the operator. "By order of the sheriff's department."

The operator looked at Loushine, and he nodded. I took him by the arm and half pulled him toward the hospital door.

"Put a tap on her phone," I told him. "Then you can release her calls. I want to know who she talks to."

"Why?" Loushine asked.

"Because in the unlikely event that she actually was involved in the shooting, she might contact her two partners."

"Oh," Loushine replied with an expression that was as cheerful as three days of hard rain.

We were climbing into Loushine's 4X4 after he made the necessary calls.

"You're wrong, you know," he said as he slid behind the steering wheel. "I did what you asked because the sheriff ordered me to give full cooperation. But you're wrong."

"Probably," I agreed.

"No, I mean it," Loushine said. "I remember this time, it was about six months after we hired her. Gretchen and I were called to a simple burglary; I was riding with her from time to time back then, doing the supervising-officer routine. It was a trifle—fishing equipment taken from a victim's shed—and I acted like it, veteran cop telling the rookie not to get excited. The victim didn't see it that way and became pretty upset at my indifference.

"After we took the complaint, we went back to the car. I was about to open the passenger door, when Gretchen suddenly drew her revolver, aimed across the roof of the squad, and yelled, 'Drop it or I'll shoot!' She was aiming at someone standing right behind me. 'Drop it or I'll shoot!' she yelled again. I didn't move an inch. Then Gretchen started counting, real slow but loud. 'One, two, three . . .' I'm standing there, praying to hear something hit the ground. Then I heard a muffled thud, and Gretchen yelled, 'Step back!'

"I turn around, and there's the owner of the shed with his hands in the air. On the ground is a crossbow. The man was going to shoot me in the back with an arrow because I didn't take the theft of his fishing equipment seriously. Later, I asked Gretchen how high she was willing to count before she pulled the trigger. She told me she knew at three the guy would drop the bow."

"And if he didn't?" I asked.

"She would have killed him at four."

"What has that got to do with this?" I asked him.

"Gretchen is cool enough," he answered. "If she wanted Michael dead, she would have done it herself. Clean. And simple. No way she would have been as sloppy as the shooters at The Harbor."

"Now there's an endorsement," I said smugly.

"She's one of us," Deputy Loushine snapped back.

"Hell, Gary," I told him. "According to TV, according to the movies, cops go bad all the time."

I meant it as a joke, but it didn't come off that way.

twenty

I loved reading Jack London as a kid, loved learning the language of nature, listening to "the voices of wind and storm." Even now I'm impressed by his violence, the violence of the unconquered wilderness, of the men and animals who call it home. Kreel County is a far cry from London's forest primordial, of course. Honeycombed with highways, roads, and logging trails, it's nearly impossible to escape man's presence. Hike in a straight line long enough and you're sure to trip upon some vestige of civilization: a snowmobile track, a power line, a Piggly Wiggly grocery store. There are no packs of starving wolves to contend with, no rampaging grizzlies. Only hunters who can't shoot straight. It's much the same in northern Minnesota where my family kept a hunting and fishing cabin—at least it was a hunting and fishing cabin before electricity, before TVs and VCRs and microwave ovens turned it into something else. Still, it's infinitely superior to existence in the concrete jungles of big-city America, where a man can live a lifetime without ever setting a foot to untrampled earth.

At my insistence Deputy Gary Loushine drove to Chip Thilgen's cabin, even though he insisted Thilgen was not at home; he'd had people watching the place for nearly two days now. The cabin was located on a small lake at the base of a heavily wooded hill and virtually surrounded by poplar, fir, and birch trees. It was difficult to see from the narrow, seldom-used gravel road that cut through the forest between the cabin and the hill. We drove past it twice. An abandoned logging trail branched off from the gravel road well above the cabin and wound its way up the hill. After our third pass we took the trail as far as we could, eventually parking the 4X4 behind another Kreel County Sheriff's Department vehicle that was hidden well out of sight. We worked the rest of the way up the steep hill on foot. At the top of the hill I paused to look at my watch. I really didn't care what time it was. But it gave me an excuse to rest and regain my lost breath.

"Coming?" Loushine asked. He wasn't even breathing hard.

"Right behind you," I told him, a false smile on my face, as I reminded myself that I was in shape, that I worked out, that I know karate and jujitsu and aikido. I just don't make a habit of climbing steep hills in the forest, is all.

We resumed pushing ourselves through the trees and underbrush until we found a small clearing with good sight lines to Thilgen's cabin. Hunkered down at the edge of the clearing was a sheriff's deputy—the one who had driven my car when I was escorted to the county line. He was watching the cabin with a pair of binoculars. He must have known we were coming because he didn't even acknowledge our presence until we knelt next to him.

"Tell me you're here to relieve me," he said.

"Sorry," Loushine said, promising that another deputy would be along shortly. "Anything?"

"Nope."

Thilgen's cabin was about three hundred yards below us. It was tiny, one of those one-story, prefabricated jobs built on cinder blocks—from that distance the entire structure looked like it could fit inside my living room. A short flight of stairs led to a narrow deck and the cabin's only door. Like the cabin, the deck was stained red. A fire pit surrounded by a circle of large stones had been dug in back of the cabin, about fifty feet from what looked like a crumbling outhouse. Beyond the cabin I could see a small patch of lake peeking through the trees.

We sat and watched for a long time without speaking.

In the forest, first you hear nothing. Then you hear everything: birds chirping, crickets singing, wind whipping through tree branches and sounding just like running water. If you're not familiar with it, the racket can be downright disconcerting. Sitting, not moving, concentrating completely on the cabin below me, my imagination began to amuse itself at the expense of my nerves. Several times I heard voices and laughter and footsteps yet saw nothing. I convinced myself that I was being watched, stalked; convinced myself that there was a psychotic killer hiding behind every bush—the same guy who escaped from the lunatic asylum in the stories we told ourselves as children . . . the one with the hook.

A hand gripped my shoulder. I knocked it away impulsively and pivoted on my heels, my hand deep in my jacket pocket digging for the Walther PPK.

Startled, Loushine pulled away from me. Then he smiled knowingly.

"Don't ever sneak up on me like that again," I warned him.

Loushine chuckled. "What do you want to do?" he asked.

"Let's go down there," I said confidently—or at least with a voice that sounded confident. Man, I was starting to behave like the Woody Allen of private investigators, much too paranoid for this line of work.

I stood and stretched. My thought was to work our way back to the 4X4 and drive to the cabin. But Loushine was already moving down the hill. The show-off. I followed, moving gingerly, picking up the pace when Loushine did. In my haste, I tripped over a root and fell headlong into a blueberry bush. I looked up. Loushine hadn't even slowed. He was waiting for me on the gravel road at the base of the steep hill when I broke through the last wall of brush. He shook his head at me like he pitied me.

"Poor little lamb lost in the woods," he muttered.

Yeah? I'd like to see how he'd manage the Phillips neighborhood in Minneapolis on a Saturday night!

We went to the cabin and climbed the redwood steps leading to the deck. I peered through the windows while Loushine leaned against the railing. The cabin appeared empty.

"See anything?" he asked sarcastically.

I knocked on the door; its lock and frame were cheaply made and flimsy. I doubted they could withstand a strong wind.

"I told you, no one is home," Loushine added.

"Shhhh!" I hushed him. "Do you hear that?"

"What?"

"It sounds like a call for help."

"Excuse me?"

BAM!

I kicked the door in.

"Jesus Christ, Taylor!" Loushine protested. "We don't have a warrant."

"Oops."

"This is breaking and entering."

"Oh, well," I said. "Since the door is already open . . ."

"This is a felony!" Loushine insisted.

The cabin consisted of three rooms, including the bathroom. The first room, a combination kitchen/dining room/living room was papered from floor to ceiling with pages that had been carefully cut from *Penthouse* and *Playboy* magazines and *Victoria's Secret* catalogs (personally I preferred the lingerie models over the nudes, but that's just me). The room also contained several bookcases filled with paperbacks with titles like *Country Club Wife, Fraternity Initiation, The Girl Next Door, The Naughty Lady,* and *Curious Cathy.* Another bookcase next to the TV and VCR contained adult videos with similar titles. I recognized one: *Debbie Does Dallas,* an oldie but a goodie. Nowhere did I see a publication dealing with the environment.

"Wow!" Loushine said from where he stood just inside the doorway.

"Man doesn't get out much, does he?" I said.

"Guess not."

"Take this room," I told him.

"And do what?"

"Look."

"For what?"

"Incriminating evidence."

"What exactly does incriminating evidence look like?"

"It's like pornography," I told him. "You'll know it when you see it."

"Yeah, but even if we find some, then what? Without a warrant, a judge would never allow us to admit it into evidence."

"Trust me," I told him.

"Trust him," he muttered. "Big-city homicide cop."

"Amateur," I muttered back.

I went into the bathroom. It was small, dirty, and stank of mildew. Thilgen had taped several suggestive photos—they were suggestive in the way a slap in the face was suggestive—to the dirty mirror fronting the medicine cabinet. I opened the cabinet. Thilgen's toothbrush, toothpaste, electric shaver, and hairbrush were all accounted for.

"If Thilgen is running, he didn't plan to," I called out.

"Huh?" Loushine grunted.

I moved to Chip Thilgen's bedroom and immediately regretted it. The small room reeked of sweat and semen, and the sordid odor made me gag. The unmade bed was soiled; its sheets looked as if they hadn't been changed in months. More pornography hung from the walls, and several life-sized posters were stapled to the ceiling above the bed.

"You're one strange biscuit," I told the absent Thilgen as I went through his bureau drawers. They were filled with clothes and assorted sex aids—manual and electric. Two small suitcases, both empty, were hidden under his bed, and the tiny closest was filled with shirts, pants, and jackets. In the pocket of the jacket hung from a hook on the back side of the door I found his checkbook. Again I concluded that if Thilgen was on the run, it wasn't something he had planned. At the bottom of the closet I discovered a cardboard box filled with his financial records: old tax returns, receipts, bank envelopes stuffed with canceled checks, and several check registers. I set the checkbook on top and carried the box back into the kitchen with me.

"Whaddaya got there?" Loushine asked, rushing to my side—anything to quit searching through Thilgen's unsavory life. He watched over my shoulder as I examined the contents of the box, paying particular attention to the checks written most recently.

"This is interesting," I said at last.

"What?"

"Nearly every check Thilgen wrote paid for monthly bills or purchases—groceries, gasoline, utilities, that sort of thing—except for these six that were made out to James Johannson."

"Jimmy Johannson is an asshole," Loushine told me. "An asshole with a record."

"Yes, I know," I recalled. "We met." I studied the check amounts. "Five checks were written for five hundred dollars each over the past nine months except for this last one." I gave Loushine a look at the carbon in the checkbook register. It was for twenty-five hundred, and it was made out the day the Buick was stolen from the Wascott fire chief.

"The day before Michael was shot," Loushine noted.

"Uh-huh."

"Let's go," the deputy said excitedly.

"Go where?" I asked.

"Go and brace Johannson, whaddaya think? Bring him in for questioning."

"On what grounds?" I asked.

"On what—?"

"What probable cause are you going to give the judge when he asks?"

Loushine gave it two beats then began to curse bitterly.

"Dammit, Taylor. You've compromised the investigation."

"Would I do a thing like that?"

"We can't use any of this shit now," Loushine told me as I returned the check registers to the box.

"Unlawful entry . . . proceeds of an illegal search . . . fruits of the poisonous tree . . ." Loushine went on like that while I took the box back to Thilgen's bedroom. He was just finishing up when I returned.

"Is this how you do things in St. Paul?" he asked.

"Of course not," I told him. "It's illegal." I smiled—and inwardly shuddered—at the thought of what Anne Scalasi would do to me if I attempted the same nonsense in her town.

"So now what do we do?" Loushine asked.

"So now *I* go talk with James Johannson. Alone."

Deputy Loushine cursed some more.

twenty-one

Deputy Loushine's directions—or my misunderstanding of them—got me all turned around. I ended up at a service station off the county road, absolutely lost. The kid manning the pumps regarded me suspiciously, and when I asked him for directions to Johnny Johannson's place, he asked, "Why do you want to know?"

"So I can talk to the man. Is that a problem?"

"Let's just say it's a small county, and it's getting smaller all the time, and I have to live in it, and I don't want to do anything that will make living in it harder than it already is."

"I just want to talk."

"There's a phone inside."

"Swell."

And people say *I'm* cynical.

A phone book was attached to the telephone stand with a chain in case someone wanted to steal it. It listed John Johannson's address as 315 Fire Road 21. Next to the unmanned cash register was a rack filled with maps going for a buck-fifty each. I stole one labeled Kreel County and took it back to my car.

No fewer than five wrecks littered Johnny Johannson's yard, the hood of each car opened to the elements. Most of the cars were rusted through, dead but unburied. I parked in the driveway next to them, thinking that my '91 Dodge Colt fit right in.

The house itself—an ancient ramshackle two-story in need of paint and a new roof—was situated at the end of a dirt road in a weed-infested clearing surrounded by a wall of trees. There was no lake that I could see, only woods. I followed a worn dirt path to the front of the house and knocked on the door. Johnny Johannson answered it. He clenched his fists and went into a defensive stance at the sight of me. It had been weeks since he had seen me last, yet he still wanted to know, "You lookin' for more?"

"Not me, sir," I told him. "I figured I got off lucky the first time."

"Then what do you want?"

"I'd like to speak with your son, James, if I might?"

"What for?" still on the defensive.

I showed him my photostat.

"I'm looking for someone," I said. "Guy named Chip Thilgen. I was told James might know where I can find him."

"James isn't in trouble?" Johannson asked.

"Not that I know of." I shrugged, acting oh-so-innocent. "Not with me, anyway."

"That's good, that's good, 'cuz Jimmy, he's had his share—if you know what I mean."

I pretended that I didn't.

"Is he around?" I asked.

"Well, now, I can't say that he is," Johannson replied. "He's out"—Johannson gestured toward the trees surrounding his home—"workin' his new dog. But I expect he'll be back anytime now if you care to wait."

I said I would and followed him inside.

Johannson offered me a cold beer, which I accepted, and led me to his workroom in the basement.

"You had me, you know," he said as we descended the stairs. "Back at The Last Chance, you had me. With them moves of yours, you coulda killed me easy. A lot of them assholes be happy to see it, too."

"Why didn't you just stay down?" I asked.

"I wouldn't give 'em the satisfaction."

I watched in true awe as Johnny Johannson gave me a tour of his workbench. He was a flytier like my grandfather, and he had all his paraphernalia meticulously arranged—in direct contrast to the rest of his home. The benchtop looked like a surgical tray, filled with a scalpel, scissors, pliers, tweezers, a dubbing needle, a magnifying glass, single-edge razor blades, an emery board, an Arkansas point file, and an eyedropper. Three different-sized transparent plastic boxes labeled THREAD, FLOSS, and TINSEL were neatly stacked atop each other. Fixed to the wall above the bench was a large shadowbox with over two dozen compartments, the compartments filled with jars and paper bags, each labeled for capes, fur, hair, hackles, hooks, and so on. An English vise was mounted to the bench. It was exactly like my grandfather's, and I told Johannson so.

"This is so cool," I said aloud, and he smiled.

"Whaddaya think of this?" he asked after opening a large wooden box lined with foam and containing about fifty wet flies. He placed one of the flies in my palm.

"Very nice," I said.

"What is it?" he asked, testing me.

I studied it carefully, examining the fly the way Granddad had taught me. The fly had a black wool body shrouded in deer hair and a fluffy turkey feather dyed black; the wing was extended about an inch beyond the shank, that straight part of the hook between the bend and the eye.

"I'd guess a black marabou muddler, except—"

"Except?"

"The hackle is dyed bright yellow instead of scarlet."

"So?"

"Shouldn't the tail be scarlet?"

"I don't know, should it?"

"It's how my grandfather tied them."

"Your grandfather still with us?"

"Eighty-six and going strong."

"Keep the fly."

"Thanks."

"Give it to your granddad, and tell 'im he should experiment some."

I smiled my sincere thanks. Johannson showed me more, demonstrating with surprisingly nimble fingers the proper preparation of deer tails; advising me how to select the correct thread for winding the hair. I'd been down there for nearly an hour when we heard three muffled shotgun blasts in quick succession.

"My son," Johannson said. He sounded disappointed.

We went upstairs. Three more shotgun blasts greeted us when we stepped outside. They were coming from the side of the house facing away from the road. We made our way around slowly. I knew I wasn't being fired upon, but the shots activated my internal fight-or-flight response mechanism just the same, and I instinctively searched my jacket pocket for the Walther PPK.

Jimmy Johannson was facing the forest, a twelve-gauge pump resting on his shoulder. He was scolding a black Labrador puppy at his feet. Next to the puppy was a small boy, a frail, skinny little thing dressed in dirty T-shirt and sneakers held together with duct tape. When Jimmy Johannson nodded, the child tossed a dog dummy with all his might at the trees. Johannson fired three shots in the air in quick succession. The dog flinched and cowered, and Johannson kicked it, cutting loose with a string of obscenities that did not seem to shock the boy at all.

"That's no way to train a dog," I said.

"Jimmy don't mean no harm," Johnny Johannson told me, but he didn't sound convincing.

"Who's the boy?" I asked as we approached.

"My grandson, Angel's kid, Tommy," Johannson said softly; then louder he called, "Jimmy! Man here to see ya."

Jimmy Johannson glanced at me without curiosity and yelled, "Pull."

Little Tommy heaved another dog dummy into the woods, and Jimmy fired three times. Again the dog cowered, and again he was beaten. I shook my head. The dog wasn't frightened by the noise of the shotgun. He was frightened because he knew the shots would soon be followed by punches, kicks, and screams. I was tempted to tell Jimmy so but held my tongue.

"Whaddaya want?" Jimmy asked after he had finished assaulting the puppy.

"I'm a private investigator," I told him and flashed my photostat.

"Minnesota license don't mean shit in Wisconsin," he informed me.

"Don't mean much more than that in Minnesota," I replied.

"So?" he asked. I could tell he was warming toward me.

"I'm looking for a guy named Chip Thilgen."

Jimmy didn't even hesitate. "Who?" he asked.

"Chip Thilgen."

"Never heard of him," he said.

"Sure you have," Johnny Johannson volunteered.

Jimmy turned on him. "If I say I don't know him, old man, I don't fucking know him," he snarled.

"I was told you and Thilgen were seen driving together just two days ago," I lied.

"Who the fuck told you that?" Jimmy asked angrily.

"Does it matter?" I asked in reply.

"It matters a lot if some asshole is putting me with this Thilgen guy," he said. "It matters a fucking lot if people are lying about me."

"It could have been an honest mistake," I ventured, not wanting to unduly anger a man with a loaded shotgun in his hands.

"Got that fucking right," Jimmy spat.

"Tell me, then," I asked cautiously, "where were you around noon the day before yesterday?"

"Right here," he said.

"Doing what?"

"Sucking on the welfare titty," he announced almost proudly. Then, "Pull!"

Another dog dummy into the woods, another three shots. The

dog laid at Jimmy's feet and began to whimper even before the man hit him.

I had seen enough.

"That's a piss-poor way to train a dog," I told him.

"Who fucking asked you?" he snapped. Then, to prove who was boss, he clubbed the puppy with the stock of the gun.

"Sonuvabitch," I muttered.

"I'll show you how to train a dog," Jimmy boasted.

He took two steps backward. The boy seemed to know what was coming because he dove out of the way. Jimmy pointed the shotgun and pulled the trigger. A round of six shot took the dog's head off.

"Play dead!" Jimmy shouted at the corpse. "Play dead!" He laughed as if the sight of the headless puppy was the funniest thing he had ever seen.

"See? The dog's trained," he told me and laughed some more.

The scene made Johnny Johannson turn pale. The boy nudged the black Labrador's body with his battered sneakers, staining the tips of them with blood. I gripped the butt of the handgun hidden inside my pocket.

"Ahh, fuck it," Jimmy said, suddenly speaking in a monotone as he zipped the twelve-gauge into a leather case. "Dog was no good. Gun shy. Can't hunt with no gun-shy dog."

Jimmy went around to the front of the house; his father, visibly shakened but saying nothing, dragged his silent grandson inside the house through the back door. When Jimmy reappeared, he was carrying a spade. Without expression—without any emotion that I could observe—he began digging a shallow grave for the dog's still-warm carcass. I waited. I don't know why I waited. Maybe it was so I could tell Jimmy something when he had finished.

I gripped the Walther inside my pocket and asked, "What's the only thing money can't buy?"

"Huh?"

"What's the only thing money can't buy?" I repeated loudly.

"Shit, I dunno. Love?"

"The wag of a dog's tail," I answered.

Jimmy sneered at me. "Fuck that."

He heaved the spade in the general direction of a large shed and walked slowly to the house. I did not take my hand out of my pocket until he was well inside.

twenty-two

The sign outside The Wheel Inn Motel read: STAY SIX NIGHTS GET YOUR 7TH NIGHT FREE. Now that was optimism. I wondered if anyone ever took the proprietor up on his offer. I meant to ask him, only I didn't like the way he smirked when I checked in without luggage, paying cash instead of using a credit card. He looked at me like I was a talent scout for a porno magazine. Still, he showed me to my room with a certain amount of pride. I don't know why. It looked like any other motel room you've ever been in except it was older and crummier. The wallpaper was faded and crumbling along the edges—large yellow flowers on a blue background. The bed and bureau were bought new in, say, 1933. And the toilet was operated by a chain. All the comforts of home. The owner told me there was no cable, and the ancient black-and-white TV took a good fifteen minutes to warm up, but the Brewers were playing on channel ten later that evening if I was interested.

I had two questions: Where could I buy a change of clothes?

And where could I get something to eat? As to the former, he directed me to the combination clothing/appliance store attached to the grocery store in Deer Lake: King's One-Stop. As for the latter, he recommended the $5.95 all-you-can-eat buffet at The Forks Restaurant and Casino, about fifteen miles down the road just this side of the county line.

Before I left, I made two phone calls. The first was to Deputy Gary Loushine, but he wasn't in. The woman who answered the sheriff department's telephones promised she'd deliver my message. The second call was to Cynthia. The voice on her machine promised she'd return my call, too.

King's One-Stop was located just off the main drag in Deer Lake, not too far from Koehn's counterfeit log cabin. It offered only a limited selection of men's fashions. I found white athletic socks (two to a package), white briefs (three to a package), a white shirt with button-down collar, and a pair of blue jeans all in less than ten minutes. What made me linger was a gray-black silk-blend sports jacket sewn in Korea by a company I'd never heard of that was marked down to $34.95. I spent five minutes trying to determine what was wrong with it and couldn't, except that the sleeves were about a half inch too short. But for thirty-five bucks, what's half an inch? I bought the jacket, the other clothes, a plastic razor, a small can of shaving foam, a toothbrush and paste, and deodorant, paying with a check. The cashier looked at me like I was challenging her arithmetic when I asked for a receipt, but I figured Hunter Truman would insist. If he didn't reimburse my expenses, I'd take my chances with the IRS.

On the way back to the motel, I listened to the music broadcast by the public station at UMD: Jane Olivor's cover of "I'm Always Chasing Rainbows." According to the missing person's form I had worked with over the past few weeks, it was Alison's favorite song. I listened to it carefully. It was peculiar, knowing so much about a stranger. I couldn't have named Cynthia's favorite song if my life depended on it.

When I returned to the motel, the owner said that a woman had called for me, a woman with an "underage voice" who promised she would call back. I swear to God he winked at me.

I had showered and changed—happy to know I was wearing clean underwear in case I had an accident—when the owner put Cynthia's return call through to me. I greeted her as "counselor" in case he lingered on the line.

I was so pleased by the sound of Cynthia's voice that I didn't say anything after I said hello; I just wanted to listen. Was she the *someone?*

Cynthia said it had been a tough day, that her caseload was heavier than usual, that she was considering bringing a few more freelance attorneys on board to assist her. But she was sure she could find time for us—assuming I didn't spend the rest of my life in northern Wisconsin.

"I'll be home soon," I predicted.

After a moment of silence, Cynthia said, "Irene Brown and Raymond Fleck were in the paper this morning."

"Were they?"

"The Dakota County grand jury refused to return an indictment, and the county attorney was forced to release them. According to the paper, Irene and Raymond are leaving Minnesota. The paper said they're getting married and moving to Oregon."

"Happy trails," I said.

"You're off the hook."

"With them, maybe."

"How's Alison?"

"Still critical, last I heard."

"That's too bad."

"Yeah," I said. Then just to change the subject—I didn't want to speak of Alison anymore—I asked, "What's your favorite song?"

"My favorite song?"

"Yeah."

"I don't know."

"Think," I urged her.

"I . . . probably . . . I don't know, 'Misty,' I guess."

"'Misty'? Really? The old Erroll Garner tune?" I was expecting something by Jewel or Melissa Etheridge, somebody like that.

"No, no," Cynthia repeated. "Not Errol Garner. The song Johnny Mathis sings."

"Yeah, he covered it," I said. "Garner wrote it. The music, anyway."

"Why do you ask?"

"It's just something I thought I should know."

Deputy Loushine was not surprised by anything I told him concerning Jimmy Johannson.

"The sadistic sonuvabitch never drew an honest breath in his life," he told me.

"He lied about not knowing Thilgen," I said. "The question is, Does he have a reason for lying, or is he just doing it out of habit?"

Loushine cursed. He had information that would bring Johannson to heel—Thilgen's canceled checks—but he couldn't use them because some big-shot private detective didn't know shit one about the rules of evidence.

"Hang it up for tonight," I told the deputy. "We'll get a fresh start in the morning."

I could hear him yawn.

"Meet me for breakfast," he said, naming a café in Saginau. "Seven-thirty," he added.

"I'll be there," I promised without complaining how much I hate getting up that early in the morning.

My next call was to Duluth General Hospital. After a brief give-and-take, the switchboard operator directed me to the Intensive Care Unit. The nurse who answered the phone wanted to know how I was related to the patient before she would release any information. I couldn't bring myself to lie and pretend I was a member of Michael's family or that I was even a close personal friend. Instead, I lied and said I was Kreel County Sheriff's Deputy Gary Loushine. The nurse put me on hold while she checked her charts. When she returned, her voice had changed considerably. It was now low and rough and filled with exhaustion. And male.

"Gary," the voice said. "Is there something new?"

"Um, sorry, Sheriff," I said; I nearly hung up when I heard his voice. "It's not Loushine. It's Holland Taylor."

"Goddammit, Taylor," Orman muttered.

"I'm sorry, Sheriff," I told him quickly. "I just wanted to find out how . . . Michael is doing"

"She's still in a coma," Orman told me.

"I'm sorry," I repeated.

A moment of silence passed between us before the sheriff asked, "You really care about her, don't you?"

"Yes," I surprised myself by answering. I'd spent weeks examining every aspect of her life, so of course I cared about her—at least that's how I justified my feelings to myself. "I only met her that one time, but it feels like I've known her all my life," I added.

"I feel the same way," the sheriff admitted. Then he said, "I don't want you calling here again."

I promised I wouldn't and hung up.

My next call was to Hunter Truman, whose reaction was surprisingly subdued as I told him that the Kreel County Sheriff's Department was giving me carte blanche in finding out who had shot Alison and why. I guess he had been looking forward to the lawsuit.

He asked how Alison was. I told him she was in a coma. His reaction surprised me again. Instead of being concerned for her well-being, he wanted to know if Duluth General Hospital—and the rest of the world—knew that she was, in fact, Mrs. Alison Donnerbauer Emerton and not Michael Bettich.

"I think they're catching on," I told him.

"Well, I guess it doesn't matter," he told me.

The Forks was located northwest of Kreel County at the intersection of two blacktops and three snowmobile trails. It was a flat, sprawling, ornate complex wholly out of place in the Northland; it had started small but had expanded every which way, until it could now boast 23 blackjack tables, 262 slot machines, and 36 bingo tables. It was simple enough to find. I just followed the bright glow in the sky—the casino had twin searchlights mounted in its parking lot, scanning the heavens for gamblers. I wondered if the Three Wise Men had felt the same way when they followed their celestial beacon to the King of Kings. Probably not.

Along with gambling paraphernalia, The Forks housed a restaurant where you could get a drink but only if you also ordered food. The waitress, who was white, told me it was "a tribal thing." The Ojibwa had suffered enough alcohol abuse in their history without promoting it themselves. I passed on the buffet. Buffets are for old people who need to see the food they're ordering—my grandfather told me so. Instead, I asked the waitress what was good and went with her recommendation of prime rib. That's when I discovered that The Forks served no Minnesota beers: no Pig's Eye, no Landmark, no Summit Ale. I brought the obvious prejudice to her attention, and she reminded me with only a hint of impatience that I could drive to the Minnesota border in an hour if I kicked it. I settled for a Beck's.

The restaurant was elevated about eight feet and looked out over a handsomely carved railing to the gambling area. Like the protesters at the church in Deer Lake, I can't bring myself to call it "gaming." Watch the intense, humorless faces of the people sitting at the tables or perched in front of the slots, and then tell me it's a game.

Still, I'm fairly ambivalent about casino gambling. It's not something I like to do. For one thing the odds are appalling; you're six times more likely to catch malaria than you are to win the big jackpot on a typical three-wheel slot machine. For another, I believe we have only so much luck in our lives, and I'm loathe to squander it playing twenty-one. But, then, I'm a fully insured, independent contractor who likes his job and has a couple of hundred thousand dollars tucked away in various IRAs. Most people aren't as fortunate. When they buy a lottery ticket or pump a quarter into a slot, they're buying something that their lives don't already give them: hope. Hope that lightning will strike, and they'll become independently wealthy and won't have to work that demeaning job anymore or put up with that terrible boss or go another year without a decent home or car or whatever. They're buying a tiny chance on a kind of *Reader's Digest* sweepstakes dream that they'll gain complete control of their lives and live happily ever after. And who am I to ridicule their fantasy and the short-term pleasure that pursuing it brings them?

Certainly there was at least one believer on the casino floor. I heard her shriek, *"Five thousand dollars!"* while I was waiting for my meal. The words cut through the crowd like a gunshot. Several hundred people became suddenly quiet; then a ripple of applause brought the volume back up as the woman danced around a dollar slot machine, hugging complete strangers who had encircled her to share her good fortune.

"Double or nothing! Double or nothing!" a woman in the restaurant shouted. I turned to look at her. She was seated six tables away, and I could see her profile.

"Hundred bucks says she blows it before the night is out," she bet her companion and laughed again. It was a joyless laugh, high-pitched and forced. I think the laugh was more recognizable to me than the face. Both belonged to Eleanor Koehn, King's wife, the "slush" Gretchen Rovick had pointed out during my first visit to Deer Lake.

Her companion scanned the eyes of the restaurant patrons as they turned toward Eleanor, and he pulled in his head like a turtle.

"What are you afraid of?" Eleanor demanded scornfully.

Her date didn't reply, and Eleanor slapped him hard. I could feel it even where I was sitting. He stared glassy-eyed at her for a moment, then swiveled his head around fearfully, looking for something, seeing nothing. She spoke softly to him, and he replied with a wide grin. She laughed again, took his face in her hands, and kissed him. While she was kissing him, she straddled his lap, her skirt hiked up to there. When she was finished, she laughed some more and called him, "My little doughboy."

"Enjoying the floor show?" the waitress asked, placing a platter in front of me.

"Better than the afternoon soaps," I told her, and she grunted. She must have alerted the management because a moment later a tall Native-American gentleman meticulously dressed in matching jacket and tie approached the table. He said something quietly, and Eleanor removed herself from her date's lap. She smiled seductively and brushed the manager's cheek with her fingertips as she returned to her chair.

"Champagne!" she called, slapping the table, rattling the remains of their dinner. "A big bottle."

Her date bowed his head and said nothing.

A bottle was brought to the table in a bucket of ice and opened expertly by the waitress, much to Eleanor's obvious disappointment. She no doubt had wanted to try shooting out one of the overhead lights with the cork. Still, whatever the manager had said must have registered because although Eleanor poured liberally from the bottle, she remained comparatively quiet.

I grew bored with the show by the time I had finished the prime rib and signaled for the tab, paying by credit card. That's when a man entered the restaurant and approached Eleanor and her date like he had been expected all along. He was a big, soft-bellied man with gray hair that may or may not have been his own. It was King Koehn. I knew it without knowing him.

After taking my receipt, I ordered another beer, deciding to wait for the second act. The waitress sniffed at me and turned away. Near as I could tell, she had no sense of humor. Perhaps she had never been unhappy enough to develop one. Either that or she simply didn't appreciate the entertainment value of a good public brawl between husband and wife.

King Koehn spoke with the clear, booming voice of a practiced politician. I could understand every word he said from fifty feet.

"There you are," he told Eleanor and slapped her date on his back. From the look on the date's mug, it might as well have been the kiss of death.

But whatever hope of maintaining his dignity that King might have entertained was dashed when Eleanor asked loudly, "What are you doing here? What do you want? Did Michael throw you out? No, no, wait. She's sleeping with the sheriff these days. No, no, I forgot. Somebody shot her. An outraged housewife, you think?"

Say what? Another suspect? I removed my notebook from my pocket and wrote Eleanor's name under Gretchen's. Then I crossed out Gretchen's name. After a moment's thought, I crossed out Bobby Orman's, too.

"Eleanor, please," Koehn said. It wasn't a plea. It was a warning. And it went right over Eleanor's head.

"'Eleanor, please,'" the woman spit back at him.

Bad move. I knew it and so did the other diners. Suddenly it felt like we were watching a tightrope walker who abruptly stops and begins to teeter back and forth, fighting to regain his balance. Suddenly it was no longer amusing. And while no one departed, you could see from the expressions that none of us were sure we wanted to see what would happen next.

"It's getting late," the date said and attempted to rise.

"Sit down, fat boy!" Eleanor screeched at him. The date sat. It was clearly a tossup as to who he was more afraid of, husband or wife.

"Slut," Koehn called his wife.

"Prick," she countered.

"Whore!"

"Queer!"

"Bitch!" Koehn screamed and pulled the near-empty champagne bottle from the bucket by the neck.

"No!" Eleanor screamed in reply and hid her head behind her arms.

I anticipated the violence. With the first volley of insults I was on the move, and by the time Koehn raised the bottle above his head to crush his wife's skull, I was in position to pull his arm back. I held it there for a moment as the champagne cascaded over

the two of us then yanked hard, wrenching his shoulder and forcing the bottle from his grip. He grunted and tried to hit me with
a backhand. I used the bottle to block him, and he hurt his knuckles
against the unyielding glass.

"You look ridiculous, Mr. Koehn," I told him softly.

"Huh?"

"All these people watching, you don't need this."

Koehn didn't move his eyes so much as an eighth of an inch,
yet he was suddenly aware of everyone around him.

"He was going to kill me! He tried to kill me, you saw it!"
Eleanor shouted to whoever might be listening.

"You're an important man in Kreel County," I reminded Koehn.
"You can't act like this."

His nod was imperceptible to anyone not looking for it.

"Call the police! We need the police!" Eleanor added.

"Now's a good time to take a walk," I said. "Clear your head."

"Call the police!" Eleanor repeated.

"She's a whore," Koehn told me. "She's ruining my life."

I didn't know if she was ruining his life or he was ruining hers,
and I didn't care, but I said, "Screw her. Life's too short."

"Who are you?" Koehn asked.

"Let's just say I've had woman troubles myself and let it go at
that."

Koehn nodded his thanks, stepped away from me, and
announced, "Ladies and gentlemen, I apologize for disturbing
your evening. I hope you will forgive me. Good night."

"Where are you going?!" Eleanor shouted at his back as Koehn
moved away. He didn't reply, didn't turn his head. "Where are you
going?!" she shouted again, louder. She was interrupted by the
manager, who informed her that her patronage was no longer
welcomed.

"I'll leave when I'm good and ready," she told him.

The bouncers on either side of the manager quickly convinced her otherwise. One gripped her elbow and escorted her to the door. The second grabbed her date by his collar, yanked him up out of his chair, and pushed-pulled him in the same direction. In sixty seconds flat their table was cleared and prepared for more genial customers.

I returned to my own table, brushing at the champagne that soaked my new sports coat, wondering what the hell I was doing helping King Koehn. The waitress was standing there. Next to her was the tall Native-American manager in the tailored suit and tie. His eyes were quiet and sure, a take-your-time kind of guy. He said, "Follow me." I followed.

He led me down a flight of steps to the casino floor and then to the door of a closed office tucked beneath the restaurant. We passed a man and woman loitering at a blackjack table as we went.

"Give me ten dollars," the man demanded.

"I just gave you ten dollars," the woman replied.

"So? Give me some more."

"No."

"Bitch."

The manager opened the door and held it for me to enter. I did. The office inside was large and neat to the point where I was uncomfortable to be in it. Even the personal items were arranged with meticulous care and consideration. On the wall behind the desk was an ancient photograph of a naval destroyer mounted in a wood frame. A small gold plate attached to the bottom of the frame identified it as the USS *Johnston*. I was familiar with the name but couldn't place it. Sitting beneath the photograph was an elderly Native-American with the sun-drenched face of an out-doorsman. He looked as though he had been through a scrape or two in his time. He nodded at my companion, who nodded back and left the office, shutting the door behind him.

"My name is Carroll Stonetree," the man behind the desk said without offering his hand. "I sorta run things around here."

"Carroll?" I asked. The name seemed as inappropriate as his voice. He looked like the warrior who had lifted Custer's baby finger for a souvenir following the Little Big Horn massacre, but he spoke with a high-pitched reedy voice that made you think he was putting you on.

"Call me Chief," he said. "That's a naval title, not tribal. I served some years in the USN."

"She seems familiar to me," I said, pointing at the photograph.

"The *Johnston*? She was lost October 25, 1944."

"Now I remember. The Battle of Leyte Gulf . . ."

"Halsey was suckered out into the North Pacific by the Japs," Stonetree added quickly, as if he was anxious to recite the tale. "He thought he was chasing the entire Imperial Fleet. As it turned out, the entire Imperial Fleet was sneaking through the San Bernardino Strait on its way to launch a surprise attack against MacArthur's forces on Leyte in the Philippines. Five battleships including the *Yamato*, ten heavy cruisers, two light cruisers, twelve destroyers.

"The *Johnston* was part of a small task force that was supporting the landings, three destroyers and four escorts. It was ordered to intercept the Japanese. We engaged three heavy cruisers in succession: the *Kumano*, *Chikuma*, and *Yahagi*. We hurt them. Hurt them bad enough to scatter their ships and buy time for Halsey to regroup. Except they killed us. Fourteen-inch shells, six inchers— they fell on us like heavy rain. One officer said, 'It was like a puppy being smacked by a truck.' We fought until every gun was silenced. We lasted two hours. Of a compliment of three hundred twenty-seven, only one hundred and forty-one crewmen survived. But we did the job, we saved MacArthur's ass; his and Halsey's. I was seventeen at the time."

"Lied about your age?"

"I had to get into the war."

"For three generations the men in my family have been either too young or too old to fight in our nation's wars," I told him.

"How lucky for you."

"I've always thought so," I admitted. "The *Johnston*, she lost her skipper."

"Commander Ernest E. Evans. He was a Cherokee. Finest man I ever knew. He shook my hand the day I came aboard the *Johnston*. He told me, us Indians—we were Indians back then, not Native-Americans—us Indians he said, we had to be twice as good as everyone else. He was ten times as good. History doesn't even remember him."

I nodded.

"Do you ever worry about your place in history, Mr. Taylor?"

"How do you know my name?" I asked, trying hard not to sound surprised.

"Must have been from your credit card," he teased. "Why else?"

"Do you take a personal interest in everyone who orders the prime rib?"

"How was it?"

"Average," I told him.

He sniffed like he didn't believe me.

"I figured I owe you for defusing what could have been an ugly situation upstairs," he informed me and held up my credit card slip. He crumpled it into a ball with one hand and tossed it into the wastebasket ten feet away. "Dinner's on us."

"Thanks," I said, waiting.

"Have a drink with me," Stonetree said. He pulled open a desk drawer and removed a bottle of Jack Daniel's.

"I've always heard Indians can't hold their firewater," I told Stonetree as he filled two double-shot glasses.

"You believe all those movie myths?"

"No more than I believe Indians are afraid to fight at night."

"Actually, that one is true."

"Really?"

"I know I never liked it," he said and raised his glass. *"L'chayim."*

"H'gun," I answered, reciting what I thought was the Dakota courage word.

"Excuse me?"

"Never mind," I said. I took a sip of the liquid; it burned all the way down. I hadn't used the hard stuff in quite awhile. "So, tell me, sir. What do you want of me?"

The chief smiled.

"You like to get right to it, don't you?" he asked.

"Not necessarily," I told him. "I'd be happy to just sit here and drink your booze and listen to a few more war stories if it'll make you comfortable. We can pretend this isn't a business meeting for quite a while, yet."

The chief grimaced at the phrase *business meeting.* "I'm that obvious, huh?"

"You don't strike me as a guy who spends a lot of time hob-nobbing with the customers."

"You got me there," the chief said, sighing. "All right. I know who you are, and I know why you're in Kreel County. I also know that Bobby Orman has given you a free hand in investigating the shooting of Michael Bettich—a development I find utterly amazing by the way."

"His deputies agree with you," I said.

"I know all these things because we operate a fairly elaborate security system here," the chief added. "We run checks on everyone who touches our business. It's a necessary precaution, I'm afraid. A lot of vultures would love to get their talons into the reservation casinos, rip us off, launder their money—you'd be amazed. . . ."

"I doubt it," I told him.

Chief Stonetree used my interruption to drain the liquid in his glass and to pour himself a second healthy drink.

"If we don't protect ourselves, the Bureau of Indian Affairs will do it for us," he continued. "We'd be back to bad meat and trinkets within six months."

He took another pull of his whiskey.

"Michael Bettich touched our business, so I had her checked out. But my security people came back with a most amazing discovery."

"Oh?" I said.

"According to them, Michael Bettich didn't even exist nine months ago. How is that possible, do you think?"

I shrugged.

"Please, Mr. Taylor," Stonetree said. "Don't obfuscate with me."

Wow, there's a word you don't often hear in conversation. I took a long pull of the Jack to give me time to think about it. As the dark liquid warmed my stomach I decided obfuscation wasn't a bad way to go.

"Perhaps Michael is not who she claims to be," I told the chief.

Stonetree laughed at my answer. "No kidding." He shook his head and added, all serious now, "Look, I don't really care who Michael Bettich is or isn't. That doesn't bother me nearly as much as something else I don't know. I don't know where her money came from. My sources tell me she only had a few hundred bucks when she arrived in Deer Lake. But a few months later she suddenly has enough to buy The Harbor for one hundred and seventy thousand dollars and give it an eighty-grand renovation. Where did it come from?"

"I don't know," I answered quickly, cursing my own incompetence. Alison had left the Twin Cities with nothing, yet six months later she has enough money for a major investment and I hadn't even asked where she got it. Dammit! The answer could help determine who'd shot her. . . .

Chief Stonetree must have seen the frustration on my face because he said, "You don't know, do you?"

I shook my head. "Do you have any theories?" I asked.

"King Koehn," Stonetree answered as if saying the name caused him pain.

"You think King and Michael are partners?"

Stonetree nodded.

"Could be," I agreed. "But if they are, they're doing a helluva job hiding it. Why does it matter?"

Stonetree sipped his drink.

"You don't want them profiting off your casino," I ventured.

"It's not that," he told me. "Obviously the more local residents that profit off our business, the better; the more tightly we are tied financially to the community, the stronger our situation becomes."

"So what's the problem?" I asked.

The chief studied me over the rim of his glass. I had nothing else to look at, so I watched him. After we got tired of each other's faces, Stonetree said, "We don't believe the tribe can afford to gamble its future on gaming, if you'll excuse the pun. The competition from the larger casinos—Hinckley, Mille Lacs, Turtle Lake—will cut deeper and deeper into our market share and our profits. So instead of expanding our gaming operation, we've been investing our proceeds in other businesses, diversifying our interests.

"We have a salmon farm now," the chief continued. "We raise

them, can them, the whole show. We recently purchased a con-
struction-equipment manufacturing plant in North Dakota. Just
the other day we initiated exploratory talks with a company that
builds snowmobiles. And we're also pursuing several other oppor-
tunities."

I asked, "What has this to do with King and Michael?"

Stonetree smiled cryptically. "I just told you."

I frowned at his answer. It seemed Chief Stonetree didn't mind
obfuscating, either.

"In five years time, we hope gaming will represent less than
forty percent of our income," the chief finally added, his voice
growing in volume as if I had just challenged his logic. Perhaps
others had.

"The tribe must be prepared for the day the gaming boom goes
bust. My God, man, we have enrolled members; every month they
cash their checks at the bank and walk out with the money in their
pockets. They don't even have checking accounts! They're not saving, they're not investing. Instead, they're spending. They're buying new homes and expensive furniture and stereo equipment and
cars and Gold Wing Honda motorcycles. I can't really blame them.
After generations of poverty, it's hard to get used to possessing
large sums of money. Only what's going to happen to them when
the bubble bursts? Who says all this is going to last?"

"No one," I answered just to be polite.

"Some tribal members don't agree. They want what they want
when they want it—like children." Stonetree shook his head violently. "They're wrong. That's why we're taking twenty percent
out of each member's check and putting it in retirement accounts
for them. That's why we're investing in infrastructure—building
a school, a water and sewer system, roads, a day-care center, a recre-
ation center, new houses. We have chemical dependency programs

and an alcohol treatment center. We're encouraging the kids to go to college or at least a trade school, paying them to attend—"

Stonetree stopped abruptly.

"But I digress," he said, embarrassed at his own oratory.

I don't know why. It all sounded quite sensible to me, and I told him so.

"Sensible," Stonetree repeated with disdain. "For a hundred years we've been a defeated people living off what the white government deigned to give us. Congress passes the 1988 Indian Gaming Act, and overnight we've become wealthy and arrogant. What's sensible about that?"

I shrugged. "It's like the saying goes: I've been rich and I've been poor, and rich is better."

Stonetree smiled. "It *is* preferable to a poke in the eye from a sharp stick, I must agree."

"Which brings us back to King and Michael," I said.

"I will pay you quite well if you can determine for me with all accuracy that King Koehn is a silent partner in The Harbor," Stonetree said.

"I already have a client," I reminded him.

"I am not asking you to compromise your client," he assured me. "I just want to acquire that one little piece of information. *Before* next Thursday."

"What happens Thursday?" I asked.

"On Thursday we go before the Kreel County Board of Commissioners and make a formal offer to purchase the civic center."

"I understand," I told him.

"No, Mr. Taylor, you don't."

And by the way he rose to his feet and lifted his glass, it was obvious he wasn't about to enlighten me. "Thank you for your time," Stonetree said. "Please keep in touch."

"Thank you for the drink and the interesting conversation," I told him.

"I hope your woman recovers soon," he said.

My woman? He thought Michael—I mean Alison—was my woman?

"Thank you," I said again. I mimed a toast to the photograph of the USS *Johnston*.

Stonetree raised his glass to me. *"H'gun."*

twenty-three

The wind-up alarm clock that The Wheel Inn provided read 5:45. I didn't like the clock. I didn't like the way it rang until I lurched out of bed and beat it into submission. I didn't like the sun, either. It was shining. And the birds were singing. Didn't they know it was 5:45 in the fucking morning?!

The lights in the bathroom were too bright, the towels were too rough, the soap bar was too small, the floor was too cold, and so was the water that flowed from the faucet labeled H. I forgot about my bruises and stretched, then remembered every one. They were now turning an ugly yellow-rust color. I looked diseased.

I cut myself shaving three times. After years of using an electric razor I had lost the knack—at least that's my story, and I'm sticking with it. My new sports coat and shirt were stained from the champagne, so I wore my other jacket and dirty shirt, instead. I packed the rest of my belongings in a paper bag with King's One-Stop printed on both sides and escaped to my car.

There was a lot of traffic on the county roads, and it infuriated me. Where were all these people going so early in the morning? Turned out many of them were going to the same place I was: Annie's Parlor, the café in Saginau where I had promised to meet Deputy Gary Loushine. The café was located on the town's main drag between two bars. Across the street was an everything-for-everyone hardware store flanked by a bank and a gift shop. I parked farther down the street in the parking lot of the Kreel County Court Building, where the sheriff's department was located, and walked back.

Annie's Parlor was doing good business. A small crowd had gathered at the PLEASE WAIT TO BE SEATED sign, including two older women who smiled benignly at me and said in unison, "Beautiful morning, isn't it?" The women were actually wearing skirts. Everyone else was dressed like they were going to cut the lawn right after breakfast—the dressing-down of America. When was the last time you were confronted with a dress code that exceeded "No shoes, no shirt, no service"?

At 7:05 Annie—who also wore a skirt—welcomed me to her parlor and led me to a window booth with a good view of the hardware store. She offered coffee while I waited for my companion, and I accepted. It was good coffee. I sipped it and wondered vaguely if Deputy Loushine had as much trouble with early mornings as I did. I passed the time by watching the traffic move up and down Saginau's main drag and listed all the reasons why I could never reside in such a small town. The list was short and featured mostly social items: no jazz clubs, no movie theaters, no professional baseball.

Deputy Loushine abruptly slid into the booth across from me; somehow he had entered the café without my seeing him. Before I could even say "Good morning," Annie was by his side.

"Coffee, Gary?"

"Thanks, Annie," Loushine said. Apparently he and the woman were old friends.

But as Annie was pouring a steaming mug, the radio Loushine wore on his belt suddenly crackled and squawked. He responded with his personal code, and a woman's voice told him to proceed to an old logging road off County Road T, three-quarters of a mile south of Road 34.

"What do we have?" Loushine asked the voice.

"It's Chip Thilgen. We found him."

Sheriff Bobby Orman was not happy. Not one damn bit. His face was bloodless, his mouth stretched downward into a long, hard frown, and his eyes fairly glistened with fury as he carefully picked his way along the logging trail toward the white Buick. Orman arrived a full forty minutes after Loushine and I did, although he had been summoned at the same time. What took him so long I couldn't say—he certainly hadn't stopped to shave. On the other hand, he had returned from Duluth at three that morning, which meant that he was operating on less than four hours' sleep.

Orman joined the knot of deputies waiting for him at the open driver's door. The deputies muttered an unenthusiastic "Good morning" but didn't look at him—or at each other, for that matter. Instead they gazed at the thick growth that surrounded them, their boots, the sky—anywhere but inside the car, where the body of Chip Thilgen was folded neatly across the steering wheel. Orman probably didn't want to look either, but he did as the deputies drifted away from the Buick and down the logging trail to their own vehicles to silently await orders.

In contrast, Loushine was excited and spoke rapidly. Only TV cops get a steady dose of dead bodies and high-speed heroics, and he was not a TV cop. How many shootings, how many murders, will a cop in a rural community like Kreel County catch in a career? Counting Alison's shooting, this was Loushine's fourth. I figured he had already exceeded his quota, and the stress was telling.

Still, he was well trained; someone had beaten discipline into him early on. Disregard the speed in which he gave it, and Loushine's report was concise and thorough. He faltered only once. That was while informing the sheriff that Thilgen had been shot in the head at close range, as was evident by the contact burns on his temple. I was relieved when I'd noted the burned flesh earlier. It meant I hadn't killed him when I shot out the back window of the car. It meant I didn't have to burden my conscience with still another dead man.

"Suicide?" Orman asked hopefully. If this was Loushine's fourth homicide, it was Orman's first.

"We found a .38 on the seat next to him," Loushine answered.

"Then it could have been."

Loushine clearly didn't think so, only he didn't say it. Instead he told the sheriff, "The .38 still had a full load; it hadn't been fired. But we have a bunch of these." He held up a plastic bag filled with copper shells. ".41 AEs."

The sheriff took the bag of shell casings and stepped away to collect himself. Loushine watched him intently. After a moment the sheriff said in a quiet voice, "He looks like he's been dead for a long time."

"Three days," I told him. "I'm betting he was popped right after the shooting."

Orman didn't respond to me. Instead he told Loushine, "Dust the car inside and out; process the latents fast. Send copies to the Wisconsin Department of Criminal Investigation. Also, see if you can get a quick grouping on the blood. . . ." We all glanced impulsively at the dark stains on the seat and floor around Thilgen's body. "Some of it might not be his. And I want casts made of the three boot impressions outside the passenger door."

Good eye, I thought.

"Of course," Loushine replied, obviously miffed. I guess he didn't like Orman telling him how to do his job.

"Something else, if I may," I said.

Orman nodded at me.

Looking directly at Loushine, I told him, "A murder victim has no assumption of privacy; you don't need a warrant to search his house." Loushine's eyes grew brighter at my words, and a smile of unexpected happiness crept over his face. You'd have thought I was sending him on a blind date with Cindy Crawford.

"I recommend that you conduct a search immediately," I added with a wink. "Pay particular attention to Thilgen's financial records."

"Good idea," Orman said. "I want to know the name of everybody associated with Thilgen—his friends, his environmentalist buddies, whoever. I want a list of everyone he spoke to in the forty-eight hours preceding his death. I want his phone records. I want a time-coded list of associate events. . . ." He spoke like he was reading from a manual.

"I'm on it," Loushine told him.

"Where the hell's the medical examiner?" the sheriff asked impatiently.

"He's coming," Loushine assured him and then turned back to Thilgen. "It would be convenient, wouldn't it?" he asked no one in particular.

"What would?" I replied.

"If Bettich was shot by Thilgen because he didn't want her spoiling the environment, harming the animals. It would make everything so . . . tidy."

Ⅲith Deputy Loushine occupied, I was stuck in the Wisconsin wilderness without a ride. Orman offered me one. We drove a long time toward Saginau. Not a word passed between us. The sheriff was whistling soft and low a tune that started out sounding like something from *Fiddler on the Roof* but ended up a meandering patchwork of disjointed notes.

I turned my attention to the trees that blurred past the window. I was not having a good time. I needed to hear a joke. I needed a stand-up comic to make me laugh at myself, take my mind off my troubles. I thought of Officer George Meade of the St. Paul Police Department, the man who had broken me in. Now, there was an entertaining guy. How long was it since we'd last worked together? Twelve years? Thirteen?

This one time we responded to a domestic, standing outside the door of a third-floor apartment listening to a husband and wife go at it over money. "You spend too much!" he's saying. "You're cheap!" she's saying. Meade knocked on the door, announced that the police had arrived, and then opened the door. The man and woman were standing in the middle of the room, a kitchen table between them. In the center of the table was a kilo of cocaine and several automatic weapons. The four of us looked at the cocaine and guns. The four of us looked at each other. Then we all looked at the cocaine, again. Suddenly, we all reached for our guns and dove for cover. It was like an umpire had yelled, "Play ball!"

They started shooting first—I remember that distinctly. We returned fire. Over one hundred rounds were exchanged. The sulfur became so thick that my eyes teared up, yet miraculously no one was hit. Not by them, not by us, not by the SWAT team on the roof or the chopper in the air—we had so much backup, you'd think it was the annual meeting of the Minnesota Police Federation.

Finally Meade yelled, "Hey, buddy, nobody's hurt yet! We can still make most of this go away!" And the husband yelled back that he doesn't want to go to jail, but Meade told him he didn't see how it could possibly be avoided. The husband thought about it for a few minutes and then said, okay, jail's fine, just as long as he's not in the same prison with his wife.

The wife heard that and started ragging the husband something fierce about being such a poor provider and how her mother had been right about him all along, and prison be damned, she didn't even want to be in the same fucking *state* with him.

He told her that that suited him down to his toes, and it was just lucky they didn't have any children that would grow up to look like her.

Eventually they tossed out their guns, and we cuffed 'em, Mirandized 'em, and moved them out to the street. Along the way the wife turned to the husband and whined, "You never loved me."

And Meade started making like a marriage counselor.

"Now, now, you kids, let's hear no more of that kind of talk," he said. "Sure you have your problems. What married couple doesn't? But you can work them out; you can make this marriage work. It just takes time and a little effort. Hey," he said, nudging the husband, "when was the last time you told your wife you loved her?"

The way the husband looked at him, you just knew he wished he'd shot it out after all.

"Ahh, the good ol' days," I mused.

"Hmm?" the sheriff grunted.

"Just thinking out loud," I said.

Orman grunted again.

After a few more minutes of silence I said, "I have a few hard questions to ask you."

"I figured you might," Orman replied.

"You know who Michael is," I told him.

"We don't have secrets between us."

"Where did she get the quarter million dollars to buy and remodel The Harbor?" I asked.

"I don't know."

"Who told her about the Ojibwa's plan to turn the civic center into a casino?"

"I don't know."

"I heard it was Charlie Otterness."

"I don't know," the sheriff repeated yet again.

"I guess you do have secrets."

The sheriff remained silent.

"Jesus Christ, how can you not know these things?"

"It never occurred to me to ask."

Either that or he didn't want to learn the answers.

I turned and stared at him. "Well, don't you think it's time we found out?"

twenty-four

I was astonished by the sheer size of the Otterness Bait and Tackle shop. A good six thousand square feet and well lit, it had thousands of old-time lures decorating the walls and rafters. And to enter, you had to walk through a small foyer embellished with autographed photos of fishing heavyweights: Bill Dance, Jimmy Houston, Roland Martin, Orlando Wilson, Al and Ron Lindner. I guess I was expecting something like the mom-and-pop bait store near my parents' place in northern Minnesota.

Just inside the shop was a huge floor-to-ceiling mural of a typical northern lake painted with a breathtaking devotion to detail—I was afraid to brush against it for fear of getting my clothes wet. An angler, proudly flaunting a brute of a walleye, stood before the mural. He was having a Polaroid taken of himself by a young photographer with the name Otterness stitched to his knit shirt. While the angler and the photographer were waiting for the Polaroid to develop, Sheriff Orman asked if Charlie Otterness was available. The photographer gestured with his head and said, "In the back." I appraised the mural one last time before heading in the direction he pointed. That's when I noticed the name R. Orman painted way down in the corner.

Sheriff Orman and I found a door next to a plastic tank swimming with shiners and stepped through it into a large storage room filled with boxes of tackle, rods and reels, electronic fish detectors, and sundry other gear stacked on rows of metal shelves.

"Don't do it!" a voice cried with some urgency from several rows over.

A second voice replied, but I couldn't make out the words.

"Charlie, get used to the idea," said the first voice. "You're dead politically."

Again came a muffled reply.

The first voice insisted, "If you try to run . . . embarrassed . . . to be humiliated?"

The volume of the second voice increased. "What do you think . . . now? That woman . . . power screwdriver."

". . . sixteen years. Let it go at that."

The voices came from an office at the far end of the room. Orman was all set to break in on the conversation, but I nudged him behind the last row of metal shelves and touched my index finger to my lips.

". . . proud man, Charlie. . . . Don't . . . this way. I appreciate . . . Nothing you can do. . . . The bitch killed you. . . . People around here . . . Selling the civic center to the Ojibwa, you sold your office."

"But I didn't tell her."

A muffled reply.

"Goddammit, Harry, you're not listening. I . . . didn't . . . do . . . it."

Harry's answer was too soft and low, and the sheriff and I began edging closer. I caught part of a sentence: ". . . people figure you let them down."

The voice that I assumed belonged to Charlie Otterness exploded. "How many times do I have to say it? I didn't tell her anything!"

We moved closer.

"Goddammit, Harry!" Otterness shouted. "You're like all the rest. You don't listen. Lookit! If I had told Michael about the Ojibwa, she wouldn't have bought the fucking resort. On Thursday you'll understand."

"What does that mean?"

The question came from Sheriff Orman. He had circled past me and was now blocking the office doorway with his frame. I came up behind him.

Charlie Otterness was taller than I was, but, then, so was just about everyone else I've seen in Deer Lake, including the children. Something in the water, no doubt. His hair was gray and combed to cover a bald spot, his eyes were watery and pale, and the flesh of his face was pasty and hung in loose folds. He looked like a man accustomed to drinking alone in the dark. He was also at least thirty years my senior, which made him forty years older than Alison.

The other man in his office was just as old and half Charlie's size—but still taller than me.

When Otterness saw the sheriff, he froze like a small animal caught in the headlights of a speeding car.

"Sheriff," he said.

Charlie Otterness reluctantly rose from behind his gray metal desk, like he was giving up cover. I didn't blame him. The way the sheriff looked with bloodshot eyes and unshaven face, he scared me, too. Judging from Charlie's voice and body language, I figured Orman was the last person he wanted to see. But it wasn't out of fear; there was something else working.

"Sheriff," Harry echoed with deference.

Orman ignored him. He only had eyes for Charlie. "Answer the question," he insisted.

"How's Michael?" Charlie asked instead.

"She's in a coma," the sheriff answered.

"Coma," Charlie repeated as if it were a death sentence—and maybe it was.

"Talk to me, Charlie," the sheriff demanded. "What happens on Thursday?"

I've been told that some primitive tribes sniff out the guilty party among a group of suspects by smelling for body odor. Others demand that suspects chew and swallow a handful of rice; if their mouths are too dry to manage it, they're in trouble. As an investigator, I'm trained to look for several physiological symptoms of lying and guilt: sweaty palms, an unusual pallor, a dry mouth, a rapid pulse, erratic breathing. Charlie Otterness? He had them all. I didn't know if he was feeling guilty or going into cardiac arrest.

"Tell him, Charlie," Harry urged.

When Charlie refused to speak, I said, "On Thursday the Ojibwa tribe is going before the county commissioners to make a formal, public offer to buy the civic center."

Apparently it was a good guess. Charlie looked as though he had just caught me peeking through his windows. "Who are you?"

"Never mind him," said Orman. "Is what he said true?"

Charlie straightened his back. "I'm not at liberty to say. You'll need to come to the meeting and find out." He may have looked like a liar, but he didn't sound like one. Chalk it up to a lifetime in politics.

The sheriff studied Charlie for a moment; I stepped back. I didn't want to distract him. Finally, Orman asked, "How much money did you give Michael?"

Charlie's mouth unhinged and fell open, his bottom jaw just hanging there until he cradled it with his hand.

"Money?" he asked. "What in the hell are you talking about?"

"You know what money."

Charlie looked at Harry and then at me. Neither of us had an answer for him. "What's going on?" he asked.

"I want an exact amount," the sheriff insisted.

Charlie's mouth worked, but no words came out.

"*How much?*" the sheriff screamed.

I flinched. So did Harry. Charlie Otterness didn't. Instead his eyes grew wide and he stepped forward, prepared to meet any attack. I realized then that despite my earlier impression, there was nothing at all soft about Charlie. He was a scrapper just like Johnny Johannson.

"No one talks to me that way," Charlie hissed.

"I'm the sheriff," Orman reminded him.

"What the fuck do I care?" Charlie pointed a finger at him. "You ain't your father, Bobby. Don't pretend that you are."

Orman leaned forward, clenching and unclenching his fists, but somehow the older man's words had deflated him; he reminded me of a balloon with a slow leak. I decided it was time to step in.

"You have a nice place here," I told Charlie.

He turned his angry gaze on me, obviously still wondering who I was. "I like it," he said.

"Profitable?"

"I make a living," suspicious now.

"Enough to invest in The Harbor with Michael?"

Charlie laughed at the question. "I get it now." He laughed some more. "You're wrong." He sat back down behind his desk and put his feet up. "You are so wrong. You'll see." He continued to laugh.

Suddenly Orman laid his hands on a metal folding chair and flung it across the office, nearly hitting Harry where he stood in the corner. The sheriff's face was flushed with anger, his teeth were bared, his fists clenched. He had jumped to the final stage of aggression—*assault is imminent*—fuck the first stages. I have no doubt he would have attacked Otterness if I hadn't stepped in front of him.

"What?" I asked.

"You know Chip Thilgen," Orman accused Charlie, pointing at the older man over my shoulder.

"Where is all this coming from, Bobby?" Charlie wanted to know. "Why are you so pissed off?" Good question, I thought. But Orman refused to answer it.

"Hey?" I said.

Orman shook his head slightly, his lips a thin line, and took three steps backward. He nodded at Charlie like he wanted me to keep at him.

"Do you know Chip Thilgen?" I asked while still watching Orman.

"Of course."

"Friends?"

Harry snorted from the corner where he stood watching the goings-on as if he couldn't possibly imagine Thilgen having a friend.

"No, we weren't friends," Charlie said. "We were on the same side on some environmental issues; he actually had some good ideas if you could get past his bullshit. But that was it."

"Was the spoiling of Lake Peterson one of the issues you agreed on?"

"No," Charlie answered. "Lake Peterson can support a fishing resort now that it's been restocked."

"When was the last time you saw Thilgen?" I asked.

"I don't remember."

I turned to face the man, leaned on his desk. "Where were you when Michael was shot, Charlie?"

"I was fishing Storm Lake. Who are you, anyway?"

"Who were you fishing with?" I asked, ignoring his question.

"I fish alone. Everyone knows that."

"No witnesses, eh?" I said. "That's too bad."

"I've been keeping a low profile. Since—"

"Since you sold your office?" Orman again, his voice way too loud.

Charlie had nothing to say to that.

"When did you stop seeing Michael?" I asked.

Charlie gestured toward the sheriff with his chin. "When she started seeing him."

"Hmph," Orman grunted.

"Did you break up because of the sheriff?" I asked. "Or The Harbor?"

Otterness looked down at his fingers splayed over his desktop, counting each one carefully. "Buying The Harbor the way she did hurt me," Charlie admitted. "I told her people would get the wrong idea about it, but she said it was her shot, and she was taking it. But that didn't break us up, and neither did the sheriff."

Orman grunted again as I asked, "What then?"

"My age," Charlie confessed. "At first she said it didn't matter. She said all adults were pretty much the same age, and in the things that counted I was younger than most of the men she knew. But it did matter. I knew it mattered from the beginning."

"Then why did you get involved with her?" I asked.

He grinned like it was the dumbest question he had ever heard. "Have you seen her?"

"She's a looker," Harry confirmed from the corner.

"I guess they're right when they say there's no fool like an old fool," Charlie continued. "I should have known she was only using me. . . ."

Like Raymond Fleck and Hunter Truman, I thought.

"But, hey, I couldn't resist. So sue me." Charlie smiled again. "I have to admit, it was fun while it lasted."

"You sonuvabitch!" Orman snarled behind me and again made a violent move toward Charlie, who sprang to his feet, ready to take him on. I made sure I was between them, my arms outstretched like I was parting the Red Sea.

Harry in the corner shook his head sadly. "Women," he muttered. "No matter how old we get, they can still make us act like idiots."

Charlie didn't hear him, but the sheriff did. He moved his shoulders like he was shaking off a heavy cloak, then pointed at Charlie.

"Don't go anywhere I can't find you," he warned.

"You won't have to look for me," Charlie replied defiantly. "I'll be here."

———

"Nicely done, Sheriff," I told him when we were outside again. "Ever think of a career in law enforcement?"

"Fuck you!"

"Yeah, right."

"Otterness is a piece of shit, and he's finished in this county," Orman told me.

"Why's that? Because he slept with your girl?"

"Get in the fucking car."

The sheriff was out of control, and I wasn't sure what to do about it. If he had been working for me, I would've had him relieved from duty. Only he wasn't working for me; we were in Kreel County, and he was the law here. I was just along for the ride.

"The mural on Charlie's wall," I said—maybe if I could remind him who he was—"did you do that?"

"Yeah."

We were on the county road now, driving well above the speed limit. Orman gripped the steering wheel too tightly for safe driving and nodded.

"So you and Charlie must have been friends at one time."

Orman didn't say.

"Behind your desk," I added. "The whitetailed buck. That's yours, too."

The sheriff's glance shifted to me and then back to the blacktop.

"It should be in a gallery somewhere," I said.

"I know," he said matter-of-factly. Then he sighed audibly and loosened his grip on the steering wheel. The car slowed to the posted speed limit. "There's a gallery in Duluth that's been wanting it," Orman continued. "But it was my first truly good painting, and I'm having trouble parting with it. It won first prize in the

Minnesota Deer Hunters Association art contest three years ago."

"No kidding?" I asked excitedly, although I had never heard of the Minnesota Deer Hunter's Association or its art contest.

"When I wouldn't sell it, a couple of backers put out a limited-edition print that made some money," Orman added, warming to the subject. "Since then I've been selling paintings through the gallery in Duluth and another one in Minneapolis. I haven't done badly with it, either."

"Did you study art in school?"

"No, no nothing like that. It's just something I picked up when I was with the Wisconsin HP. The watch commander was into it, and he encouraged me to sketch with charcoals and then he critiqued my work. He said it showed promise. But I didn't get real serious about it until I moved back home."

"How many paintings have you sold?"

"Seventeen in the past two years."

"Is that good?" I asked stupidly.

"Yeah, it's good. Better than most."

"How long does it take to paint a canvas?"

"It usually takes me three, three and a half weeks to put something together. When I work, I work real fast and furious. I don't have the luxury to sit down like an artist who works full time. I can't paint every day. Sometimes I'll go weeks without touching a brush. It depends on business. When the county is quiet, I paint. When it isn't . . .

"You'd think painting would be a nice outlet, even therapy," he continued. "You'd think I'd be able to come home, take off the gun and badge, and forget about what happened that day. Only it doesn't work like that for me. I try to create these quiet worlds filled with loons swimming lazily under a full moon. But when the real world is noisy, it shows in my work; my paintings become loud, and the loons are frightened away. Lately it's been getting worse. The breakdown of families, drugs, alcohol abuse, growing poverty—Kreel County isn't Mayberry anymore. I haven't painted in two months."

"Ever think of doing it full time?"

"What's that supposed to mean?" he asked sharply, but the sheriff knew what I was saying.

Just to be sure, I added, "Any damn fool can wear a badge and carry a gun, but how many can do what you do?"

"You don't think I should be sheriff?"

"Do you?"

He didn't answer.

"Why did you become sheriff?"

"Sense of duty, I suppose. I figure I owed it to my father. And my grandfather. It's what they would have wanted."

"My father was a businessman before he retired," I told him. "One of the high muck-a-mucks. And I think he wanted me to follow in his footsteps. But he never said so. Instead, he encouraged me and my brother to do whatever we wanted. He only had two rules: Do the best that you can. And enjoy yourself."

I gave Orman a few moments to reply. When he didn't, I asked, "Are you enjoying yourself?"

"I acted like a fucking idiot back there, I know that. You don't have to rub it in. You don't need to give me speeches." After a few more moments of silence, he added, "I was jealous"—as if that excused everything.

"Well, I've heard artists are supposed to be emotional."

"Shut up, Taylor," he told me.

I didn't. "What's next?" I asked.

"I'm not quitting just because some city boy doesn't like how I run things."

"I meant what do we do next about Michael."

"Oh." Orman hesitated a moment, then announced, "King Koehn."

"Oh, goody. Are you going to throw his chairs around, too?"

"Shut up, Taylor."

This time I did.

twenty-five

Angel Johannson asked us to wait for a moment. "Fuck that," Orman said. He pushed past Angel's desk and strode purposefully to King's closed office door. He opened it hard; if it had been locked, I have no doubt he would have kicked it open. I was beginning to suspect that the sheriff was wound way too tight for this line of work.

"I've been expecting you," Koehn said evenly from behind his desk.

I was standing behind Orman. Angel was crowding in behind me. If her boss was calm, she decidedly was not.

"Should I call the police?" Angel asked. Orman looked at her and smiled, but there was no humor in his expression. Angel hesitated, then slowly went back to her desk.

With very little effort, the sheriff's smile became a sneer. He planted himself in a chair in front of Koehn's desk. "You were expecting me?" he asked, making the question sound like an accusation.

Koehn gestured with his thumb at the telephone. "Charlie

Otterness called to tell me you were running amok; he's probably calling everyone else in the county, too. I'm afraid you're skating on very thin ice, my friend."

"You're not my friend," Orman retorted.

"Yes, I am," Koehn insisted. "I'm the one who got you your job, remember?"

Orman pulled the badge off his uniform shirt and tossed it violently on Koehn's desk. "Fuck the job."

Koehn stared at the badge for a moment and then glanced up at me. I thought the sheriff's gesture was a little too theatrical, as well, but I remained silent.

"What is this shit?" King asked.

The sheriff flushed a deep crimson and sprang from his chair. He leaned on King's desk. King pushed backward; the wheels on his chair carried him out of Orman's reach.

"You're this close," Orman warned, holding his thumb and index finger a quarter inch apart.

I took a few cautious steps forward, wondering what was next, when Orman abruptly snapped upright. He turned his angry gaze on me, and for a moment I envisioned the picture of the white-tailed buck hanging in his office, scarcely believing this lunatic had painted it. Orman looked like he was working hard to rein in his anger. After a moment he barked at me, "I'd just as soon beat the shit outta him right now. But maybe you can talk to him. . . ." Orman glanced over his shoulder at King. "I'll be waiting outside." With that he stormed out of the office—but not before retrieving his badge and slipping it into his pocket.

"I think we might have made a mistake hiring Bobby," Koehn told me once the sheriff was gone. I didn't say if I agreed or not.

Koehn's office was paneled with redwood and featured dozens of photographs, most of them pictures of King shaking hands with people I've never seen before. The desk was larger than it needed to be, and the rest of the furniture seemed expensive, although I noticed a small sticker on the base of a crystal lamp: FABRIQUE A TAIWAN.

"I know you," he told me, recognizing me for the first time. "Last night at The Forks."

I nodded.

"You did me a good turn," King added. "I appreciate it."

I nodded again.

"Who are you, anyway?"

I told him my name. I told him why I was with Sheriff Orman.

"That's not right, is it?" he asked. "A PI working for the sheriff's department."

"It is a bit unconventional," I admitted.

Koehn grimaced as he rocked from side to side in his swivel chair. "Things have been turning to shit over there for a while now. People complaining about this or that . . . He's not his old man, not by a long shot. But Bobby's my problem. What can I do for you?"

"Tell me about last night."

"What's to tell? It wasn't the first public disturbance caused by my wife, that's for sure."

"She accused you of sleeping with Michael Bettich," I reminded him.

"She'd accuse me of having an affair with Hillary Clinton if she thought people would believe her."

"Is it true?"

"Sure, me and Hill are like that," he said, crossing his fingers.

"Sidesplitting," I told him.

Koehn frowned. "Everyone is so serious all of a sudden."

"Homicide just doesn't crack people up the way it used to."

Koehn's frown turned into a grin. At last, someone he could talk to.

"Did you sleep with Michael?" I asked.

"No. But it wasn't for lack of trying."

"She led you along, then blew you off—is that how it worked?"

"No." Koehn smiled. "Michael was up front about it from day one: No screwing around. She said she'd learned her lesson about sleeping with people she worked with."

"But you hit on her anyway," I suggested.

He held up his palms. "Nothing ventured, nothing gained."

I settled into the chair in front of King without asking permission. "The thing is, what you did or didn't do doesn't matter as much as what your wife thinks you did or didn't do," I told him.

King smiled like he'd had a lot of practice. "You think Eleanor did it?"

"What do you think?" I asked.

"I think Eleanor is delighted that Michael stole The Harbor from me; it gives her something to needle me with, and if Michael is killed, Eleanor'd lose her weapon."

"Interesting relationship you have."

"It has its ups and downs," King admitted.

"Why stay married?" I asked.

"We love each other."

For a moment I was convinced he was putting me on, but the smile on his face told me otherwise. The man was serious.

"Whatever works," I said and changed subjects. "You sold The Harbor to Michael."

"Common knowledge," King said.

"Then you got pissed off when news of the casino leaked out."

"I did."

"You claimed she ripped you off."

"Absolutely, she did."

"And that made you angry."

"Indeed."

"And you vowed revenge."

"Civilization is built on trust," King answered, continuing to smile even as he rubbed his face. "Trust of your neighbors and business associates, trust of your government, trust of your police. Trust. You need trust. Trust is everything. Trust is essential. Without trust, what do you have?"

"Mistrust?" I suggested.

"You have chaos," he told me.

"Ain't that the truth," I said.

"Mike betrayed my trust. I'm going to make her pay for it."

I noticed the future tense.

"How are you going to do that?" I asked.

"Hey, that's what lawyers are for."

I flashed on Hunter Truman. These guys were made for each other.

"It was suggested that you and Michael are actually partners in The Harbor deal. That you put up the money for her to buy it."

"Why would I do that?" King asked.

"So you can profit from the casino without alienating all the customers, employees, and business associates who are vehemently opposed to it—people who might boycott your other businesses."

"That's nonsense," Koehn insisted. "Course, now that you mention it, it's not a bad idea."

"How much did Michael pay for The Harbor?" I asked.

"One hundred seventy. She got it cheap."

"Who handled the loan?"

"No loan. She paid in cash."

"Cash?"

"Actually, a cashiers check."

"Where did she get the money?"

"It never occurred to me to ask."

"It didn't?"

"Hey, don't ask, don't tell. Besides, the check was good. What did I care where it came from? I was relieved to be unloading that white elephant." King sighed dramatically. "Little did I know . . ."

"I'd like to see your business records," I told him.

"Do you have a warrant?"

Of course I didn't, and I wasn't likely to get one.

"I don't mind chatting with you off the record like this," he added, still smiling. "But c'mon, Taylor. I'm not stupid."

"Refusing to cooperate might make the sheriff angry," I told him.

King thought that was pretty funny.

"I'm the guy who can have Bobby Orman fired with a phone call," he reminded me.

"Did it work?" the sheriff asked when I joined him outside. He was leaning against his cruiser.

"Did what work?" I asked.

"Did I frighten King enough to get him to talk?"

That brought me up short. "Good cop–bad cop? You were playing fucking good cop–bad cop?"

The sheriff smiled his answer.

"What? You see that on *NYPD Blue* or something?"

The smile disappeared.

"All you succeeded in doing was to piss the man off. He's probably on the phone getting you fired at this very minute."

The reproach made the sheriff angry. He yanked open his car door and said, "Get in." But I had seen enough. Way too much, in fact. I had only one more suspect on my list, and I didn't want the sheriff bungling the interview.

"I'm not going anywhere with you," I said more harshly than I should have. "I think you're way over your head, Bobby." I refused to call him Sheriff. "I think you should get the Wisconsin DCI up here right now, before you botch this investigation more than you already have."

The sheriff was inside the car, gripping the steering wheel now. "Are you finished?" he snapped.

"No, I'm not finished." I was on a roll. "You could be the best investigator in America. You could be Anne Scalasi. It doesn't matter. You should still hand off the case. You're too emotionally involved. You shouldn't be doing the things you're doing."

The sheriff was furious. I could actually hear his teeth grinding as I scolded him. And when I was finished, his mouth started moving like he had something to say. It took him a while to get it out.

"I love her," he told me.

"That's my whole point," I told him.

"You love her, too."

"I don't even know her," I admitted bluntly—probably for the first time.

But the sheriff hadn't heard me. He was too busy slamming his car door, gunning the engine, and peeling out of Koehn's parking lot, leaving a trail of exclamation points behind him.

twenty-six

"Hey, stranger." Ginger greeted me when I entered The Height. "What can I get you?"

"Nothing," I said.

"If you don't mind my saying so, Taylor, you look like you could use a drink."

"I'm too tired to argue with you," I sighed. "Okay, give me a scotch. A double. Neat. And I'll want to eat the glass, too."

"Coming up."

Ginger set the drink in front of me, and I started to sip it.

"So, have you figured out who shot Michael, yet?" she asked.

"We expect an arrest within twenty-four hours."

"Seriously?"

"No, that's just the stock reply to that question. Listen, is there a cab or a bus I can catch to Saginau? I need to get my car."

"We can give you a ride."

I turned to find Ingrid standing directly behind me, her lustrous blond hair spilling over the shoulders of a heather-gray twill wrap dress with a sweeping skirt and a neckline just deep enough to stimulate the imagination. Lonnie Cavander, the blues-singing Ojibwa, was standing next to her, but I'll be damned if I can remember what he was wearing.

"I don't want to be any trouble," I told her, desperate to keep my eyes above her chest.

"No trouble," she said. "I have to head in to see my accountant. Lonnie's coming to keep me company."

Lonnie smiled and gave Ingrid's shoulders a five-second massage.

My first thought was that two's company, three's a crowd. But I didn't give in to it.

"I'd appreciate it," I said.

"Thirty minutes?" Ingrid asked.

"I'm at your convenience."

Ingrid smiled her breathtaking smile and left through the EMPLOYEES ONLY door. Lonnie followed close behind.

———

A half hour later the three of us were riding in Ingrid's white 1997 Sebring convertible. She drove at only five miles per hour above the posted speed limit, but with the top down it seemed much faster. She wore black sunglasses, and to minimize the damage to her hair, she had wrapped a black scarf over her head, knotting it tightly beneath her chin. Lonnie Cavander sat next to her. I sat in back, leaning forward and turning my head to catch their conversation over the wind.

"Do you really expect an arrest within twenty-four hours?" Ingrid asked.

I flashed on Jimmy Johannson. "It's possible," I said.

"Who?" Lonnie asked.

"I really shouldn't say," I told him. "But I doubt anyone will be surprised."

"Not King?" Ingrid asked.

"No, not King."

We were halfway to Saginau. The county road dipped and turned and suddenly we were motoring past The Harbor.

"I still feel awfully guilty about all this," Ingrid said.

"Guilty about what?" I asked.

"The Harbor."

"What about it?"

Ingrid didn't answer. Instead, she turned her head and looked at Lonnie. Her eyes weren't visible behind the sunglasses. Lonnie shrugged.

"You think?" Ingrid asked.

Lonnie shrugged again.

"What?" I asked, intrigued by this silent passing of information.

Ingrid's chest rose and fell with a sigh that I couldn't hear over the wind.

"It's my fault," she said.

"What?" I leaned in close so I could hear better.

"I'm the one who told Michael about The Harbor," Ingrid confessed. "I'm the one who told her the Ojibwa were buying the civic center across the highway."

"You?"

Ingrid nodded.

"How did you find out?"

"I told her," Lonnie said.

"Are you privy to the tribe's business dealings?" I asked him.

"Carroll Stonetree is my uncle," he told me.

"You're kidding," I said.

"My mother's brother."

"He told you that the Ojibwa are building a new casino?"

"Not exactly," Lonnie answered.

"We kept that part from Michael," Ingrid added.

"What part?"

Ingrid's chest rose and fell again. "Michael was talking about how she wanted to become an *important* part of the community," Ingrid explained. "But the way she said it, it reminded me of King. She didn't want to become a part so much as she wanted to *own* a part, to run a part. And it annoyed me. I realize now that I was just being petty. I see myself as a big fish in a small pond, and I didn't want any other big fish coming around.

"So one night we were talking and I mentioned that The Harbor would make a good investment, the kind of community investment she was looking for. I told her the Ojibwa were negotiating in secret with the Board of County Commissioners to buy the civic center across the highway and turn it into a casino. I told her I would buy The Harbor in a heartbeat myself, only I didn't have the money. So she bought it."

"What's wrong with that?" I asked.

"The Ojibwa are not going to build a new casino," Lonnie told me. "The tribe has no intentions of expanding its gaming operations."

"Why then—"

"The tribe is starting a company to build recreational boats," Lonnie explained. "The civic center would make an ideal factory for it."

"And you knew that?" I asked Ingrid.

"Lonnie told me," she said.

"But why keep it a secret?" I wanted to know.

"Because the company will be in direct competition to King Boats, Koehn's bread-and-butter company," Lonnie said. "The tribe wanted to secure the civic center location before King had a chance to use his political ties to squash the deal. And the county commissioners wanted to keep it a secret because they knew if King did scuttle the deal, they'd be stuck with the civic center for all time."

In his own obfuscated way, Chief Stonetree had told me all this the night before—but I was being too obfuscated myself to see it.

"The entire county is up in arms thinking you're building a casino," I reminded Lonnie.

"Think how happy the people will be when they discover that we're not," he said, smiling. "When people discover that we're actually bringing honest manufacturing jobs to the region, I expect we'll become quite popular."

"With everyone except King Koehn," I suggested.

"I doubt he'll appreciate the competition," Lonnie agreed.

"That's why you've been content to allow all this casino nonsense to go on," I figured out loud. "To keep King in the dark as long as possible."

Lonnie nodded.

"Shrewd," I told him.

"That's what they'd call it if a white company made it happen. I'm real curious to hear what adjective they'll apply to us."

So was I.

"Then Charlie Otterness was telling the truth," I said. "He didn't pass insider information."

"No," Ingrid agreed. She added, "I feel really, really guilty about that. But everyone will know he told the truth when the Board of County Commissioners meets in formal session and the Ojibwa make their bid."

"And Michael?"

"If she works at it, I bet she could make The Harbor go," Ingrid predicted. "With a boat factory across the way, she'll have a good lunch crowd if nothing else. Probably a good happy hour, too."

"But she won't have the business a casino would bring in," I noted.

"I won't, either," Ingrid said in her defense.

I leaned back in my seat and watched the back of Ingrid's head as she guided the Sebring into Saginau. Suddenly I didn't like her as much as I had before. Or Lonnie. Or the chief. Suddenly I didn't like anybody because of what they had done to Alison.

They had stolen her dream.

At least that's how I saw it.

"Drop me at the county court building," I instructed Ingrid. And she did.

We were all surprised when we pulled into the parking lot. It was filled with deputies donning Kevlar vests and checking weapons.

Ingrid and Lonnie were curious but not enough to ask questions. They drove off, leaving me standing next to my car. I was curious and not shy about it.

"What's going on?" I asked no one in particular. Gary Loushine heard me and answered as Sheriff Bobby Orman stood behind him and listened to every word.

"We searched Chip Thilgen's house," the deputy told me. "We found financial records that indicate that Thilgen wrote five checks to James Johannson for five hundred dollars each and a sixth for twenty-five hundred. Each of the five-hundred-dollar checks were written the same day as a reported farm break-in or animal liberation that Thilgen had been accused of but not charged with. The sixth check—the twenty-five-hundred-dollar check—was written the day before Michael Bettich was shot."

I nodded, pretending I didn't already know this.

"Jimmy Johannson is well known to us," Loushine added. "He has a significant record. So we checked his fingerprints against a set of latents we lifted off the Buick, including an index finger we found on one of the shell casings. We examined them on the optical comparator. There's no mistake."

"The perpetrator is James Johannson," Sheriff Orman announced, reminding me of Jack Lord in *Hawaii Five-O*.

"James Johannson," Loushine agreed.

They were both smiling.

"So what do you expect from me?" I asked. "Applause?"

twenty-seven

Sheriff Orman was acting like Joe Professional now—perhaps he thought he had something to prove.

"We have an hour of daylight left," he estimated, glancing at his watch.

"Yes, sir," said Loushine.

"I want everybody here. Now."

"They're here," Loushine said.

Sheriff Orman nodded.

"This is going to get ugly," I muttered to myself.

I was impressed by how grim and unsure the deputies appeared as they awaited their instructions—so unlike my former colleagues in the St. Paul Homicide Unit. This was not something they wanted to do, and not wanting to do it put them at risk. Loushine moved among them, grinning, even cracking a joke or two. He managed to illicit a few chuckles, a few smiles that faded fast. But the overall mood didn't change, and I could see that he was as concerned as I was.

I didn't know any of these men, these strangers. I didn't know if they were properly trained for this kind of action. I didn't know how they would react. I knew only that they were scared. And that was reason enough for me to adjourn to the beer joint down the street. Besides, it wasn't my job. I was a civilian. I shouldn't have even been invited to the party. But then the sheriff asked, "You coming, Taylor?" in a voice loud enough to be heard by all of his deputies.

The men stopped checking their weapons, stopped donning their body armor, and waited for my reply. And suddenly I felt responsible for them, for all of them, as if my refusal to join the posse would make them more afraid than they were, and that extra load of fear would be too much for them to carry.

Loushine whispered something to the sheriff, and Orman replied, "No, it'll be all right."

"You're the boss," Loushine said and joined the others who waited for my answer.

"Wouldn't miss it," I said, smiling just as big and brightly as I could.

And we tell our children not to succumb to peer pressure.

Thirty minutes later I sat on the hood of the sheriff's cruiser about a mile from the Johannson homestead while he deployed his men. I could hear the low rumble of his voice but not what he was saying. By my estimate, we had thirty minutes of daylight left.

"I'll tell you what we used to do," I announced. "When we could, we would take our suspects at dawn. Hit 'em hard and fast when they were still too groggy from sleep to put up a fight. It was standard procedure."

No one was listening.

"I was out there yesterday," I recalled. "Johannson's father and his young nephew were in the house. Have you considered them?"

No one was listening.

"Hey, I know! We have the barn. We have the costumes. Let's put on a show."

"Quiet down, Taylor," Loushine warned.

"Deputy, this is small-town amateur night," I countered.

He looked at me like he knew I was right but said nothing. A moment later, the sheriff joined us. His deputies had scattered, some in cars, to encircle the house down the road. He looked at his watch. "The teams will be in position in ten minutes. Then we move."

"Move? What do you mean, move?" I knew what he meant, I just wanted to hear him say it.

"We're going to knock on the front door."

"Sheriff, the man has an UZI semiautomatic carbine. He can fire twenty-five rounds before you can say, 'Bless me father for I have sinned.'"

"You're not frightened, are you, Taylor?" Loushine interrupted.

I studied him for a moment. He was busy checking the load in his service revolver. It wasn't necessary. I had seen him check it twice before. But it gave his hands something to do, and it was an excuse not to look me in the eye.

"I'll be standing right behind you, Deputy," I told him.

Sheriff Orman slapped a gun into my hand. A Smith & Wesson .38 Police Special, Model No. 64: three-inch barrel, thirty and a half ounces fully loaded, serrated-ramp front sight, square-notch rear sight, square butt, satin finish, six shots—as efficient a close-encounter killing machine as you'll ever find and a stunning improvement over the Walther PPK in my pocket. Yet I looked at it like I had never seen one before in my life.

The minutes dragged on, giving me plenty of time to think, plenty of time to contemplate what I was expected to do with the .38. I was expected to point it at a man and squeeze the trigger. Simple, right? Yeah, sure. That's why I have nightmares, because it's so simple.

It is not as easy to kill a man as TV and the movies would suggest. Living with it later is even harder. You don't brush it off and go out for Chinese like the actors in the cop shows: "Hi, honey, I killed a couple of guys today; what's for supper?" I know. I've killed men. Four of them. I've replayed my encounters with them a hundred times in my head, carefully editing each tape until any alternative action was clearly impossible. I memorized their rap sheets until I convinced myself that their deaths were an almost preordained consequence of their lives and my involvement a kind of destiny. Yeah, I know it's self-deluding bullshit. But a man has to sleep.

Now I was being encouraged to kill again.

And I was willing.

I stuck the .38 in the waistband of my jeans and pretended it wasn't there, concentrating hard on the advice George Meade had given me my first day on the job: "Don't think too far ahead."

When his deputies were in position, Orman cautioned them over the radio to play it safe and ordered them not to shoot unless Jimmy Johannson tried to break through.

"If there's any shooting to do, I'll tell you," he said. "Remember, surprise is what we want. If we do this quick and clean, we won't have anything to regret tomorrow."

"Please, God," Loushine prayed.

I wished I had said that. I believe in God as much as anyone who doesn't make a living out of it, which is to say I believe in Him more at some times than others. It's true we haven't exactly been on speaking terms since my wife and daughter were killed. Still, one would hope He wouldn't hold that against a guy. I found myself searching the quickly darkening sky for a sign that He approved of tonight's activities. There was none. Just as well. A divine revelation right then would have been particularly disconcerting.

"Ready, Taylor?" the sheriff asked.

"Yeah," I answered and squeezed into the back seat of his cruiser with another deputy. Orman and Loushine sat in front.

Fear is the most transient of emotions. It cannot be sustained at a high pitch for more than a few minutes at a time. I was terrified as the sheriff pulled off the county blacktop onto the gravel road and drove the mile to Johannson's place. Yet I was calm by the time his wheels hit the dirt driveway. I took in everything, seeing much more in that first instant than I had in several hours the day before. There were actually six wrecks cluttering the yard, not five—four on the left of the driveway and two on the right. The wreck closest to the house on the right was a rusted out pickup, the hood open to heaven like all the others. About ten yards in front of Johannson's door was a shrine to the Virgin Mary. Her statue was perched on a large rock and surrounded by smaller rocks and brightly colored flowers. About twenty yards to the left of the shrine were three oil drums. A siphoning apparatus was attached to the middle drum. To the left of that was the large shed.

I was out the door and making a low run to the pickup before the sheriff's cruiser came to a halt. When they got out, the sheriff motioned his deputy far to the left, near the shed. Then he and Loushine approached the front door. The lights above the door and the shed were burning, and the sheriff had left his headlights on. I was leaning across the pickup, the .38 trained on the front door. Yet even though I was watching it, I was unprepared to see it fly open and Jimmy Johannson dash out, squeezing off God knows how many rounds from the UZI as he ran to the oil drums. The sheriff and Loushine retreated to the cruiser. The other deputy found cover behind the shed. I stayed where I was. I didn't fire.

At the first sound of shooting, two cars pulled into the yard from opposite directions with lights and sirens. Johannson pinned them down, giggling between bursts as his submachine gun turned the vehicles into scrap. I wondered how many magazines he had.

The sun was down now. The only light was man-made, all of it concentrated on the drums and the front of the house. I heard several handguns and a single shotgun blasting away from outside the circle of light as Kreel County's finest returned fire. But I couldn't see anybody except the deputy at the shed.

I crawled from the front of the pickup to the back. The sheriff was crouching behind his cruiser. He was in a bad spot and couldn't get a shot at the man behind the drums without exposing himself to return fire. Loushine had a better line, but he, too, was exposed, on the ground behind a maple tree.

I returned to the front of the truck. Johannson was in a good position. The way the drums were arranged, he was protected from the front and the sides. To take him, I would have to maneuver behind. But there was no cover until I reached the shrine. Dammit, I knew this was going to be a mistake.

I caught the eye of the deputy at the shed and rotated my finger vigorously in the air, motioning for covering fire. He stared at me for a moment, probably wondering what kitchen appliance I had become. But he caught on quickly and raised his hand for me to wait. He reloaded his revolver and nodded.

I dashed away from the wreck, holding the .38 low. Several guns fired at once. I couldn't see the deputies, but they could see me. I circled around the shrine, brought up the .38, and squeezed off two rounds.

Something punched me in the left shoulder so unexpectedly that I actually looked around to see what it could have been. Suddenly, a voice sang out loudly, "I'm hit!" I recognized it immediately. It was mine.

I crept back behind the junker. Nausea climbed into my throat, and trembling in my legs forced me to sit on the ground. My right hand went to my shoulder, and I realized for the first time that I was no longer holding the .38. Where the hell was it? I searched the ground as best I could in the darkness but didn't find it. Wasn't that the damnedest thing?

I felt warm; sweat beaded up on my forehead. Yet my teeth were chattering. I took my hand from the shoulder. It was wet and sticky. That's when I fully realized I had been shot. I'd been shot before, so you'd think it wouldn't have taken me all that long to catch on. But it did. Go figure.

I took my handkerchief and pressed it against the wound with the idea of stopping the bleeding, but I could tell by the warm dribble down my side that I was doing a poor job of it. Then the shoulder began to hurt. The pain actually cleared my head, and my trembling eased, and I didn't feel so much like vomiting. I wondered how bad my wound was and tried to stand, as if that would make it all better. I couldn't make it and I felt red hot tears of rage in my eyes. What a piss-poor turn of events this was!

The shooting had continued unabated, but I didn't notice until a dark figure sidled up to me behind the truck. My first guess was wrong. It wasn't God. It was Johnny Johannson.

"Hi," I said, like I had come across him unexpectedly while out on a stroll.

"This won't do. I'm going to stop it."

"Stop what?" I asked him, confused.

He reached next to the bumper and picked up the .38. So *that's* where it was. He stood and walked slowly toward the drums. I used the truck to pull myself up and watched him. At about twenty feet he leveled the .38. At ten he squeezed the trigger three times. The bullets pounded Jimmy Johannson in the back. He threw up his arms, dropping the UZI; he spun off the drums and fell. The sheriff and Loushine closed in quickly, followed by a half dozen deputies. They circled Jimmy, all of them pointing their weapons at him except Loushine. He eased the .38 out of Johnny's hand and moved him away. By the time I staggered to the circle, the sheriff was cradling Jimmy's head and yelling at him.

"Why did you shoot Michael Bettich?"

"My . . . lawyer," Jimmy sputtered, calling for his constitutional rights even at this late date.

"Your lawyer can't help you now. Who were you working for? Tell me!"

"My lawyer," he said.

And then his lights went out.

I sat on the back seat of the sheriff's cruiser while Loushine removed my jacket and shirt. He was gentle but too slow, prolonging the agony.

"I've been hurt worse," I told him.

"I doubt it," he said.

"No, really," I insisted. "I was shot in the leg once."

I would have told him more, but he wasn't listening. Instead, Loushine was picking around the edge of the wound as I worked to keep from fainting. It was high on the shoulder, higher than I had first thought.

Other deputies offered to help, but we ignored them. Orman came to the car and said he was sorry I was hurt. We ignored him, too. The bleeding had stopped, but I couldn't say whether it was because of Loushine's efforts or because I had simply run out of blood—my clothes were soaked through.

When Loushine pronounced me ready for travel, he slid behind the steering wheel. I excused myself first, walked a few feet into the woods, and threw up. I was trembling again, and I had a difficult time getting back to the car. The deputies turned away, averting their eyes, apparently embarrassed by my show of weakness. Screw 'em. I sat in the back of the cruiser. Loushine buckled me in and shut the door because I couldn't. It was a swell ride to the hospital.

twenty-eight

"You chipped the hell out of your collarbone," the woman doctor told me. She seemed happy about it.

"Will I live?"

"Not if you keep going on like this. You have a lot of scars, my friend."

She was right about that. And I was well past thinking of them as trophies: Say, did I ever show you my dueling scar? I've risked my life many times, certainly more times than I should have, and after each episode I was left with the same nagging question: Do I have more past than future?

The morning light was streaming through the half-closed blinds. I had slept some the night before after the doctor had attended my wound, but I could've used a lot more. I thanked the doctor for her consideration and settled in for a long nap. But she wasn't inclined to leave. She replaced my chart in the plastic tray attached to the door and sat next to me.

"Michael Bettich is dead," she said.

The news hit me so hard, I thought I had been shot again.

"Dead?"

"Four forty-two this morning. Duluth-General said respiratory failure, of all things."

I heard her words, but I didn't know what they meant.

"There were so many other things that could have killed her," she added.

I still didn't understand, and my face probably showed it.

"They said there was nothing that could be done."

That last part got through. Only I didn't know how to respond. My emotions concerning Alison were all ajumble. I knew too much of her history and not enough about her. So I stared blankly at the doctor, hoping she would tell me how to act.

"I told the sheriff. He didn't take it very well. I guess he was in love with her."

But I wasn't. I didn't love her. I was infatuated with the image I had created for her, that was all. And the image was incorrect, anyway. I didn't really know Alison. We had spoken only a few words to each other.

"What will make you go away?"

"Tell me why, that's all. Tell me why you went to all the trouble."

"It's a long story, and quite frankly, I see no reason to share it with you."

"Who was she really?" I wondered aloud.

"Michael?" asked the doctor.

"Her name was Alison," I told her.

"Who are you talking about?" the doctor asked, laying the palm of her hand against my forehead, determining if I was suddenly feverish.

"I guess it doesn't really matter."

I was woken by the light that fell across my face when the hospital room door was opened. "Are you sleeping?" a voice asked. The voice belonged to Gretchen.

"No," I told her.

She came in, limping on crutches, letting the door close behind her.

"Turn on a light," I told her.

"No lights," she said.

We sat in the dark without speaking for—I don't know—it seemed like a long time. In the dark a minute can be an eternity. Finally I said, "I'm sorry about Alison." I didn't know what else to say. I still hadn't been able to sort it out.

"We buried her this afternoon."

"So soon?" It was only yesterday that I'd heard she had died.

"There wasn't any reason to put it off."

"Her parents?"

"We buried her under the name Michael Bettich. That's the way she wanted it."

"I see."

We went a few more minutes without speaking until Gretchen announced, "Sheriff Orman resigned. He's moving to Duluth. He said he was quitting to paint full time."

"Good for him."

"Yeah."

"What about you?"

"What about me?" Gretchen asked in reply.

We fell silent again. I liked Gretchen in spite of everything. But not so much that I was willing to conduct long conversations with her in the dark.

"Christ, Alison," she said after a couple of minutes, her voice filled with pain and tears. "I don't need this, I really don't."

Then the door was open and she was gone.

I was dressing in new blue jeans, white shirt, and gray sports jacket. They were gifts from Acting Sheriff Gary Loushine. It was the least he could do, he said.

"In my profession, you have to be smart or tough or lucky. Preferably all three," I told him. "Lately I have been none of those."

"Well, if you decide to quit the PI business and get a real job, you could always work for me."

"No, thanks," I told him. He was sitting on my bed, paging through *People* magazine. "How's the investigation progressing?"

"What investigation?" he asked absentmindedly while glancing at a photo of Nicole Kidman.

I was amazed.

"The investigation into the murder of Michael Bettich!"

Loushine shrugged. "Case closed."

"You're kidding."

"The UZI we took off Johannson: It fired the bullet we found in Bettich. And Thilgen. We have Johannson's fingerprints. What more do you want?"

"How 'bout why," I answered.

"Thilgen made a lot of threats against Michael. Thilgen had paid Johannson to do his dirty work in the past; he paid him for this job, too."

"Why would Johannson then shoot Thilgen?"

"He was afraid Mr. Chips would give him up."

I took the magazine from Loushine's hands and set it on the bed. Once I had his full attention, I told him, "When I was at St. Mark's Elementary School, Sister Agnes told us a cautionary tale: Two cars loaded with teenagers were on the highway driving toward each other at high speed. The first car had its high beams on. The driver of the second car flicked his lights to warn the first driver to dim them. The first driver didn't. So the second driver said, 'I'll show him,' and turned on his high beams, too. The drivers blinded each other, they hit head on, and everyone in both cars was killed."

"What's your point?" Loushine asked impatiently.

"If there were no survivors, how did Sister Agnes know what really happened?"

Loushine patted my shoulder and smiled.

"Taylor, do me a favor. Get out of town."

Hunter Truman was in the lobby of the Saginau Medical Center, arguing over my bill. He paid it, but not before he threatened the cashier with litigation.

We left together. I drove off in my car, and he followed in his. We stopped at the Field of Hope Cemetery not far from The Harbor. It was a lonely place, little more than clearing among the trees, partially hidden from the county road. We found Alison's grave near a stand of maples. She was buried under a marble stone that read BETTICH and nothing more. The flowers had already withered.

"Dammit, Taylor," Truman said. "I told you to make sure that they knew it was Alison. Now I'll need to have the body exhumed."

I didn't answer. Instead, I strolled to a small bench, the kind you normally find next to a tee on a golf course. Truman joined me.

"I blame myself for everything that's happened," he said, trying mightily to sound conciliatory.

"So do I," I told him.

"You do?" He acted surprised by my callousness.

"It worked out exactly the way you had planned, didn't it?" I added.

"The way I planned?" Truman asked. "What are you talking about?"

"It would clinch things if it was you who defended Jimmy Johannson on an assault charge in Minneapolis last year."

"Who?"

"It'll be public record and easy enough to check," I warned him.

Truman spoke slowly, cautiously.

"What if I did?" he asked.

"I expect he was very grateful. Let me guess. After the verdict he pumped your hand and said, 'Anything, you need, anything at all, you call ol' Jimmy.' Am I right?"

Truman didn't say if I was or I wasn't.

"You were Dr. Bob Holyfield's divorce lawyer, too, weren't you?"

"What are you suggesting?" Truman asked.

"Nothing that can be proved," I admitted.

And then Truman smiled. "That's right."

"It was the money," I continued. "Everything could be explained somehow except for the money."

Truman eyed me carefully.

"The fucking money," I said. "I gave it a lot of thought while in the hospital. Let's see if I finally have the facts straight: Dr. Bob wanted to divorce his wife and take up with his mistress, Alison. But he was afraid his wife would leave him a pauper. So he devised a way to secretly transfer all his liquid assets to Alison—with your help, I have no doubt. At least a quarter of a million dollars. I don't know how he did it, but it's been done before.

"Only Alison had no intention of hooking up with Dr. Bob once his divorce was final. Tie herself to that arrogant creep? Not a chance. She decided to take the money and run.

"So she very deliberately created a new life for herself while just as deliberately ending the old one. She framed Raymond for her murder. I don't believe she had anything against Raymond, she just needed to fake her own death so no one would come looking for her, and Raymond, with his record, was the perfect fall guy. And you have to admit, she did a helluva job. The blood was an inspired touch. And the snowstorm? Manna from heaven. As a result, the authorities were convinced Alison was buried in a shallow grave somewhere.

"Except you didn't buy it, did you?" I continued. "You and Dr. Bob. That's because you knew about the money. But you couldn't say anything, not without revealing your own fraud. So you hired me. And when I convinced myself that Irene Brown killed Alison, you put the note on my windshield to make me think otherwise, to keep me looking—you knew where I was having lunch that day. Damn! I should have seen it then.

"But I didn't. So I kept looking for Alison. I kept looking until

I found her. Only the money was gone by then, spent on The Harbor, with no way for you and Dr. Bob to recover it. But you anticipated that, too, didn't you? That's why you brought Stephen Emerton into it. How much did you offer him? A third? He hated his wife so much, I bet he settled for less."

Truman didn't answer.

"You brought Stephen into it because even if Alison was pretending to be Michael Bettich, she was still legally married to him; if she was killed, all her assets would go to him. That's why Stephen was willing to risk casting suspicion on himself by admitting that Alison had had an affair with a doctor she had previously worked with; that's why he dropped a hint that she could still be alive—so he could claim a piece of the action later. He was much smarter than he had pretended.

"After that the three of you just sat back and waited until I found her, knowing that I wouldn't quit until I did. And when I did find her, you discovered that there was a trigger in the neighborhood already primed to do your killing. How lucky for you."

"Interesting theory," Truman told me.

"You'll never get away with it," I warned him.

"If what you say is true—and I most emphatically deny that it is—we already *did* get away with it, Mr. Taylor. And since you are without a shred of evidence to support these outrageous allegations, I strongly suggest you keep your fucking mouth shut or I'll slap your ass with an injunction and sue your brains out. By the time I get done, you'll be taking your meals with the other derelicts at the Dorothy Day Center."

"How are you going to get a court order to exhume Michael's body without my testimony?" I wondered. "How are you going to prove it actually is Alison buried down there to claim her property?"

"I have your written reports," Truman reminded me. "They

should be sufficient for our needs. Unless you testify that they're phony, of course—and lose your license in the process. Are you willing to do that?" Truman was smiling triumphantly. "I didn't think so."

He stood up. "Good-bye, asshole. Don't forget to send me a bill."

He started toward his car and was halfway there when he stopped and looked back at me.

"Oh, and one more thing," he called. "Hiding Dr. Holyfield's assets from his wife? That was Alison's idea. I just thought you should know."

I should have hated him, but I didn't. I should have hated Dr. Holyfield and Stephen Emerton, too, but they didn't seem worth the effort. Instead, I convinced myself that sooner or later they would all get what they deserved. Life would settle with them, just as it had with Alison. It was something I needed to believe.

I gazed at the bright, cloudless sky as I returned to my car, realizing for the first time that I had not heard the sound of a jet engine for over a week, hadn't seen any planes at all. The realization depressed me, although I couldn't tell you why.

After seating myself behind the steering wheel, I took Alison's photograph out of its envelope. When she had been just a voice on a cassette, a face in a photograph taken years earlier, I found her fascinating. And Cynthia and Bobby Orman were right: I had fallen a little in love with her. But now I was surprised by how ordinary she had become. A common thief with just a dash of uncommon flair.

I tore the photograph into pieces too small to reassemble and littered them on the ground.

twenty-nine

I watched Cynthia stretch, pushing against the edge of my redwood picnic table, first one finely chiseled leg, then the other extended behind her. Watching Cynthia move, especially in jogging shorts and tank top, was like an ice cold beer on a sweltering summer day: always a pleasure.

She had asked me to go jogging with her, but I had declined, using my still tender shoulder as an excuse—although it certainly hadn't bothered me when Cynthia and I were together the night before. But it was such a beautiful day, why ruin it by getting all sweaty and out of breath? Instead, I wished her well, sprawled out in my hammock, and read my *Sporting News*. It was hard going. I kept thinking of Alison. And the men who had killed her.

I told Anne Scalasi and Chief Teeters what had happened in Deer Lake. They didn't take it well. Teeters threatened to arrest me for obstruction. Anne just wanted me to go away for a while. But at least Teeters wouldn't be haunted by the one that got away. And Scalasi would be able to replace the red tab in her murder book with a blue one.

"There's not a damn thing you can do about them," Cynthia said after I told her the story. "You have no evidence, nothing that's admissible."

"I could kill them."

"But you won't."

"No, I won't," I agreed. "Alison was dirty. That's why she was hiding. She knew what she was getting into. It's just that—"

"You want justice for her."

"I don't know from justice," I admitted. "What the hell is justice, anyway? If you have a working definition, I'd like to hear it. I just want . . . I don't know what I want. A happy ending, I guess."

"Oh, Taylor, you of all people should know better. Not every story has a happy ending. Some of them just end."

She was right, of course. The world is what it is, not something else. That's one reason why I have so little patience with peace demonstrators. But I didn't feel any better about it.

I hadn't read more than a dozen pages of the *Sporting News* when Cynthia, mopping her forehead with a towel, returned to my backyard, carrying my mail.

"This ought to improve your mood," she said guardedly and handed me an envelope with Hunter Truman's return address. It contained a check for $12,800—thirty-two days' work, counting my time in the hospital, one of the longest cases I've ever investigated. However, Truman had decided to ignore my $1,982 expense invoice, and I debated suing him before finally deciding against it. It would probably give him too much pleasure.

"Who's Rosalind?" Cynthia asked.

"Hmm?"

"Rosalind Colletti," she repeated, handing me a postcard.

A jolt of adrenalin electrified my body at the sound of the name. I sat up, my legs straddling the hammock, and snapped the postcard from Cynthia's fingers. On one side was a spectacular photograph of the Split Rock Lighthouse overlooking Lake Superior just north of Duluth. The other side had my address, a Duluth, Minnesota, postmark, and this message written in long hand:

Dearest Taylor,
    I've been told your first aid saved my life, and for that I will
be eternally grateful. But you know, despite what Oscar Wilde

had to say on the subject, living well is not always the best revenge. Sometimes dying is.

Rosalind

"Who's Rosalind?" Cynthia repeated after I had read the post-card for the fourth time.

She'd done it again! I'll be damned, she'd done it again! Sheriff Orman must have helped her . . . managed to get to someone in the hospital. . . . And when Truman and Emerton and Dr. Bob exhumed her body only to find that there was no body . . .

"Is it a secret?"

"Hmm?"

"Who's Rosalind?"

I smiled. I couldn't help but smile.

"Just the girlfriend of a painter I used to know."

"She says you saved her life?"

"Nonsense," I said.

And then I started to laugh. I laughed long and heartily until Cynthia was compelled to join in even though she didn't get the joke.